WITHDRAWN

www.hants.gov.uk/library

Tel: 0300 555 1387

Hampshire
County Council

Love
YOUR LIBRARY

shaw

C016535344

ALSO BY MICHELLE HODKIN

THE MARA DYER TRILOGY

The Unbecoming of Mara Dyer

The Evolution of Mara Dyer

The Retribution of Mara Dyer

First published in Great Britain in 2017 by Simon & Schuster UK Ltd
A CBS COMPANY

Originally published in the USA in 2017 by Simon & Schuster BFYR,
an imprint of Simon & Schuster Children's Publishing Division

Copyright © 2017 Michelle Hodkin

This book is copyright under the Berne Convention.
No reproduction without permission.
All rights reserved.

The right of Michelle Hodkin to be identified as the author of this
work has been asserted by her in accordance with sections 77 and 78
of the Copyright, Design and Patents Act, 1988.

1 3 5 7 9 10 8 6 4 2

Simon & Schuster UK Ltd
1st Floor, 222 Gray's Inn Road
London
WC1X 8HB

www.simonandschuster.co.uk
www.simonandschuster.com.au
www.simonandschuster.co.in

Simon & Schuster Australia, Sydney
Simon & Schuster India, New Delhi

A CIP catalogue record for this book is
available from the British Library.

PB ISBN 978-1-4711-7141-3
eBook ISBN 978-1-4711-7142-0

This book is a work of fiction. Names, characters, places and
incidents are either the product of the author's imagination or are
used fictitiously. Any resemblance to actual people living or
dead, events or locales is entirely coincidental.

Printed and bound by CPI Group (UK) Ltd, Croydon, CR0 4YY

Simon & Schuster UK Ltd are committed to sourcing paper
that is made from wood grown in sustainable forests and support the Forest
Stewardship Council, the leading international forest certification organisation.
Our books displaying the FSC logo are printed on FSC certified paper.

the Shaw Confessions VOLUME 1

the becoming of noah shaw

MICHELLE HODKIN

SIMON & SCHUSTER

For the lost boys, and the girls who find them

the
becoming
of
noah
shaw

Caveat Emptor

TRIGGER WARNING FOR SUICIDE, HOMICIDE, assault with a deadly weapon, assault with a deadly mind, harm to others, harm to self, disordered eating, disordered thinking, disordered feeling, disordered being, body shaming, victim shaming, shaming of every kind, dark humor, ill humor, shitty humor, maiming, miming, death of teenagers, death of adults, death of authority figures, death of inconsequential red shirts. Also sex. But if you need a trigger warning for that, you're reading the wrong book.

Part I

Rather than love, than money,
than fame, give me truth.

—Henry David Thoreau, *Walden*

My dear friend,

Sincere apologies for my lack of
correspondence, but the journey has been long
and, as of late, rather fraught.

You did admit that this would not be an
easy . . . venture, though I must confess
that I did not expect that to mean I would
arrive in Calcutta as one of only three
survivors of the steamer Ceres.

The first man to go missing was a
merchant; no man aboard could speak to the
manner of his disappearance, and prior to our
voyage he was unknown to the captain and
crew, all steady-seeming fellows. A search
of the ship was conducted, and when he was
not to be found, the captain concluded he must
have fallen overboard in the night.

When the captain vanished eight days
later, no one aboard could say the same.

The Ceres left London with twenty-one
men aboard, including myself. As advised,
I have concealed the true nature of our
venture to all who would ask, even members

of the Company. I expect to be questioned,
come morning, about the events of the past
two months, and all papers are in order.
I have told my wife little more than was
necessary—that I believed this journey would
prove prosperous, and I do still hope that to
be the case, though it is not my fortune but
my fate—and that of many others—I hope
to improve. Though only you are aware of that
truth.

Yours Respectfully,

S. S.

1

CONQUER OR DIE

WE ARE A TEARLESS, TINY CROWD, WE survivors of David Shaw.

Imagine it: five of us gathered like a wilting bouquet, my grandmother the lone thistle standing.

Next to her, my grandfather softly droops under the grand dome above us, painted by some hideously famous artist centuries ago. This is quite literally our ancestral home, built in the fifteen hundreds by Henry the Somethingth. Grandfather, a.k.a. Lord Elliot II, was once a strapping, reed-backed but jolly Englishman's Englishman. Hunter of pheasants, of foxes, but not of fortune—that he inherited from his father, who inherited it from his father, and on it goes. Now, however, he sags beside my grandmother, half of his face twisted into a permanent grimace after a stroke two years ago. I tried to heal him when that was a thing I realised I could do. It didn't work. I still don't know why.

His light blue eyes are clouded over and staring at noth-ingness as he leans on his cane, his hand trembling. My grandmother can't quite disguise her pleasure at the optics of our black-frocked family standing on the grand staircase of the grand entrance as we pretend to wait for the cars in full view of the mourners passing by on foot. Never mind that my grandfather can't do steps—Lady Sylvia could not care less.

Imagine, if you will, a sharper, crueler version of Maggie Smith, and you'll have some semblance of an idea of my grand-mother. Add an unhealthy dose of botulinum toxin, and there's your visual.

Standing beside the remains of my family, I've never felt more like a stranger. My stepmother, Ruth, grips my sister Katie's hand as the valet helps my grandfather descend to the car—for my sister's sake more than her own. My stepmother seems quite fine, actually, enduring this hideousness as if it were any other day with my grandparents—she's had years of practice being a lowly American, and my father's second wife at that. My sister, however—her ocean blue eyes are dull and clouded, staring at nothing, and dressed in black, she looks mostly dead herself; she hardly notices when my stepmother breaks away to head to the chapel on her own. We should be going with her, but my grandmother insisted on this arrangement (separate cars for second wives), and Ruth either didn't care enough to protest, or knew better.

The eighteenth-century chapel is on the grounds of the estate, only about a half a kilometre away—its spire pierces the English sky (grey, sunless, speckled with the occasional crow). A carefully landscaped wood helps obscure the twelfth-century ruins of the abbey that preceded it. Grandmother finds the ruins unsightly, unsurprisingly, but the National Trust entered into an arrangement with some skint ancestor or another—maintaining castles isn't cheap—and thus prevented her from fucking up that which should not be fucked with. I'm rather sentimental about the ruins—as a child, I halfheartedly attempted suicide there now and again, always returning from post-tourist-hours expeditions with knees winking with cuts, and the occasional fracture or two.

"All right, children." My grandmother clasps her hands together as the car comes to a stop. "The carriage will begin the procession once everybody is assembled at the chapel. All you need do is wait until the casket is carried inside, then sit in the front left pew. Is that understood?"

My father's affectless, emotionless voice is echoed in hers, and she speaks as though it were not her dead son we were gathered here to mourn, but rather a play we're about to put on. If I were capable of feeling anything at the moment, I think I might hate her.

"Yes, Grandmother," Katie says.

My turn. "Understood," I say.

"Perfect." She arranges her and my grandfather's iron hair, along with his suit. The chapel doors are open, and a small crowd awaits the carriage hearse within and without. The valet exits our now-idling car to help my grandfather, and when the door opens—

The air is swollen with sound, more heartbeats than I can count, the threads of at least a hundred pulses quickening, the air itself seeming to inhale and exhale with each breath taken behind the stone walls. I can hear the tiny hearts of birds—crows, pheasant, pigeons, distinct from the hawk slicing the air above us. The knotty-wood-and-iron door opens, and it's like cracking open a hive of bees—whispers and coughs and echoes, every note bursting and lurid. An old, dull impulse to place my hands over my ears and scream like I (very occasionally) did when I was a boy arises, but my ears were never the problem. My mind is.

What it usually feels like to be me:

The sounds I shouldn't be able to hear skim off the surface of my mind. Everything is white noise until I focus, until something seizes my attention, but this, right now—it's nothing like that. This feels like an assault, a mess of sounds, like being surrounded by instruments being smashed. It's distracting enough that I hadn't noticed the dozens of heads twisted over shoulders to glance at our Long-Expected Party. And lo, among them stands Goose.

The volume of the noise blurs my vision for a moment—crowds are always awful, but it's especially worse today—and Goose is nothing more than a fall of blond hair and an open smile, flanked by the smudges of Patrick and Neirin. There's a thunderclap of a hand on my shoulder. "Hard luck, mate," says Goose, his voice deep and rather astonishingly resonant, rising above the din.

"We're so sorry," Patrick follows. A simple nod from Neirin.

Those three faces, none alike in dignity or feature: Goose light and lanky and loud; Neirin dark and soft and innocent; and ginger red and freckled Patrick.

Patrick and Neirin seem frozen in time—their faces the same as they were nearly three years ago when I left Westminster. I see snapshots of memories with their faces: Goose flashing his middle finger at me in Yard; Patrick rolling his first cigarette with ferocious concentration; Neirin scratching at maths problems, his face pinched with concentration.

And then me, holding a champagne sabre, spraying hundreds of pounds' worth down open throats. Putting my cigarette out in the horsehair pancake to the collective horror of the teachers and students assembled for the Greaze, and the four of us snorting lines of coke Patrick shyly produced from his pocket, off his iPad in his father's study.

We were not a foursome. For that, we'd need to be bonded by secrets, and I shared none of mine. Secrets cut you off from everyone else, so I would always suggest the vast majority of our exploits to mask that I never could quite connect with them in the first place. Insert a stifled sob here, would you?

A forked tongue clicks beside my ear. "It's almost time," my grandmother says, looking at the valet for confirmation, then at my stepmother. With a tiny crunch of a nod she looks ahead, toward the manor house, toward the old stables, ancient but fortified over the centuries. From the gate, four glossy Friesians emerge, a driver in a top hat commanding them, and my father's coffin encased in a black wood and glass hearse behind.

I can't see all that well from here—my head is still fizzing with sounds, whispers and coughs and everything else. But not Mara.

The way she sounds, the way she's always sounded—like one discordant note, twisted just enough to affect the notes surrounding it—is impossible to ignore. An aural fingerprint, distinctly her own, distinctly Mara. The first time I heard her, I never wanted to listen to anyone else.

I look and listen for that note as the horses' hooves knock the ground in a steady, dignified trot, their large hearts pumping solidly with the effort. I can almost feel their boredom as they approach, which is why, halfway down the path, the ripple of terror and rage in their bodies reverberates in mine. They break their gait, stopping, stamping—one backs up, another sidesteps into another horse. Then one of them rears, nearly snapping the harness. The colour of Katie's face is ash, her heartbeat racing the way the horses want to.

"It's all right," I say reflexively, and my sister snaps her head toward me and slits her eyes. There's anger there, fighting for a place beside her sadness. Today is changing her, has changed her already.

My grandmother holds tight to my grandfather's arm, her face a mask of placidity as her blood ices with anger. She looks to the priest, who says something to the people in a vain attempt to calm them, because the horses begin to thunder toward the chapel, eliciting screams despite being several lengths away. I can feel the power of them in the ground. They're about to turn sharply to their right, cracking into the woodlands just before they do it, just before the hearse overturns.

I know what they're going to do before they do it, because at that moment I hear Mara, see her running toward us, diagonally through the hedges that enclose the gardens and past the Atlas fountain, and as her path begins to converge with the carriage, the horses blaze with panic. My eyes meet Mara's, and she stops short. Looks at the horses, then back at me.

It's her they're terrified of. I know it, she knows it, and so she vanishes as swiftly as she arrived.

I don't wait for anyone to calm the horses, or for the pall-bearers to fetch the coffin and bear it toward the church. I turn away from the priest, attempting to usher everyone away from the scene and into the chapel, and manage to slip away unnoticed. I glance back just once before I reach the woods, long enough to see Katie's glossed head moving through the doors, her eyes vacant, her arms held by Ruth and my grandparents before the last knot of bodies passes inside. And then I turn away from them all, away from my father, away from the sodden remains of my family, to Mara.

2

BE NOT SIMPLY GOOD

PAVED ROAD TURNS TO GRAVEL TURNS TO DIRT path as my mind runs on seeing her again. We've barely had a moment alone since arriving in England—my grandmother fought the idea of her presence at the funeral, and Ruth tried to broker a deal: England yes, funeral no, but I held fast. I miss nothing about my father—he tortured people I care about, and Mara most of all. It felt right for her to bury him with me. To be rid of him together.

It's been less than a year since Mara first asked about my family; I've become closer to her than I've ever been to any of them, but here, today, now, I can't help but wonder if she's ever regretted it. Of course our meeting had been engineered, though we didn't know it then, and probably couldn't have done much differently if we had, but if she could go back . . . would she have wanted to know me if she'd known where I would lead her? What I would lead her into?

The first time she asked about him, we were on our way from my house to our first date, and, unsurprisingly, he wasn't home. Only my stepmother was.

"So where was Daddy Warbucks this morning?"

"Don't know, don't care." Mara looked a bit surprised at that, and I remember being rather surprised at myself—I'm usually not so obvious. "We're not close," I finished, hoping to end that particular line of questioning.

"Clearly," she said. Her eyes were on me, and she said nothing else—she waited expectantly for me to keep going. I hid behind sunglasses instead.

"Why doesn't your mother have a British accent?"

"She doesn't have an *English* accent because she's American."

"Oh my God, really?" I'd known the girl for half a second, and she loved giving me shit from the very first.

"She's from Massachusetts," I said. "And she's not actually my biological mother." Mara knew nothing about me, and all I knew about her was that she'd been the only survivor of some calamity that claimed three lives—and that I heard her voice in my mind the night that it happened, despite her being thousands of miles away. The second I saw her, I needed to know her. Which, I suppose, meant letting her know me.

"My mother died when I was five and Katie was almost four," I said neutrally. I probably added some version of the standard *It was a long time ago, I don't really remember her* line. I waited for her to offer the expected platitude, but she didn't. So I decided to tell her the truth—some of it.

"Ruth spent high school in England, so that's how she met my mother, and they stayed friends at Cambridge." I searched for my pack of cigarettes almost reflexively, placing one between my lips as I told Mara about my parents' and stepmother's brief flirtation with civil disobedience. I still smoked in front of Mara then—I'd started at eleven and realised I could exhale through my nose like a dragon. Seemed like a good enough reason at the time.

I went on with carefully worded backstory for a bit, and when I finally risked a glance at Mara, she was curious. There was even a slight upturn at the corners of her mouth. I remember wanting to shock her, so I told her my mother was stabbed to death, thinking that would do it.

A thing I loved about Mara immediately, though—she looked back at me completely without pity.

"At a protest," I added. Her brows drew together, but the wide-eyed look of horror mixed with *Poor baby!* I'd expected to see was nowhere to be found.

So I kept going. "She made my father stay home to watch

Katie that day, but I was with her. I'd just turned five a few days before, but I don't remember it. Or much of her at all, really. My father won't even mention her name, and he loses it if anyone else does."

"Ruth came back to England when she heard about my mother. She'd said at one point, when I was older, that after my mother died, my father was useless. Couldn't take care of us, couldn't take care of himself. Literally, a disaster. So she stayed, and they got married, even though he doesn't deserve her, even though he'd become someone else. And here we are now, one big happy family."

That was what I remember telling Mara that day—more than I'd told anyone, certainly, but not quite the truth.

The truth is that I do remember when my mother died.

I remember her funeral: the air heavy with flowers, my grandmother's perfume, and the picture they'd had of her in the chapel, wearing a cream-and-black-striped jumper, her blond hair pulled back in a messy ponytail at the base of her neck. The sleeves covered her hands, and she had her chin resting in one of them, her eyes crinkled at the corners, and she half smiled, quite deviously, at the camera. "You have her smile," people said, and I remember looking into the casket at her face, wondering if that meant I'd taken it from her, and the wave of guilt that descended on me then.

Her eyes were closed, her skin waxy, her body fitted poorly into a dress I never remembered her wearing. My father had sat solemnly beside me, spine ramrod straight, his typically clean-shaven face now shadowed with days of stubble. Ruth wept openly as she stood beside the priest and spoke about Mum. I could hardly hear words through her sniffles and sobs.

My father, on the other hand—his face was nothing. He held Katie on his lap, and she was uncharacteristically quiet, her blue eyes looking bluer in her pale face, which looked paler in her little black frock and Mary Janes. Ruth wept until she couldn't speak, and the priest, looking stricken at the open display of emotion, helped her down to her seat. She sat down beside me and took me in her arms, but I shook myself free. The room was filled with candles, tall ones, taller than I was, some of them, and I watched the wax drip onto the petal of a flower and wondered how much longer I'd be sitting there in that room with the thing that was and was not my mother.

I remember the moment she became that thing.

I remember the little gasp she made as someone pushed past her, and her head bowing forward before her hand loosened around mine.

I remember the red flowering her shirt under her jacket.

What I don't remember is the face of the one who stabbed her. I don't remember screaming for her or crying. And as I watched her dying, I don't remember a look of surprise on her face or fear in her eyes, or seeing any sadness in her at all.

I remember seeing relief there, instead.

3

THE TONIC OF WILDNESS

WHEN I FINALLY SEE MARA, SHE'S NO longer in sight of the chapel. She's a small Brontë character silhouetted in black, standing in the shadow of a marble tower on top of a high hill; the mausoleum containing centuries of Shaw remains, perched between and overlooking the woods and the ruins. My absence in the chapel and presence on the grounds goes either unnoticed or undealt with, because no one stops me.

I stride alongside the man-made river that pulses through the grounds. The absence of sound vibrates inside me the farther I get from the chapel. The air is thick, and even the water seems to die beneath the spot where my girl stands.

Mara bows over the bridge, her hair cascading over her shoulders as though it's reaching for the river. She casts a slim shadow over the water. "I didn't think," she says, possibly to herself.

I stand next to her, resting my elbows against the old stones. "About?"

"The horses."

"Why would you? I didn't. If it's anyone's fault, it's mine."

Her face is in shadow—I can't tell what she's thinking, and I can't hear her either—the air is unnaturally still, and my mind is as quiet now as it was loud before.

"Are they okay?" she asks.

"The horses? I'm sure they're fine."

"The humans?"

"I'm sure they're fine too."

"Are people freaking out?" A breeze ripples her curls and the water.

"The English don't really 'freak out.' But I'm sure the guests are quietly aghast."

She tilts her face to me, finally. Her eyes are impenetrable, but a slice of sun hits her shoulder, I feel her warmth through her clothes, then the softness of her skin as her fingers glance over my hand as we lean over the bridge together.

I don't know what she's thinking, but all I can think is that I want her against me, around me, enveloping me. I slide my hand around her waist, my fingers slipping beneath the waist-band of her skirt, searching for skin.

She raises her eyebrows. "Won't you be missed?"

I press her to me, bending so my lips graze her ear as I speak. "Probably. Ask me if I care."

"Do you care?"

"Not even a little."

By the time we reach the mausoleum, Mara's breath is quick, her skin dewy. I pull her under the cold marble dome, between the columns that surround it, and press my mouth to hers, insistent, demanding. She softens against my lips, melts, and every moment is bursting—the hot slide of her tongue in my mouth, the bite of her teeth into my lower lip, and then the stiffening of her bones and muscles as her body pulls away and the tension in mine rises to a ferocious ache.

"Noah, we shouldn't—"

"Shouldn't . . . ?"

A resigned exhale. "We shouldn't be here."

"That's precisely why we are here," I say. I break away for one agonising moment, and the door creaks as I push it open and guide her inside.

The mausoleum is quite large, the size of a grand studio apartment in New York, perhaps. There's a short marble altar in the centre, with Latin words and carved figures of the Four Ages of Man on each side: *Infantia. Adolescentia. Virilitas. Senectas.* I push her gently against *Virilitas*, but she pushes back.

"It's your father's funeral."

"Well aware," I say, leaning to kiss her neck. When she doesn't move, I ask, "Do you find this inappropriate?"

"It's . . . unusual," she says.

"Would you like to go back?"

"Would you?"

I answer by raising her hips onto the altar and stand between her parted knees, her pleated skirt hitched up to reveal the paleness of her thighs. A slow glance slightly downward.

Her eyebrows lift as her lips part. "Are you serious?"

"Deadly."

She bites her lower lip. "I don't want you to regret not being there."

"Won't," I say, slipping one hand beneath her shirt.

"How do you know?"

My mind returns to my mother's funeral, my father staring at her coffin with dead eyes. "My father died the day my mother did. A monster took his place."

"I know, but—"

"No, there's nothing else. No one else. He's gone—he can't hurt anyone anymore. There's no one and nothing in our way." I pause, resting my fingers on the clasp of her bra. "We should celebrate."

A laugh escapes her throat. "Not really your style."

"No, but it is yours."

Wide eyes slit into a cat's slant. She bows her head, conceding. "Has anyone ever told you you use sex as a coping mechanism?"

"Yes, why?"

"Oh, no reason." A pause fills the air. Then Mara arcs her body toward mine, her lips toward mine, and softly flicks her tongue into my mouth.

I'm split open with desire, happiness. We smile against each other's skin, and I inhale the salt-sweat smell of her, kiss her again, on her throat. Collarbones. Her hands thread through my hair and mine reach her chest—she gasps, and the sound alone has me spinning with heat. It's been only hours since I've looked at her this way, but it could be years, centuries, for all that it matters. I'm starved for her, all the time, even now—I want every part of her, to devour her, to inhale her, but I also want her slowly; to see her, to listen to her, to listen inside of her, and so I force myself to stop. To trail my fingers slowly over the soft skin of her thighs, and pull back to see her expression.

Just looking at her face unmoors me. Cheeks flushed, skin shimmering, lips red and swollen with kissing, her head is tilted back, throat arched under the dome. But she can feel me watching her and reels her head back up, takes my hands, and pulls them onto her hips. The sound of her silk skirt sliding up against her silk skin is like silver on crystal.

Who is she? Who is this girl who would allow me to do

this, here, now? And how am I allowed to have her?

I kiss the inside of each knee and up, farther, the roughness of my cheek raising redness on her skin. Then she grips each of my forearms, rocks herself back, and in one agonising, shimmering moment, one of her hands reaches beneath the hem of her dress, between her legs. Then her underwear slips to the ground.

A sharp hitch of breath. Mine. My head tilts down to kiss her skin, all of it, every bit I can reach. Just as I feel the warmth of my breath meeting the warmth of her body, my mind seizes.

I'm not looking at Mara—I'm looking at a reflection in a distant, black, stagnant puddle below me. At a reflection that isn't mine. And then I jump to meet it.

4

THE DIRECTION OF HIS DREAMS

HERE IS NO SOUND, NO AIR, AS THE ROPE strains against someone's neck. Fingers claw at my throat—no, *his* throat—trying to undo what he's done. Then, the thoughts—his thoughts, his voice—storm my mind.

Help me help me help me help me help me help me help me hel—

Above me, worn stone opens to grey sky as a murder of crows takes flight overhead. It's the last thing I see through his eyes before I hear Mara scream my name.

I am in my body again, staring up at the veined white marble ceiling of the mausoleum, not at the sky, not at dark, wet stone. I see Mara in front of me, not emptiness.

"What happened?" Her voice is panicked, urgent, and I realise then that I'm gasping for air.

"Someone—" Someone what? My neck is still raw, and I reach for the rope that was just there.

"Did you see something—"

Images flicker behind my eyes, final still frames the boy captured before he died. Ruined stone, handmade tiles. A dead pigeon, a pile of feathers and bone in the corner of the . . . tower. He hung himself in a tower.

"He didn't want it," I say, knowing it without knowing how.

"Who?" Mara's hands cup my face. "Noah, what happened?"

I steady myself on the altar, and my eyes fall on the heavy wooden door, opened just a crack. "He killed himself *here*."

Mara is off the altar now and braced, her body humming with adrenaline. "Who?"

"I don't know."

"Where?"

"The ruins," I say, leading her to the door.

I've never been able to hear anyone's thoughts before. Gifted, Afflicted, Carriers, whatever the fuck we are—when one of us is dying, or about to, I feel what they feel—their pain and terror connects us. And I see what they see—enough to find out where they are, usually, but never with enough time to actually help them. I've grown used to failing them after I've seen and felt, and so many die—there's an emptiness that bleeds in from the edges, fills up the space where Feelings should be. I don't even feel guilty anymore—if it happens and I'm in public, I beg off and either invent an excuse (*Sorry, PMS*) or deflect and say/do something assholic. It's exhausting, being a witness, being a fraction of a victim each time—and there have been more that Mara knows not of. I don't lie to her (much), but I sweep dark things into the darkest corner of my mind so I can be with her, enjoy her, feel and see and hear her, because it's too late for them. I can't keep these memories in that corner forever, but I can close the door on them and step back into the present.

But not today. This one—he was different. I was in his mind—I *was* him, for the slightest moment. Completely dispossessed.

I'm so consumed still that I don't even realise that Mara's taken over leading us to the ruins until sound overwhelms me.

The air is clotted with sobs, panic, confusion—Mara can hear it, feel it too. It tightens her body, coils her muscles, and I realise she's holding my hand to soothe *me*, not herself. When I look away from her, I'm rather shocked to see that we've already crossed the bridge.

The gravel path forks toward the chapel and toward the ruins. She's tugging me toward the chapel—we're close enough now to see the crowd filing out. The volume's dialled up again, and a wave of exhaustion licks at my body.

I step back, pulling Mara closer to me. "Other way," I say, turning from the crowd. We wind back through the wood, avoiding eyes and ears, but something squirms in my spine the nearer we get. We push past dark spiky woven branches—Mara scratches her cheek on one. The only sound is that of twigs crunching beneath our shoes, and I'm grateful.

And then we're there, standing in the shadow of the old abbey. The smell of cold, damp earth and wet layers of leaves hooks onto childhood memories and tries reeling them to the surface of my mind. I slide them away so I can see what Mara sees instead.

Her head tilts up. "This place is . . . bigger than I thought it would be. Up close."

"Bigger on the inside," I say. She nods absently.

We cross beneath a carved archway, and our footsteps echo on the stone, spiralling off against the flying buttresses. The sound rings in my teeth. If I didn't know this place so well, I wouldn't have found him as quickly.

A massive, grassy courtyard opens up to our left, but I turn right instead, past a row of stone stumps that were once columns, toward the old bell tower. Water trickles from somewhere, and a high, rising call sounds above us, like a warning. I look up just in time to see the arc of a sparrowhawk's wing in the corner of my eye before I see *him*.

Mara's gait is steady, panther-sleek, neither disgusted nor

afraid. I shouldn't be either, but there's a smell coming off him. I can taste it in my mouth, acrid and wild.

Fear.

I put my hand out to stop her, but my hand catches air.

The body is still swinging, barely. That's what I notice first. Then the slight trickle of blood from his nose that runs over his lip, his chin, before the droplet falls to the still, dark puddle beneath his body.

Something in my stomach flips. I ignore that warning call again, skittering off the tower, and approach Mara. She's standing so still I'm not even sure she's breathing.

I've seen dead bodies before. The boy and girl Jude killed at Horizons to show Mara and me how willing he was to kill, full stop. Same age as us, throats slit, blood and urine staining the sand beneath their bodies, and I was immune to it. I saw-heard-felt only Mara. And there were others, but again, next to her, they didn't register. Their soundlessness was nothing because Mara's notes spiked higher.

This boy, though. There's horror here. A violated dignity that scrapes at my skin. I force myself to look, to ignore the hollowness of him beating at my ears, a black hole of sound, pulling everything around us into silence. *Including* Mara. I hear her breath from the outside, steady and even, but nothing else. No heartbeat, no pulse, no *her*.

"*Noah.*"

I startle at her voice. "What?"

"Do you know him? I asked you twice. You were staring off at something else." She turns her head, and I follow the line of her gaze. It stops at a bloody mess of white feathers and bone. A hawk's kill. A dove.

"What's wrong with you?"

I shake my head. "It's not me, it's him." I force myself to look again. His fingers are beginning to blue, like his eyes—open, like his mouth, slightly parted as if he's about to speak. The rope creaks; the sound of it fills my head.

Mara's voice, then. "Yeah. I feel it too."

"What?" I ask.

"He's like a block of ice," she says curiously.

"You *touched* him?"

"You know better," she says. It's true, she would never have done. Evidence. A defence lawyer's daughter then and now and always.

"Here, come closer." She puts her hand in mine and feels me stiffen, ignores it. We approach him again together.

She's right. The cold spirals off him, chilling the air, as if he'd been dead for days instead of moments.

"Do you know him?" she asks me again, enunciating each word.

I can't answer. My eyes keep bouncing off his face, registering only the smallest of details, refusing to assemble them into a coherent picture. It doesn't make sense, this hollowness, my resistance, that feeling of warning in the air, pushing back against me.

"I'm not sure," I say. There's something familiar about him—he feels like someone I *should* know, though that doesn't make any sense.

Mara's head turns to the side. "People will come," she says.

They should be coming already. Had it not been for the commotion—the horses, the coffin, everything—they might've even seen it happen.

That's what he wanted. He *wanted* to be seen.

I step backward, away from him, away from Mara, my feet carrying me through arches and passages I didn't know I remembered. Mara calls after me, but I'm drawn forward anyway, trying to hear his last thoughts instead of her voice. My footsteps echo against the stone until I stand before an iron gate.

It's open. It shouldn't be. I know this gate, stood before it as a boy, had to steal the key to get past it to the steps. But now it's open, creaking with rust as I push through and climb the stairs. Moss and lichen grow on the damp stones, but I don't slip—I remember this place, and when the staircase ends I know exactly what I'll see.

I step out onto the ledge. If I look down, I'll see the knot where the boy tied the rope his broken body now swings from.

But that isn't what I see when I look down. I see Mara's face. And fear upon it.

5

THE DESPERATE COUNTRY

YOU SCARED THE SHIT OUT OF ME," SHE SAYS once I've climbed back down. I take her hand too tightly and begin snaking our way out of the ruins.

"Did I?"

"My 'Stop! Don't! Come down!' shouts didn't give it away?"

"Wasn't listening." I'm still not, quite. There's a gated exit that should bring us closer to the house without being seen. I'm sure my absence hasn't gone entirely unnoticed, but I'd rather my presence with Mara, here, remain so.

"I was screaming," Mara says. Her voice sounds distant behind me.

"Sorry." I duck under a low hedge archway that opens up to the old stone stable and falcon mews.

She frees her hand from mine. *"Sorry?"*

"You seem rather put out."

"You're being an asshole."

"I am rather good at it."

Mara stops, forcing me to turn back. She shifts on one foot; a branch snaps beneath her pointed Oxfords. "Why did you go up there?"

"Where?"

Her expression transitions from annoyance to worry. "Noah. The bell tower. The one you just climbed down from. What's going on with you?"

"Nothing," I lie. "I just wanted to see . . . what he saw. More than I could when he was dying."

"You could've fallen." Her face is as hard as the stones around us.

"Didn't though. And wouldn't have." I reach out to touch her cheek, expecting her to shy away, but she lets me. "I know this place, Mara. I wanted to find out what I could, while I could."

"Did you?"

"Not yet," I say, sliding my hand down her arm before I take her hand again.

The snorting and stamping and screeching of horses and birds follows Mara as we move through as quickly as we can to the service entrance (previously known as the servants' entrance). The door is locked.

I remember going through as a child, exploring "Below Stairs"—the old kitchen, servants' quarters, all of it as separate and unequal from the manor above as though it were part of a different world entirely. Which it was. Is.

"We have to go in through the hall," I say, arcing my head around. It'll mean the grand staircase, the great hall, the centre of the house, the centre of attention.

"The great hall," she says.

"That would be the one."

"Where literally everyone else at the funeral will be?"

"Indeed."

"No other way?"

"Lots, but we need to get there now. That's the fastest, so."

Mara squeezes my hand. Knows I've been wounded, somehow. She'll ask later, but for now, silence.

Until there isn't.

The house vibrates with noise. Everyone at the funeral has been corralled inside, and more cars are arriving by the moment, emptying old moneyed couples onto the gravel drive with rather alarming precision. We enter the house with one of them, me wishfully expecting to hear a stern, sombre *Thank you for your condolences, but the wake has been postponed*. Except we don't hear it. Instead, the fire's roaring, and a table has been placed in the centre, tyrannised by flowers and condolence cards. Servants are carting the Fortnum & Mason towers back to the sitting rooms, closed to visitors but today open for guests.

As we walk through the hall past the growing crowd, my grandmother walks among them, talking loudly about the weather, the tea, anything of absolutely no consequence she can grasp at, anything to avoid the unpleasantness of a suicide spoiling her son's funeral.

Because she must know of it by now—Grandmother is omniscient when it comes to the family, and this is her domain. She could have postponed this display, but instead she's probably called in favours to either postpone the arrival of the police or keep them out of view. If there's one thing she will never tolerate, it's scandal.

And whatever ears she's whispered in, whatever words she whispered—they're causing the desired effect. There's a surge of sounds hammering inside my head—quickening heartbeats, forced laughs—but I can't discern anyone talking about the boy, what happened to him, who he was, anything. People know something's wrong, but they don't know what it is yet—and likely won't, until they're able to whisper and gossip about it from the comfort and anonymity of their homes. How very English.

As soon as I think it, my grandmother appears. "Noah Elliot," she says with a clenched smile. "Darling," she adds for good measure, "we've been looking for you."

"I apologise," I say, matching her forced politeness with insincere regret.

My grandmother pauses, obviously debating whether to accept it or demand an explanation for missing the funeral. But that would mean causing a scene in front of Mara. My grandmother turns her steel blue eyes on her. "I must steal my grandson from you now. But please"—she gestures ever so graciously—"have some tea, a bite to eat—rest for a bit. I can have Allegra make up a bed for you in one of the downstairs rooms."

Mara opens her mouth to respond—to refuse, surely, if for no other reason than it being the middle of the bloody day—but I intervene. "I agree, sweetheart." Mara's expression is filled with such obvious incredulity at my use of *that* expression, it's nearly impossible to bite back my laugh. "Have a lie-down. It's been a trying day. I'll find you in a bit, just . . . make yourself at home."

A tiny smile at my extremely awkward code for "Go forth and find out what in fresh hell is going on." She nods and manages to feign a yawn. "You'll have to excuse me. I'm . . . overwhelmed?" She looks at me for approval, and gets it.

"Of course," my grandmother says, a lift in her voice whilst she takes my arm. And then I'm steered away, flicking a winner's grin over my shoulder at my girl. It takes a moment to register that I've been shuttled into a side corridor cordoned off from the public, filled with some of the many marble busts of past generations of Shaws, casting long shadows that slice the marble floor.

The staccato rhythm of my grandmother's heels halts once we're alone. "Noah," she says, casually brushing something from the shoulder of my suit. "It's time to discuss your inheritance."

6

SILVER FETTERS

THAT SENTENCE ECHOES UNDER THE ARCHED ceiling as though the statues themselves were repeating it.

Your inheritance. An inheritance. The inheritance.

The sun shines dimly from the mullioned, arched windows, transforming the wrinkles that fold my grandmother's face into a mask of light and shadow. She'd be almost cartoonishly frightening if she weren't standing beside a Greek statue of a smiling naked boy astride a ram.

"Is it really? The time?" I ask.

Chin lifted, she begins walking again. "Today has not gone as planned, I'm quite aware. But there are things that must be discussed, things that cannot wait."

There isn't any point in arguing. I want nothing to do with my father or what he's left behind. What he's done to me, Mara—it's more than enough. I needn't even say it—I can thin my smile and listen as my grandmother speaks and ignore whatever she says.

She walks ahead beneath the high, lonely ceilings, turns sharply to the left, where a bank of what must surely be unused rooms lie in wait for occupants who will never arrive. One of them gets lucky—my grandmother turns a gleaming glass knob, opening the door to a time capsule from the eighteenth century. The ceiling mouldings are tipped with gold, highlighting every carefully carved curve and corner, helped along by a drapey crystal chandelier fitted with actual tallow candles (unlit). Instead, the light comes from the lit, gilt-framed portraits in every size and shape. Everything in the room is perfectly preserved, arranged, to accommodate guests in waistcoats and corsets—not the Asian woman in business casual sitting in front of the fireplace. She seems so out of place that I blink, and she seems to disappear, then reappear the next instant.

"Noah, dear, allow me to introduce you to Ms. Victoria Gao, your father's attorney." Ms. Gao crosses the room to shake my hand, looking far too young for the grey bob that frames her face.

"She's here to inform you of the"—my grandmother, for

the first time, appears to scrabble around for the right words—
"responsibilities that you now possess as heir to your father's
estate."

I'd thought I was prepared for this, but the word "heir"
brings me up short. "Why isn't Katie here?"

"Your father named you as the executor of his will, once
you turn eighteen."

In just a few months, then. The air seems to flare with heat,
blazing. "I'm not sure I understand. Katie—"

"Your father expected you to provide for your sister as you
see fit, but he expressly prohibits the transfer of executorship
to your sister until she's reached twenty-five years of age."

"I'm not even eighteen—this makes no sense."

"Mr. Shaw, it isn't my job to question my clients' final
wishes."

"Then what is your job?"

"To make sure they're granted," she says, and holds out a
thick envelope. I put it on a side table inlaid with what was
probably ivory. Fuck this shit.

"Fine." I turn to my grandmother. "Am I free to go?" She
glances quickly at the envelope on the table and then at Ms.
Gao, whose expression remains placid.

"Not quite, I'm afraid," my grandmother says. "Your father
was our only child, which means that he was our sole heir.
He refused to use his title when he married your mother, but
never formally disclaimed it," she says with an ugly curl to her

mouth. "But that's all over and done now. You can reclaim the title of lord." She hits the big smile button. "And you may inherit our entire estate in addition to your father's."

"What about my sister?" My voice is new and rough-edged. "She loved our father, he loved her, she loves you, you love her—why is she being excluded?"

"She's only fifteen, dear."

"So? She's far more dedicated to preserving my father's legacy than I am."

That earns a sharp-edged smile. "Your grandfather and I are less concerned with your father's legacy than we are with the *Shaw* legacy. Your sister will marry, take her husband's name, no doubt, as will her children. Whereas, yours—"

"Grandmother," I say with a frozen little grin. "This is a difficult day for everyone. Why don't we leave this for another time? We're all exhausted, and there's the *incident* to think about."

Her eyebrows twitch at the word, but that's all the acknowledgment I need to know that I've struck a nerve. Which I consider to be an invitation to continue. "We should be thinking about practicalities now, not an unknowable future."

An expression of surprise, and dare I say, approval? "Yes. Well. That is a very mature suggestion, dear. Very well, then." She stands and smooths out her dress, pats her hair—nervous tics. I've thrown her, which makes me wonder how much she thinks she knows of me, what she may have heard in the few years since I left home. And who might've told her.

"I'll join your grandfather—I expect you'll be along soon?" She turns to Ms. Gao, who offers a bit of a nod. Then, to me, "I'd like to introduce you to the manor's curator. She'll be the one to tell you everything you need to know about the estate. If you happen to run into her before we meet again, do come and find me so I can make a proper introduction. She's wearing a red suit." Grandmother punctuates her sentence with a sniff, playing painfully to type.

"Of course," I say.

"Splendid. I'll leave you to it." She drifts slowly out of the room, as if waiting to be called back at the last second.

Ms. Gao does not approach the side table where the envelope lies, but indicates that I should open it. "In that envelope you'll find your father's personal financials—his liquid and real property assets, his wishes relating to Euphrates International Corporation, and—"

With my grandmother out of the room, I'm free to interrupt her. "Ms. Gao, I'd like to be very, very clear—I want nothing to do with my father. Including his money." Her expression is glass. "Give it away, burn it, I don't care. Give my sister what she needs and take the rest for yourself if you like." Still nothing. "Do you understand me?"

"Perfectly." She stands straight and still. "But what you're asking is impossible, legally. The funds have been automatically transferred into an account in your name. The account numbers, everything you'll need, is in that envelope. Ignore it if you like, but what belonged to your father is now yours to do with it what you will. You, and no one else." She stands and leaves the room, leaving me alone with the poisoned fruit of my father's poisoned labour.

The idea of touching the envelope repulses me. I intend to leave it there, to leave the room, the manor, the estate, everything behind.

But I don't. I take it and open it, skimming my father's last will and testament before something else catches my eye at the very end. The ghost of my father smiles as I read it.

Dear Mr. Shaw,

My sincerest condolences on your great and terrible loss. Naomi was a treasure; it was one of the great honours of my life to know her, and an even greater honour to teach her.

Your wife had a brilliant mind, of course, but it was her ferocious heart that struck me upon our first meeting. I thought I was prepared for it, but the extent of her gifts took even me by surprise, and mixed with the passion of her convictions, anyone in her orbit would find him or herself helpless to resist.

If she had been a lesser person, she could have used her gifts to indulge impulses and man's inherently selfish nature. Instead, she gave her life to give life, and not just to your children.

My position prevented me from getting to know you—we met only once, for the very briefest of moments, and you had quite a lot else on your mind then, rightly so, as your son was being born. As I know you've begun to suspect,

Noah is indeed special, in ways I'm afraid I can't begin to explain. It is the unfortunate nature of my own gifts that I am so limited in what I can say, but please know this: Your wife did not die in vain.

By the time you read this, I'll have left Cambridge, and we are not fated to meet again. I urge you to spend what time you would otherwise waste on searching for me with your son instead—he needs you, and the world needs him.

Your wife has bequeathed to you the greatest gift. Don't let her death be in vain.

Most Sincerely,

A. L.

7

A BLUNDERING ORACLE

WHEN I FIRST MET THE PROFESSOR, I was with Mara at a botanica in Miami, and he was masquerading as a Santeria priest (which I would've preferred). Abel Lukumi a.k.a. Armin Lenaurd a.k.a. whoever the fuck he is, in reality, is nothing more than a Gifted con man. He used my father, my mother, and will use me if I allow it. Before he vanished, my father explained, quite insanely, that he believed I would have to kill Mara because of Fate and Destiny, or else she'll inevitably kill me in some unspecified way. After that horror show, I received my own letter, as did Mara. Mine was from my mother, written to me before she died. Mara's was from the professor, but the message to both of us was the same: The die has been cast. Your role has been written. Be the hero and play it, or there will be no happy ending for either of you.

I made a decision that day, and it seemed I'd have to make another. I tear the professor's letter in half.

Fate is bullshit. Destiny doesn't exist. If I want a happy ending, I'll have to write it myself.

I find Mara poised in the middle of a balcony that rings the great hall. People in black swarm inside the house and then march out of it like ants. Mara has been pacing, tigerlike, between the two groups—I stuff the will and letter back in the envelope before I call out to her.

She rushes over. "Noah, I know who he is." She notices the envelope in my hand. "What is that?"

"Shit my dad said, essentially." The professor is rather a sore subject with us. "I'll explain later. What happened?"

"So, after you and your grandmother left, I tried to find my way out of the house so I could go outside and see what was happening with the body, but this place is Labyrinth, and I never made it." A look of clenched frustration, then a deep breath. "I was trying to get out of the house, and I ended up hitting a dead end—a staircase roped off with a little sign that said 'private' or whatever. Obviously, I stepped over it."

"Obviously."

"I ended up in this older part of the house—the rooms

46 · MICHELLE HODKIN

looked completely different," she says, glancing behind her shoulder at the great hall. "I ended up under the stairs? Beneath the stairs?"

"Below Stairs, do you mean?"

Her eyes light up. "Yes! Below Stairs. I ran into this complete caricature of an old English person who said his name was Bernard—he pronounced it *Bernerd*, by the way—"

"Naturally."

"He works for some charity, I think—preservation, maybe?"

"The National Trust?"

"Maybe? I think he said something else. Anyway, he told me I wasn't supposed to be down there, of course, and I played the dumb American."

"Not very well, I imagine."

Her mouth lifts into a half smile. "I start apologising, saying I got turned around, and that I was with you, and his eyes twinkled with this old-man-who-doesn't-get-to-talk-to-anyone-but-today's-his-lucky-day twinkle, and he pompously starts giving me a tour of 'Below Stairs.' Muttered something about rumours and 'that boy.' Right," she says, nodding as she registers my expression. "He's the first—maybe the only person I've met—to even mention him. So of course I ask, 'What boy?' And then he acts like he didn't hear me, telling me hundred-year-old stories about maids catching your ancestors having affairs, whispering about whose children belonged to whom, instead."

"But you kept on."

"No one has ever been more interested in the shit Bernard has to say. As far as Bernard knows."

"You looked up at him through your dark lashes, face full of wonder."

She grins. "Which makes him more enthusiastic and less willing to let me go. He starts showing me things that old valets and lady's maids and other indentured servants squirreled away—two-hundred-year-old kids' toys and these small trunks inlaid with silver and probably, horribly, ivory, so I start having a panic attack."

"Wait, are you joking?"

"No, I mean, sort of. It was a thing—the dumb-American game didn't seem to be working, so I worked up to the scared-little-girl game." She lifts her shoulders into a shrug. "I wanted to find out if he knew anything that actually *mattered*, but he sits me down and tells me to breathe."

She hates being told to breathe.

"I fucking *hate* it when people tell me to breathe—it's like telling me to smile. Like, *you* breathe."

"Dare I ask whether Bernard survived your encounter?"

"Fair question. I took pity on him because he's eight thousand years old."

"Generous."

"Indeed," Mara says, mimicking my accent. "Anyway, I started going on about how upset I am about your father, and *what happened* at the funeral, and then I go shivery and whisper, *Sixth Sense* style, that I saw the whole thing. He licked up everything I offered him, and then begins telling me, 'in strictest confidence' how 'The boy is the great-great-grandchild of a house maid that served your great-great-grandfather.' There are pictures of him somewhere, a portrait in the house. There's all of this stuff that goes back centuries, he said. Your family kept everything."

"Did he happen to add anything helpful, like, for example, where?"

"Yeah, no. He talked about servant records and family trees and shit being *here*, in the house, but *where* here, he didn't know. But he did give me a name."

"Need I ask?"

"Sam Milnes. Familiar?"

I shake my head.

"He's apparently also the great-great-grandson of the old groundskeeper, but his G3 was fired as soon as they discovered the lady's maid was pregnant, and moved south to do something else, I don't remember, and Sam's dad is a chef at a pub about an hour away from here. *Not* at the funeral."

"His father wasn't? Mother?"

"Nope. No one in his family. I asked specifically."

"Bad blood?"

"Bernard mentioned something about a rumour that he wasn't the groundskeeper's kid, that *someone* in the family knocked her up, then sent both of them packing to hide it." She shrugs one shoulder. "Or some other shit happened so long ago that no one cares about it anymore."

"Maybe Sam cared," I say, looking past Mara for a moment. I thought I spied a spot of red behind her. A red suit, perhaps?

"Or he knew something? I don't know. Why was he *here*?" she asks herself.

"He had the key," I say absently, trying to find the red-suited curator.

Her forehead scrunches. "What key?"

"To the bell tower he—the tower we found him in. That part of the ruins is only accessible by staff of the house and the Trust. He had the key, somehow, to unlock the gate."

"It—you don't think it's the same key his family would've had, do you? I mean, it's not like they had safety regulations in the . . ."

Great-great-grandfather. I do the maths. "Eighteen hundreds?"

A flicker of something passes over Mara's face, quick enough that I'm not quite sure whether I've imagined it.

"The gates are old—don't know when they were put up, but I couldn't get past them as a child. And I did try. Some of my first lock-picking attempts, in fact."

"Maybe we should go back and check?"

Maybe. Probably. But I need to check on something else, too. The professor's letter is scratching at my mind—as Father surely intended, for some undoubtedly twisted reason. And I don't want to bring it, or him, up with Mara. I'm entirely sure he's full of shit, and she—well. She's not. I can't give her any reason to think about him. We've been there before, and I know where it'll lead—with her wondering if she should leave me. For my sake—for my life, rather. But my life means nothing without her in it, so. Unmentioned the professor shall remain.

"Why don't you go back to find out what's happened with Sam?" I ask her.

"Okay," she says slowly. "But don't you think the English CSI equivalent is swarming the scene?"

Doubtful—my grandmother would pull whatever strings available to make sure they're doing whatever it is they do without being spotted by the guests. "Why don't you find out?"

Her head tilts. "Me? As in, just me?"

"I still haven't found Katie. I want to talk to her before we go."

Mara nods, but there's a wariness to her. I'm an extraordinary liar, but she knows me too well.

"What, you don't want to be alone?" That'll get her blood up.

"I don't care about that," she says with a slight lift of her chin.

"It's all right if you don't. I wouldn't."

"I'm *fine* by myself," she insists. "I just don't really know where I'm going."

"Right. I'll go with you back to the tower, but see if you can't find someone here who'll tell you whether the police have got here yet. I'll meet you back here as soon as I find Katie."

She's quiet. Not hurt—a bit annoyed, I think, but there's more to it than that. What, I don't know.

I fit my hand around her cheek, thumbing her bottom lip. "All right? I won't be a minute."

She nods, biting the tip of my thumb. Not softly, either.

I lean toward her, letting my lips graze her earlobe. "I'll be back very, very soon."

And then I leave her at the balcony, glancing back once and adding an arrogant grin for good measure before I take the stairs two at a time, past the great hall, past the thrumming masses of people and the silent statues, and head Below Stairs myself.

8

THE ENTERPRISES OF ANOTHER

I MEANT TO LOOK FOR BERNARD, OR FAILING THAT, the curator—one of them must be able to tell me more about Sam, which seems nearly as important as filling in the headspace the professor's letter is currently occupying. I find Goose instead, languidly rolling a cigarette in the doorway of a small, spare servants' bedroom.

I wouldn't be at all surprised if this were a postcoital smoke, the object of his brief affection tucking himself back into his pants or her shirt in some corridor. His heartbeat is thunderous, and my mind tilts under the weight of the buzzing throng of mourners above us.

"Neirin and Patrick split off," he says without looking up.

"Off to study for something. Good little Westminster boys they are. They send their condolences."

"Accepted," I say, masking the strain in my voice. "And you?"

A lift of one shoulder. "Bored. You?"

"Same," I lie.

"And how long are you planning to remain in your home country?"

"As briefly as I can arrange. We'll leave as soon as Grandmother releases us from her clutches. Tomorrow, if I have the chance."

"Not a prayer," Goose says, grinning.

"Where are you off to after this?"

"Family's in Cornwall whilst the weather holds." He lights the cigarette, cupping his hand around the flame. "Or Father is, in any case. Mother's claimed the London town house in what promises to be the beginning of a spectacular divorce."

Goose, a year older than Patrick, Neirin, and I, was a fellow boarder despite the local family, same as I. Tumultuous childhood he never spoke of but others whispered about. Obviously, I sympathise. "Sorry, mate."

"I'm not." He blows out a curl of smoke. Casual tone betrayed by his rapid heartbeat, the tightness in his frame, the sharp, quick chop of his breath between drags. "Thought I'd go for a Gap Yah," he says, taking the piss.

"Where to?"

"Undecided," he says with a classic scowl-smile I've only ever seen on him. "Thailand's pedestrian. Thought of skipping about the world, but it's exhausting just thinking about it." His face twitches into mischief. "Perhaps I'll join you in New York."

"Who says I'm heading to New York?"

"Your girl. Overheard her conversation with your stepmother, I believe."

Perfect. I'd hardly spoken to Ruth of my plans myself. I really should find her. And my sister.

"She's quite something," Goose says, sweeping me back into the present. "How'd you meet?"

"My stepmother? I thought everyone knew that story."

"You're really not that clever, you know."

"You love me anyway," I say, leaning against the wall. "We met at school."

"That pit in Miami?"

"The very same."

"I'm guessing she's the reason you lost touch."

And there it is. "About that—"

"You don't need to explain," Goose says, which is brilliant, because I can't explain, at least, not in any way that would be satisfying.

"I'm sorry. Truly."

"No worries, truly. We've all been busy, haven't we?"

That's a word for it. "Tell me about you. Your life."

He barks out a laugh. "It's my life. Same shit, you know. Was going with El for a while—"

"El? You've crushed on her since she was at St Margaret's. Bravo, chap."

Being back here makes me feel like the child I was when I used to visit, a regression I'm not particularly keen to experience. And yet here we are, ribbing each other the way we had at Liddell (House. The school divides its students into houses. Yes, like Hogwarts). I wonder a bit why Goose stayed after Neirin and Patrick left—the real reason. But if I ask, he'll never say.

So I ask instead, "You still together?"

Shakes his head, blows out smoke, his body loosening. I can hear it, his joints relaxing, eyes drooping closed. Feigned boredom, actual sadness, a fading discordant note in the speeding, roaring mixture of sound that has me feeling bruised and exhausted—and sad—myself.

Goose is as homeless as I would be, without Mara. And I can actually *hear* how shittily he feels about it. Which must be why I say, "Come with us."

A cock of an eyebrow.

"To New York."

"And do what?"

"Whatever it is people do during their gap year. Observe the American people. Learn their savage customs."

"I've been hearing rumours about this mysterious thing called a Brazilian arse lift?"

"That . . . is something some do, yes."

"Intriguing." His cigarette is mostly ash, and he smothers it against the bottom of his bespoke shoe. If his family didn't have quite the fortune mine does, they weren't short by much.

"Where'll you live?" he asks me.

"Don't know yet."

"Manhattan?"

"Might do." Though it's always felt like walking through a hive, with stacks of people reaching for a smear of sunlight and a glimpse of water. I don't love it the way Mara does, but then, I don't know that I love anything the way she does. She's on a different spectrum entirely. A human one, basically.

"You'll have to buy a penthouse, you know," Goose says thoughtfully.

"Naturally."

"With terraces and all that."

"Of course."

"Disgustingly expensive."

Back to money. Family's or father's money, each with strings attached—psychological if not legal.

"Highly likely."

"Well, let me know when you decide," he says, and stands straight. The notes in his voice swirl in little eddies as he moves. I'm hyperaware of everything today in a way I'm not usually. "Might join you after all."

"You can fly over with us. I'll send you confirmation when we book it."

He holds out his hand to shake mine. "Good chap. Done then." His heartbeat turns a bit faint for a moment. "You're sure, mate?"

For some reason, I am. And say so.

"See you at Heathrow, then," Goose says lightly. He thinks I mean for a week, month tops.

"Manchester, actually," I say.

"Fuck."

"More convenient."

"True," he says, and stands. "Well, mate, apparently I've got a flight to pack for."

"Goose," I say. He pauses in the doorway.

"Pack to stay for a while."

"Shall do. And, mate?"

I raise my brows.

"I really am sorry about all this." He pauses. "About your father."

I'm not. But this is England, so I thank him rather than saying so. Once he's gone, I reopen the will. And ignore the torn letter, though I can't quite bring myself to bin it. The last thing my father did before he died was decide what I should have, and that included this. The words are imprinted on my mind.

She gave her life to give life, and not just to your children.

Don't let her death be in vain.

I take the stairs up, bypassing the hall and doing my best to avoid absolutely everyone. My father had no love for what I am, for my so-called Gifts. Everything he'd ever done for me was actually for my mother, who loved the promise of me so much she was willing to sacrifice her future for it, for which he never forgave me. He's the one who forced me to choose between killing the girl I love or her brother, more like family to me than he ever was, and *he's* the one who walked away from us—not just me but Katie, and Ruth, never to be seen or heard from again. Until, of course, he turned up dead, having stabbed himself in the neck with a shard of glass. Officially, it was suicide. Unofficially . . . I suppose we'll never know, and I can't help but smile when I think of what my grandmother must've gone through to bury the *scandal* as deeply as she's done. One would think a family would want to know the truth about how their loved one died, but the fact that my father was found on the anniversary of the date my mother was killed seemed to be enough for them. And the fact that there was, reportedly, a suicide note. I haven't seen it, and honestly don't care to. He deserved what he got, however he got it.

My mind skitters back to that letter. He couldn't resist this one last fuck-you, could he? I can give away his money, I can burn down his life's work, but he knew I wouldn't be able to throw out this letter. Not till I find out what it means. And

I can't do that without digging through the past of House Shaw, and for that I wish for the first and only time that my father could be alive for one more moment—so I could spit in his face.

Part II

All houses wherein men have lived and died
Are haunted houses. Through the open doors
the harmless phantoms on their errands glide,
With feet that make no sound upon the floors.

—Henry Wadsworth Longfellow, *Haunted Houses*

9

THE WORST VICE BETRAYED

TWO BRUTAL DAYS PASSED BEFORE I WAS released from England. Family obligations kept me from spending any meaningful (and by meaningful I mean alone) time with Mara, and so I tried to spend the hours with Katie, but she wanted no part of me. She knew how I hated our father, and now she knows she's been left out of the will.

"David had this all arranged for a long time, Noah," my stepmother said when I finally got around to speaking to her about it. She'd flipped through the will and shrugged. "It's classic *him*."

"What's that?"

"Even at university, it was so clear that he was trying to *be* his family and escape his family at the same time." She'd gestured to the statues everywhere, the painting on the dome of the great hall. Scenes of angels and gods, Greek and Roman figures looming in every corner of the house and grounds. "Our house in Florida?" Ruth asked. "Notice any similarities?"

She was right, of course. Exactly, obviously right. He'd arranged it the same way—on a smaller scale, obviously. But the resemblance was clear. Painfully so.

"David doted on Katie when she came along, of course, but from the moment you were born, he treated you like a grown man, grooming you for . . . all this. Your mother," her throat closed over the word. "Your mother drew that out of him like poison from a wound, rolled it up into a little ball, and threw it away. When she was—when she died," she says, swerving away from *murdered*, "the poison crept back in again. Little by little." She sighed. "He really should've been in therapy."

If she only knew.

My stepmother and my sister were already well provided for through trusts established while my father was living—I had one myself, actually—and Ruth insisted that she didn't want anything else, wouldn't take anything else. The will was more symbolic than anything, she said—a passing of the torch and responsibility and all that, not so much a Gringotts vault full of gold. Pity me.

As Ruth and Katie had decided to live in Florida—my

stepmother for her veterinary practice and my sister for, God knows why, honestly. Friends, a boyfriend, perhaps? Regardless, good-byes were said, our plane boarded, and then Mara, Goose, and I embarked for our return home, and Goose's sojourn from his. I told Mara Goose would be starting off his gap year in New York. I hadn't mentioned that I'd invited him to live with us, but what could go wrong.

She promptly fell asleep on my shoulder upon takeoff in any case, and we were all staying in hotels for the moment anyway, so. Plenty of time.

Throughout the seven-hour flight, plans spun through my head, and I began e-mailing with Ms. Gao. As Mara says, wanting something doesn't make it real. But sometimes, money can. Today, it would.

Duffels shouldered, we three handed them off to the waiting driver when we landed at JFK, and Goose split off from us to the Gansevoort ("Spectacular pool"). Mara was visibly thrilled to be here—Daniel's already in the city, creating some groundbreaking individualised study colloquium at NYU or something, lured by a full scholarship and the most posh room and board situation the American higher education system has on offer. As for the rest of her family, they've been planning to move back up to the Northeast with him, to be together after, well. After their Miami experience, shall we say. Long Island instead of Rhode Island, this time; her father's found a job with one of his old law school mates, and Joseph's enrolled at a private school, and as far as they know, Mara will be spending what should be her senior year auditing classes in the city and going to therapy to try and transition back to normalcy—is what Jamie told them. I think. We should probably get our stories straight. Or fuck it, hakuna matata.

We're dropped off at the Plaza Athénée at eight in the morning, blinking dully beneath the pink and orange sky. Mara is pale, exhausted—she slept on my shoulder on the flight as I typed, but fitfully. I watch her, the membrane of her eyelids a light purple, her dark lashes curled and fluttering with dreams. I wondered what was happening behind those eyelids, under her dark waves of hair, inside that head. She never did manage to get back to the ruins, and I never did manage to find out more about Sam, but it doesn't matter.

I'm heir to the Shaw estate. Ms. Gao's sole occupation is to take my orders as I give them. But my desire to give Mara everything is greater than hating myself for taking what my father made, and used to torture her.

The documents—his, my grandmother's—I feel polluted when I touch them. But I can do things now that they never would, make choices they would never make. Try and fix what my father had broken, help the people he hurt. So sign the papers I do. In a week, the revolution would begin, and I can find out everything I never wanted to know about my family if I choose. But for now . . .

We're whisked into the hotel, glimmering chandeliers

above, the papered walls bursting with rich colours, and Mara hardly notices that we don't formally check in. Everything's been handled already.

"Oh my God," Mara says, collapsing onto the bed, splayed out like a starfish. I unbuckle one of her boots, then the other, letting them drop to the floor. Peel off her socks. She flips over onto her back to watch me with artist's eyes, then arches up so I can slide off her jeans, blinking dreamily.

I've seen her in the middle of the night and the middle of the day, with makeup and without, with her hair done up and when it's been unwashed for days. I've seen her in jeans and in silk and in nothing. I would gladly spend the rest of my life just looking at her.

Thankfully, I'm allowed to do more than that. I climb up her body to take off her shirt, and the feel of her skin makes me ten times more awake.

And then I see what she's wearing underneath. Her chest is cupped in black edged with ivory lace, her arse in cheeky boy-shorts that match.

"Do you like them?" she asks, her voice soft, her eyes closed now.

"Not enough to keep them on you," I say, reaching to unfasten and tug, but she doesn't move.

"Mara?"

No answer. Her breath is deep and even. I bounce lightly on the bed just to confirm it, and, yes, she is in fact asleep.

With a heavy, pathetic sigh, I get up to close the curtains so the sunlight doesn't wake her, and pull the comforter up over her body. I bend down to kiss her cheek and whisper, "You're a mean girl, Mara Dyer."

She smiles in her sleep.

10

THE AMUSEMENT OF MANKIND

HER MOBILE RINGS IN THE EVENING—WE'VE both slept away the day, it seems.

"Who?" she moans, her voice hoarse. She makes no move to get it, so I untangle myself from her limbs and search her discarded clothes for it to no avail.

"Nightstand," she mumbles.

My carefully cultivated look of disdain is completely wasted on her, as she's thrown her arm over her eyes.

A glance at the screen reveals the caller. "It's our favourite bisexual Jewish black friend."

"Which?"

I try handing the phone to her and she waves it away. "Can't. Exhausted."

"It's jet lag, not Ebola."

"That doesn't even make sense," she says, awake now. "Just answer it."

I do, whipped dog that I am, and put it on speaker. "Hello, you've reached the winter of man's discontent."

"That's Mara's line. Did you throw her into the Thames?"

"I'm afraid not. She's here, sleeping."

"Well, wake her up! I need her."

"Then come over and rouse her yourself," I say just as Mara snatches the phone from me. Speaker still on.

"Hey," she says. "What's going on?"

"Hijinks. Gang's all here."

"Who?" I ask, as she says, "Where?"

"Me, Daniel, Sophie. Frank."

Sophie being Daniel's girlfriend. She made it into Juilliard, thankfully, as he's so besotted with her he might've followed her if she'd gone somewhere else.

"Who the devil is Frank?"

"Restaurant between Fifth and Sixth on Second."

"We should invite Goose," I say to Mara. She nods.

"WTF?" Jamie says. "You want to eat goose?"

"You'll like him," Mara says. The strap of her bra slips down her shoulder as she gets up, pulls on her clothes from yesterday.

"When'll you be here?"

Mara glances at me over her shoulder. "Car or train?"

"Either."

"We're taking a car," Mara says. "So maybe nine?"

"We'll entertain ourselves at the bar while we wait."

"Mind-fucking the bartenders of New York already?" I ask.

"Why waste a good mind-fuck on drinks?"

"With great power comes great responsibility."

"Exactly. Now get your asses over here before I tell the staff it's your birthday and have the restaurant sing when you walk in." The call ends before I can respond. "Twat," I say to the phone.

Meanwhile, Mara's begun rummaging through my luggage, and for the briefest of moments, my stomach drops. The will is somewhere in there, and the letter, and the moment I realise she might see them, and read them, is the moment I realise I don't want her to. I will tell her. Just . . . not yet.

"I'll dress myself, thank you," I say, trying to edge in ever so casually. Which bag did I put the documents in? I can't even remember.

She shrugs. "Okay. If you wear the blue stripey shirt, I'll have sex with you later. But it's up to you."

"Will you hand me my bollocks when you get a moment? They're in one of your bags, I think."

She looks at me with doe's eyes and a shark's smile as I dress. On our way out, we catch our reflection in the mirror.

the becoming of noah shaw · 71

Mara rises to tiptoes and nips at the lobe of my ear before whispering, "Good choice."

We get to the restaurant just before Goose does. He exits a cab, and I glimpse a pair of long, crossed legs dangling inside. A burst of female laughter erupts before the door slams.

I arch my eyebrows, and Goose says, "Those Brazilian arse lifts are in fact a real thing."

Mara looks from him to me, back to him again. "What am I missing?"

"Nothing. Your arse is perfect," I say, squeezing it.

A roll of eyes and a swing of hips and she's inside the restaurant, which is bursting with people. It didn't sound nearly this loud over the phone—even without my ability, I'd hardly be able to hear anyone over the roar. As it is, my head feels spinny.

"All right, mate?" Goose asks, and I nod quick. Not good that he noticed.

"Sister!" I hear Daniel's shout above the rest, see his tall frame unfold from behind a long table. Mara hugs her brother gently, then Jamie fiercely.

"I missed you," she says over the noise. "Both of you." I'd probably say the same, if I wouldn't rather die than admit it.

"It's only been a week," Daniel says.

"I know. But it felt longer. England's weird."

"Is it?" Goose asks her.

Jamie notices Goose for the first time. "Noah," he says, eyes remaining on my sort-of-childhood friend. "You came bearing gifts."

"Hey," Daniel says, reaching up to shake his hand. "I'm Daniel, Mara's brother."

A nod and smile. "Goose. Noah's Westminster plaything."

A bat of Jamie's lashes. "So all of my English boarding school fantasies *are* true."

"I'm Sophie," Daniel's girlfriend says with a bright, open smile, the corners of which reach the tips of her nearly white blond hair.

"What kind of a name is Goose?" Jamie asks, feigning interest in the champagne sweating on the table, which he pours into Goose's glass before I take it and fill ours.

"The kind of name one earns at English public schools such as ours when one engages in the sort of ill behaviour we have."

"So a nickname, then?"

"One doesn't divulge the origins of such a name. Removes all mystery."

In point of fact, I couldn't even remember the origins myself. He was just always . . . Goose. Of course, he was Alastair Greaves in truth, but no one has ever called him that in my hearing.

Jamie turns to Daniel. "I can't really imagine whispering 'Goose' in bed, can you?"

A firm shake of Daniel's head. "Not even dignifying the question with an answer."

"Now, did you do something *to* a goose to earn your moniker?"

Goosey pretends to think about it for a moment. "Not so much 'to' as 'with,' I'd say."

"The goose verbally consented," I say.

Daniel turns to Sophie. "I post- and preemptively apologise for literally everyone at this table, for everything they've said or are going to say, for the rest of the night."

"Apology accepted," she says, kissing Daniel on the cheek.

"I think you have competition for your most-disgusting-couple award," Jamie says to Mara.

"We're not disgusting," Mara says, then pauses thoughtfully. "We're . . ."

"Smutty?"

"Yes!"

"I do have other friends," Daniel says to Sophie.

Mara raises her glass. "But only one sister."

"I will drink to that." Daniel clinks his glass to hers.

"So what are you all doing in New York?" Sophie looks at each of us.

Jamie lies first. "Early admission to NYU."

Sophie's eyebrows scrunch together. "That's . . . I didn't know that was a thing," she says slowly. "So you graduated from Croyden early?"

"Yes," Jamie says, his voice distinct and resonant now. The Jedi mind-fuck at work. "Mara and Noah too, in point of fact." It's the party line we're towing—Mara's family swallowed it eagerly. They want to believe; Jamie just helps them along.

Sophie nods, grins broadly, erasing all signs of scepticism. "And you guys"—she looks at us—"Are you going to stay here too?"

Mara's nose wrinkles with her smile. "Yeah," she says, turning to me. "I think we are."

"What are you going to do?"

I look at my girl. "Whatever we want."

11

WHAT YOU SEE

WE CLOSE DOWN THE BAR AND FORM A quivering circle on the street. The scale ranges from tipsy (Jamie and Sophie) to piss drunk (Mara and Daniel). Goose is solid, having inherited his tolerance from a long purebred line of alcoholics. I'm a blaze of energy standing between him and Mara, listening to the rumble of the subway beneath us and the footsteps/heartbeats/chatter of (mostly) students far more pissed than we. The moon hangs in the faded blue sky, and I feel a hundred times awake.

"Cab?" Jamie asks us. I realise then I've no idea where he's been staying.

"Train," Sophie says. "I'm in Lincoln Center."

Daniel shakes his head. "Come back to Palladium with me? I'd feel better if you didn't go home alone."

"Some of us have to get up early." Do I detect a sliver of resentment beneath that formerly cheery soprano?

"Then I'll go with you."

"We'll all go with you," Mara says. I can tell she doesn't want to let Daniel go quite yet. She looks to me for agreement, and I give it. After a fashion.

"We'll come for the ride, though Sophie volunteers as tribute to hold your hair when you vomit," I say to Daniel, and he's not so wasted that he can't glare. "We can all take the F."

A sceptical, slow stare from Mara. "How do you know?"

"While you were sleeping I memorised the MTA transit map."

"Really?"

"No," I pull her into my waist. "But you get carsick, so, I'm calling it. Goose?"

"Whatever, mate. This is your town."

Jamie snorts. "I can take the F too, so. I'll make sure you . . . toffs . . . don't get lost."

"A-plus use of 'toffs,'" Goose says brightly.

"Wait," Mara draws out the word. "Where are you staying?"

"Aunt's." Jamie's voice is clipped. A shiver ripples through Mara, and something closes off behind Daniel's eyes. I don't miss the exchange that passes between them—but it's hardly the time to ask.

We walk to the F, noisily (Goose), quietly (Daniel), nervously (Sophie), pensively (Jamie). Mara's melting into dead weight in my arms.

"How much did you drink?"

She holds up three fingers.

"Did you eat?"

"Mmmhmm." Lying.

"We're going to have to work on her," Goose says, tipping his chin toward Mara. "Unless you prefer them unconscious now?"

"Were you always such an incredible cunt?" I ask.

"Yes."

"How did I miss that?"

"You didn't."

Jamie cuts in. "If I'd had to guess, between the two of you, I personally would've thought Noah would be the one with a predilection for geese. He does love animals."

"Mm, no," Goose says. "That's the Welsh. And sheep."

"An ugly stereotype," I say.

"Did you know," Mara says to Jamie, "that Wales is a whole different country?"

Jamie looks me in the eye. "She is very drunk."

"They have their own language! It's crazy!"

"Never," Daniel says slowly. "Mix. Alcohol. And. Jet. Lag."

Mara pats her brother's shoulder. "Thank you, Gandalf."

"I prefer Giles! We've been over this. Tolkien is problematic."

"Maybe. Who cares? I love him anyway."

"That's the title of your Lifetime movie," Jamie says, "*I Love Him Anyway: The Mara Dyer Story*," and even I start laughing, because it's fucking brilliant.

Mara manages to give him the finger and descend the stairs to the subway simultaneously. I'm quite proud.

We're swallowed by heat beneath the city, as well as about a dozen New Yorkers milling about on the platform, still clinging to the edges of the night. Mara leans against me, Jamie flirts rather bizarrely with Goose, and Sophie and Daniel settle into a quiet but relaxed silence as I observe what the East Village at two a.m. has to offer; a birdlike girl with wide-set eyes, headphones far too large for her blond head, standing at the very end of the platform. A woman in a black suit, typing furiously on her laptop in one of the bench seats. There's a somewhat round student in bright blue jeans and a gold cardigan with another boy—bearded, curly haired—tugging at his jeans and pulling him in close for a kiss. Farther down, a guy our age looks down the tunnel. He's not tall, but holds himself as though he wants to be. He's thin but soft-looking, somehow, and quite pale. He stares at the tunnel, waiting for the train like everyone else, I think—until I catch him watching *me*. His eyes are a startling, unclouded blue. I hold his gaze until it slides past me, into shadow.

Each person is thinking a thousand thoughts I'll never know, living lives I can only pretend to invent, and then wonder what, if anything, they see and think when they look at me—at us, my eyes flickering toward Mara's for less than a second. Are we the students we're pretending to be, exhausted from drinking too much and laughing too loud and dancing too hard tonight? Or aimless gap-year wanderers, on our way to the next adventure? Are Mara and I girlfriend/boyfriend? Not husband/wife, surely?

The air belowground is dead and feverish, until it isn't. At first I think, astonishingly, that I might've had too much to drink—the world seems to tilt, and darken, and a rush of noise fills my skull.

Then, strands of blond hair whip in front of my eyes, lash at my skin, and I know it's happening again.

I feel someone else's fear, someone else's shame, the searing light of the oncoming train on her retinas, and the ground gives way to air as she jumps. She screams before she dies.

Dark, sharp pain condenses, a collapsing star. I see her last view before her eyes shutter forever. The stinging light, dingy metal—hear the screech and horn and sparks on tracks coming on so fast I can't breathe.

And this time, again, I know her thoughts, as I knew Sam's. The last ones. The feeling, hearing, seeing isn't new—that's always been there, all along, part of my (dis?)ability. But this.

I'm cut down by the words in her head: furious unstoppable terror pain shame and—

I'm back inside myself, my mind belongs to me again, but it rings with her agony. Jamie's voice has risen above the rest—time's passed, because there are police, clearing everyone out. My thoughts are divided; part of me notices Sophie weeping, Daniel getting sick, Goose stunned, and Mara, beside me, her voice mist-smooth through it all. The rest of me is with Beth—

Beth. That's her name.

Was her name.

"Noah." Mara's voice reaches me from the filth of the tunnel, from the freeze-frames of metal and rust and excruciating light, and I manage to stand and look up. Which is when I realise I hadn't been standing—I'd been slumped against a pillar. My eyes skim past Mara, she's blurred and shivering, as is everyone else. Or no, not everyone. That boy—the amphibious-looking one, is somehow in focus. He's staring right back at me.

I open my mouth, and my jaw aches. Mara's soft fingers are on my rough cheeks, bringing my face to look at hers. Her skin her eyes her curls her lips form my name but they don't quite form *her*. It's as though she's hyper-pixelated, almost.

"I saw—"

"Shh. I know."

"I felt her—"

"I know."

She begins to come back into focus. "Mara—"

"Don't talk. You're hurt—your head hit the concrete—"

"I'm fine." I'm not.

"Can you walk?"

Can I? "Of course." I reach up to clasp her forearm and see . . . writing. On my own arm.

Letters, numbers. My bones are ringing with echoes of Beth's last . . . everything . . . and my own senses are completely overwhelmed. I blink, hard. The writing is still there. It takes a bit to realise that what I'm seeing is an address.

Jamie, Mara, and I are last to ascend the stairs as the police attend to the mess of what was once a girl, once a person, once like us. I move by focusing on the heartbeats around me—Jamie, fast. Mara, hard.

Two more. A look across the tracks again. The boy is gone.

I look down at my arm again. The address is still there.

12

A FACT OF THE IMAGINATION

THE PURPOSE-DRIVEN LIFE. IT'S WHAT WE'RE supposed to want, or do. Carpe diem, that shit.

Thing is, I don't have one. Beth, however, did.

I hear her voice in my mind, feel her last memories written in her script, somehow, in the grey folds of my brain. Beth's Top Five Greatest Hits:

One: Her ninth birthday party, a gulf of a pool, a juicy sun, girls cracking open with laughs, her father's warm face.

Two: Eleven years old. Piano recital, fingers skimming ivory, notes perfect, gorgeous, the feel of heart-bursting pride.

Three: First concert. Her mother, the cool-cool kind, all

real, all love. Stevie Nicks provides the score.

Four: First kiss, first love. I'll say nothing more—that belongs to Beth. Only her.

And five: Discovering her Gift. The thought is there, but her Gift itself is vague, gauzy—I can see the brand of the piano she played at her recital, the closed-up hole in her father's ear where a stud used to be, but I can't get at her ability. Each time I try, another detail from just before her death reveals itself; the white scuffing on the tan leather strap of her tote bag. The edge of a tattoo peeking out from the cuff of her sleeve. A slight smear of blood on her first knuckle.

All I'm truly left with, really, is this: the absolute certainty that she didn't want to kill herself. She didn't want to die. She didn't want to jump.

But she did.

Those suicides weren't the first I've witnessed. I've thought about my own, to the point where as a child the *Peter Pan* quote "To die will be an awfully big adventure," felt like a taunt. But there had been others, other Carriers, other Gifted. A Swedish girl who slit her wrists in the bath. A boy in America who left the car running in his parents' garage. There had been only the two, and they were like and not like me—they did want to die, and they *could* die. I felt what they felt, but also an urge not just to help them, but to join them. Sometimes, particularly when this was all new, it felt like I *was* joining them. Like connections were forming, new nerves were firing, drop cloths were being pulled from dusty furniture.

Confession: What I understand that They—most everyone, really—don't, is that suicide isn't an act of selfishness. Sometimes the hurt/pain/shame/loss is so much, so constant, and with no guarantee that it'll ever dissolve, sometimes the cost/benefit analysis of life/death truly feels like it'll only ever work out in in favour of death. I never knew the names of the boy and girl who killed themselves before, but I felt what they felt as they died. It was like—imagine the best moments of your life. Then try to subtract them. Subtract every ounce of joy you've ever experienced. Erase every happy memory you've ever had.

I couldn't hear what they'd been thinking as their lives drained from their bodies, but I could feel their relief. They didn't want to hold on. They were happy to let go.

But not Beth. Not Sam.

This is what people who have never wanted to die don't understand: the worst thing for those of us who do is feeling like we have to live when we don't want to. We have to do things we don't want to. We have to be where we don't want to be. What we want is nothingness, numbness, because that seems better than living a life of quiet desperation. Quiet desperation is torture.

Others pretend at happiness for the world while they struggle alone in the dark, gushing with friends and wives and children whilst knowing the world is broken, that it can never be fixed. They know it and can't unknow it—they can't let go either. They want to, though, more often than not.

But Beth does not—*did* not—feel that way. She didn't think that way. I feel her feelings still, as the underground spits us up into the semidarkness of the East Village, each of us rippling with the impact of her death in our own way.

Mara's hand is in my hair as I lean my head back against the cracked leather seat of the cab we eventually decided to take. I try and reach for memories of Sam, because I feel a pattern forming, the design of something I don't have the vision to understand, but Mara's presence is distracting.

She wants to talk about what happened and I . . . don't. Because talking about them means talking about myself and how they're different from what I am. How they weren't missing what I'm missing. They weren't hollow. They didn't exist because they had no other choice. They hadn't grown up as I had, acting careless and reckless because on some level I felt I had nothing to lose. They didn't see the world through a lens in which every scene contains a door marked EXIT, a door I'm unable to open.

They lived because they wanted to. Up until the end, when they were poisoned by a . . . nothingness.

But where did the poison come from?

Where did the *address* come from?

Mara will want to know what I know, and I'll have to find

a way to tell her about Beth and Sam without telling her I wanted to save them and follow them at the same time.

And then there are those words.

Don't let her death be in vain.

Those were the words the professor had written to my father, words my father left to me—the words were *meant* for me. Before I was even born I was saddled with a burden I never asked for, never would've wanted, and don't know what to do with now that I've got it.

These are the thoughts that sizzle and smoke until my mind is coated in a stale layer of misery. I hadn't even noticed that Mara had taken me to the hotel, up to our room. She doesn't turn on the light—the curtains are open, only the gauzy layer beneath is drawn, and the moon shines through them, outlining her hands, her arms, as she pulls off my shirt, hers, then both of us into bed. My eyes are wide open, staring at dark. She's a soft curve behind me, hooking her arm under mine, her hand on my chest, her head curled against my shoulder.

"Something's wrong."

"Yes."

"Are you okay?"

My voice is scraped out. "Are *you* okay?"

"You're hurt." I hear the shadow of something growing in her mind.

"I'll heal."

She lets out a breath, but tightens around me. "That's not what I'm talking about."

"I always do," I say flatly, ignoring her.

She's silent, all of her. I can't even hear her heartbeat. Something's wrong indeed.

I turn to face her, her eyes blurred with sleep and sadness. I cup her cheek, kiss her forehead.

"I love you," she says.

I remember Jamie's words and smile just a bit as I tuck her head beneath my chin. "That is your misfortune."

In truth, though, it's mine.

13

CASTLES IN THE AIR

THE ADDRESS VANISHES THE MORNING AFTER. If Mara'd seen it, she'd have mentioned it, but she doesn't, and the moment when I should have is long past. Another confession: I don't want to talk to her. From the first, Mara was curious about my ability, as was I about hers. She wanted to experiment, to test each other, which is well and good if one experiments killing/healing nonsentient creatures, in theory if not in practice. (A badly executed excursion to the Miami Zoo comes to mind—I'd thought Mara's belief about her ability was a manifestation of her survivor's guilt. She proved me very, very wrong.)

But when she first understood what comes along with my

particular affliction—seeing others like us when they're in pain—her first thought, quite literally, was to hurt herself to see if I'd then have a vision of her, through her eyes, and feel what she felt.

She'd only pinched her arm then, but when I asked her why all those months ago—

"When you first told me you saw me, in December, in the asylum— you said you saw what I was seeing, through my eyes," she had said. *"And when Joseph was drugged, you saw him through someone else's eyes—the person who drugged him, right?"*

She was right. She was right because *she* caused the asylum to collapse, and my particular affliction only allows me to see what's happening from the perspective of the one causing said pain and/or terror.

"But you didn't have a—a vision just now, did you?" she'd asked. *"So there's some factor besides pain. Don't you want to know what it is?"*

I said yes. I lied.

It *had* been true, once, when it first started. I wanted to know more, why I could do what others couldn't and *couldn't* seem to do some of the things normal people could (ex: getting drunk on occasion would've been fun). I even thought I could help the people I'd been seeing—else why would I have the ability to see them? But I never managed it. I was either unable to find out who and where they were, or I found out just after they died.

So I stopped looking. Until Mara. She was the first person I'd ever met that I'd seen in that way, and at first I wanted to know why.

Now I *do* know why, and the price of that knowledge is too high.

I've felt Mara dying beneath my skin. I felt her terror when Jude, that mad dog belonging to my father's mad scientist, forced her to slit her own wrists. Felt the steel bite into her skin, her dizziness from the loss of blood, felt her cheek hit the dock when she collapsed, while I was in another state playing private detective.

"You were trying to help," she had said. *"You were trying to find answers—"*

But I didn't need any answers. *"I need you,"* I told her then, and it's even more true now.

She has a curious mind and I love her for it, but not enough to lose her to it. Not enough to risk her. I need to work this out on my own.

And so it is that I lead Mara, Daniel, Goose, and Jamie to One Main Street in Brooklyn, taking the long way along the waterfront beneath the two bridges. I assembled them all under the pretence of "Shit went down, let's decompress," with the actual goals of (a) moving out of the hotel; (b) moving the people I like in with me, and (c) doing it as quickly as possible with as many of them as possible, so no one'll notice my absence when I unpack what I've had sent from Yorkshire.

It's dusk when we meet, and the sun-dipped clouds in pinks and yellows render us as jewelled figures in an old painting. The lights are on in lower Manhattan, but not everywhere. A fairy city, it looks like. And then we're here.

The five of us look up at the DUMBO clock tower, whereupon the doorman lets us in, shows us to the lift.

Four pairs of eyes on me.

"What are we doing here, exactly?" Jamie asks.

I put the key in the lift and press the Penthouse button. "Taking a tour," I say.

"Of . . . ?"

"Of the clock tower."

"Um, why?"

"Because." The doors to the lift open up to a sleek white hall with double doors at the end of it. I key the lock and—

"Welcome home," I say.

"Holy—" Jamie starts

"Shit," Daniel finishes. Not a swearer, he.

Mara swoops in, taking in the four clock faces that invite the glittering, jagged skylines of New York inside. There's so much new coming at her, at all of us—I'd seen only pictures, sent by Ms. Gao's assistant, approved by me—that did not do this place justice.

A sheet of frosted glass falls away and every detail leaps at me, separate and vivid. The crackled cigar colour of the ancient tufted leather couches I'd had bought from some estate sale in

Yorkshire. The amber Edison bulbs with brass fittings warming the cold steel and glass interior of the loft. And my library. My books line shelves reaching at least twenty feet in the air, with an old-timey rolling ladder on rails to reach them. The books were all I could think of when the assistant e-mailed to ask what I wanted the flat to look like. I had no idea *what* I liked aside from books and music. Every choice I'd made with my father's money had been reactionary—the clothes I wore (an affront to him), the car I drove (teenage rebellion). So I told her I liked old things, things with history. Everything in the flat had come from somewhere else, had belonged to someone else, used and then sold or discarded, and now it belonged to me. Rather like using family money I hadn't earned—I had the chance to create something new with it, to take something that was theirs and make it mine.

Ours. Mara is biting her lower lip in a smile. She gets it, she knows. The others don't, not yet.

"What is this place?" Jamie asks.

"The flat I bought with my father's blood money. Do you like it?"

"Blood money?" Goose asks. "Bit dramatic."

Jamie breezes past me. "Is it?"

Mara's cringing, and Daniel makes the cutoff gesture at his neck as his eyes flick to Goose.

I've spent so little time with anyone but us, it's easy to forget what they don't know. That will take getting used to. It was good to have Goose around though. Again, that feeling of taking something from my old life and weaving it into this new one. One I'm trying to want to stay in.

I'll make Goose work. Somehow.

Daniel's in one corner of the space, standing by the grand piano, skimming a hand over the keys, his body twisted to look out through the clock at the Manhattan Bridge. Goosey's found the bar, copper and glass and well stocked. Jamie's flopped onto a sofa, eyeing the projector and original Nintendo and Super Nintendo consoles (assistant's idea, must've been). Mara stands with me, gripping my hand.

"When did you do this?"

"Days ago?" Feels like weeks, years since my father's funeral.

Jamie peeks over the couch, his face open, curious. "Heir to the Shaw estate?" The question perks up Daniel.

"Seems so."

Each of them processes my answer differently. Daniel's heartbeat intensifies when he moves over by the library, God love him.

Jamie's mind . . . is a mystery. But he's hanging on my words, turning them over. Calculating their meaning, for what purpose, I don't know. The pendant he wears is nearly identical to the one Mara's grandmother left her, the one my own mother left me. Half-sword, half-feather, cast in silver. It's invisible beneath the collar of his T-shirt. But it's there. Jamie got a letter from the professor as well and threw in his lot with the man—if he can even be called that, ancient as he claims to be—who serves no master but himself. I've no interest in being anyone's tool. My own neck is bare. Mara's, too.

"How many bedrooms?" Jamie asks.

"Six, I think."

A hint of smugness. "Going to fill them with Dyer-Shaw babies?"

Mara's already nodding as she twines our fingers together. "We're thinking of a spring wedding—we'll both be eighteen. Right, honey?"

"I don't remember proposing."

Mara takes my hand. "Noah Shaw, will you impregnate me immediately?"

Daniel's shaking his head. "Ew."

Jamie lifts a hand. "Seconded."

Goose, from the kitchen. "Are they always like this?"

"The language of love," I reply. "Actually," I say to Jamie, "I bought the flat for all of us."

Genuine shock from Daniel. Polite interest from Goose. Scepticism from Jamie.

"Catch?" he asks.

A shake of my head. "None. Truly." Which is a bit of a lie, but. To Daniel and Goose, I say, "Goes for you as well. It'd be brilliant having everyone here."

"The Never-ending Party," Goose muses. "I'm into it."

Jamie's eyes follow him. "I could *get* into it . . ."

Daniel sighs. "Pass, but it's really nice of you to offer."

"Really?" There's disappointment in Mara's voice. "Are you sure?"

"NYU bribed me with housing I couldn't refuse. Or I could, but, I'd like to be able to walk to class, since I actually plan to go to college this year."

"Hey." Mara's offended, genuinely.

Her brother raises his hands. "You're going *next* year. And everyone knows that your senior year of high school, which this is supposed to be, is pointless."

"Exactly. We're just skipping the classes we'd be skipping anyway," Jamie says. "And eliminating the adult supervision." Pointedly, to Mara: "I know how you love eliminating adult supervision."

"Cheers, as Noah would say."

Daniel ignores them. "You really deserve a break, Mara, after . . . everything. Seriously. It's your moral obligation to have fun."

"That's me," she says deliciously. "Moral."

Goose glides out of the kitchen with glasses and a £700 bottle of Caol Ila. Well done.

"Shall we?"

"I shall," I say, allowing him to pour. We all do, in point of fact.

Pride is not an emotion I'm much familiar with, but at that moment, I think I feel it. Watching my girl and my friends like this, knowing I've made this moment. Chose these people to fill it with: Goose, from my past; Jamie, my present; Daniel, the brother I wish I'd had. I feel a steady flickering of happiness, separate and apart from being with Mara. The world is shifting before my eyes into something else, fitting into outlines I want to remember for however long I'm supposed to live. We're taking on the shape of something, newborn and primitive. There's a lightness, strange and alien but welcome, as we drink and laugh. But beneath it, always, is a vein of . . . separateness. Daniel and Mara are family. Jamie and Mara are best friends, bound by an experience I was responsible for but not part of. And Goose, familiar though he is, is still farther removed from me than the rest of them.

Everyone's toasting and laughing in the living room, and, as planned, I take my leave, heading up the steel-and-glass staircase leading to the second floor. I don't want to turn on the lights, as I'm not quite sure what can be seen from downstairs and what can't, so I wander blindly, not sure which room I'm looking for until I find it.

It's chaotic in here, with unopened boxes piled up on the edge of a riveted metal desk. I step over and around trunks of different sizes and ages; some centuries old, probably. Everyone's still talking downstairs, and loudly, so I close the door and turn on the light.

Not about to start with the boxes. They look like banker's boxes and likely contain financials and other shite I've no interest in at the moment. And the trunks—I'm wary. I've already spent enough time in the company of my father's ghost. I'd prefer someone else's.

A small trunk stands out from the rest, edged in silver and gold with a host of names engraved on the front—all female, I can't help but notice. I open it and discover what appear to be congratulatory letters from what appear to be former conquests of some former relative.

Amusing, but not helpful. I look for a different one, hoping one will stand out, and one does. I cross the room; it's battered but modern, something one might see at a military supply shop. Doesn't look like something my father would've ever used—doesn't appear Shaw-ish at all, which draws me to it. I slide my fingers beneath the hinges to lift the lid, only to find that it's locked. Always something.

Returning to the desk, I open the drawers, all empty but one. Inside is a thick padded envelope filled with keys of every shape and size and, again, age, but one stands out. I feel like I know what's inside the trunk before the lock turns.

My mother's things have been packed away here by hands unknown. I recognise some of the books—Singer, Kerouac, Bukowski, and sifting through them I find *Le Petit Prince*, of course. I wonder if the photograph of Little Me is still inside, so I open it, flip through pages until the book itself settles on one, as if the spine had been cracked there, as if the book had been splayed out for years. My mother's highlighted lines:

"To me," she said, "you are still nothing more than a little boy who is just like a hundred thousand other little boys. And I have no need of you. And you, on your part, have no need of me. . . . But if you tame me, then we shall need each other."

The words call Mara to mind. Downstairs, oblivious to where I am, what I'm looking for—I'm not quite sure I know myself. Connections, I suppose. Between Beth and Sam. Between them and me.

I halfheartedly open my mum's other books. Pictures slide out of them, many of her and friends—rarely do I find one of her alone. There's this rare, magnetic thing about her that transcends the two dimensions of the photograph and catches me under my breastbone. It's nearly impossible to look away.

Most parents, when asked why they want to have children, say that they want to raise a child to be happy. To be healthy. To be wanted. To be loved.

That is not why I had you.

Those are the words she wrote me, from the letter the professor had and sent to me. They're branded in my memory. Her handwriting, elegant and frantic script:

Do not find peace.

Find passion.

Find something you want to die for more than something you want to live for.

Fight for those who cannot fight for themselves.

Speak for them.

Scream for them.

Live and die for them.

That was what she wanted for me. Not happiness. Not peace.

I shove her books back into the trunk, lock it, and pocket the key.

She certainly got her wish.

14

PLEASURES AND PAINS, THEIR KINDS

As I leave the office, I run into Mara on the stairs.

"You," she says.

"Me."

"You vanished."

"I did."

"Pretty quickly."

"That obvious?"

"To me," she says, then rises on her toes to kiss me . . . or to look past my shoulder at the now-closed door.

"What's in there?"

"I had some stuff sent over from England."

"Stuff?"

"Papers and things. All the laughing and drinking down-stairs made me a bit homesick."

"Liar."

"I take offence."

"Keep taking it," she says. "What were you doing in there, really?"

She knows me too well. "I thought I might go through some of it, see if I can find anything mentioning Sam's family."

"Did you? Find anything, I mean?" Her eyes dart from me to the door again.

"Not tonight."

She tilts her head toward the stairs. "Everyone left while you were gone."

I take a step closer to her. "Did they, now."

"Goose went back to the Gansevoort for another night or two, and Jamie went back to his aunt's. He's going to think about it."

"About . . . ?"

"Moving in." She narrows her eyes. "You invited him to live here, remember?"

"Sorry, I'm rather tired." I regret the lie as soon as I speak it—Mara sees through it immediately.

"What's going on, Noah?" She twists a finger in the hem of her T-shirt, dark grey with a brontosaurus pictured below the words THEY'LL NEVER FIND US.

I run my hand through my hair. "I don't know."

"Are you ever going to tell me? What you saw?"

"Yes."

"When?"

"Tomorrow."

She bites her lower lip, but she's really biting back words. I close the space between us and kiss her before she can speak.

Her body is stiff at first, but she begins to melt in seconds. Just as she reaches for the back of my neck, I pull away and ask, "Have you seen the rest of the flat?"

A single shake.

"Would you like to?"

A single nod.

"Follow." I turn away from her and pass the office without opening the door.

We turn the first corner. "How many bedrooms did you say there are?"

"Six."

"Which one's ours?"

"Tonight, all of them," I say, and stop. She crashes into me and I catch her, pulling her hair gently, leaning to kiss the hollow below her ear. "And the living room." My hand slides up under her T-shirt. "And the dining room."

She bites my lower lip. "The pool table."

"The kitchen," I say as she rakes her hand through my hair.

"Show me."

Breaking apart is excruciating. I grip her small hand tightly enough to shatter it—she's holding mine just as hard. I don't even need to turn on the hall lights—the moon and the city are bright enough to guide us.

We take the stairs again to the top floor. There are two rooms; only one has a bed, I know, because the other, I tell Mara, is to be her studio, if she wants.

"What I want is *you*," she says. She pulls me inside the bare room, the ceiling punched through with three skylights. The night is clear enough and we're high up enough to see stars.

I tug her back out. "Come."

"I'd *like* to, but—"

"Cheeky," I say, and open the next door. "Careful, or I may have to punish you."

"Why didn't you say so?" she says, seeing the white bed in the centre of the room, surrounded by view. She pries her hand from mine and backs up against it. There's a large beveled glass floor mirror in one corner of the room, reflecting the city. Reflecting us. She glances over her shoulder at it, then me.

"You've thought of everything."

"I'm sure I don't know what you mean."

She hitches up onto the bed, her fraying denimed legs dangling from crossed knees. "You know I know you like to watch."

I reach her. Uncross those legs. "I do."

"So"—her voice juicy with malice—"watch."

I lean in to kiss her, and she pulls her head away and gently pushes me back. "Nope. From there."

Ladies and gentlemen of the jury, how could I ever love anyone else?

She slays me, slipping out of her shirt, the city lights kiss her skin but I can't, not yet. She lies back on the bed so I can see the rise of her breasts as she lifts her hips to slide off her jeans. The clink of the button on the wood floor rings in my ears.

Down to a simple black bra and plain black boy-shorts and she's still wearing too much. We both are. I start to pull my shirt up and over my shoulders until I hear, "No."

I hear her breath and blood moving under her skin, a spiralling ache that matches mine, and it gives me a kick of surprise—it feels like ages since I've heard her last. Watching the fast rise and fall of her chest, I know she's as tortured as I am. The power of her fizzes my blood, the lure of me burns hers.

This is not our first time, but it's our first time *here*, in this place that's ours, in this new age of us. And even though every second with Mara is different, this is different from even that. She knows it too. She takes off what she'd left on, and the swollen air between us weighs a thousand pounds. My muscles strain under the pressure of not touching her, but when she reaches up for me, I say no. I do what she did, but instead of extending that excruciating wait, I climb onto the bed. Even in the dark I can see her flushed cheeks, her berry-stained lips parted, the few scattered freckles that dust her cheeks. I don't touch her skin, but I fill my hand with her hair, and let the strands that look like double helices fall from my fingers, the dusky city light making the few amber strands in her dark hair shine. I'm getting high on the scent of her, when she says, "We're home."

If I'd been standing, her words would have brought me to my knees. She touches me first, pressing her palm against the back of my neck.

Her touch throws off sparks of colours I've never seen and notes I've never heard, and I slide her beneath me and press my mouth to hers. The feel of her tongue sings high in my ears, but her body is low and purring. When she moves, I move with her. She shimmers with heat, that tortured ache rising in both of us as I get drunk on the taste of her. The sounds she's making are dizzying, and when I hitch her long, lovely, coltish limbs around my waist, she's shivering and—

If I believed in God I would pray, beg, anything to stop time, to live in this moment with her forever. Tonight is a perfect thing in a broken world, and she is the queen of it. Her pleasure, searing white, arrows through mine, and I would let the Earth ice over to keep the sun from rising, but after hours of her, it rises anyway, sunlight staining our sheets, our skin. After, I fall asleep with Mara in my arms.

I wake up in someone else's mind.

15

UNIMPROVED END

It's a boy, this time. His longish mouse brown hair lies on the pillow, sideways, as was my view, which was slitted. His brain is clouded, heavy, and the stench of sick permeates his nostrils.

On his nightstand, among books and pictures and empty glasses, are clusters of bottles; phenobarbital, Klonopin, Benadryl, alprazolam, Vicodin, and clorazepate. Who knows how many he took? He probably doesn't even know himself. He just recognises the feeling in his stomach, and in his head, and he's trying not to throw up again.

I can't hear his thoughts, but after the others, a space has opened up in my mind, and I try and cast around for something, anything, to tell me who he is. Why he's doing this. *Where* he's doing this so I can—

"Noah!" Small fingers grip my shoulders, bruisingly hard. The film of his reality slips, and when I open my eyes, it's Mara's face that I see.

"What's wrong?" I ask her, sitting up. I feel sluggish, hazy, but *here*. Normal.

Her face becomes mask of disbelief. "You were having a nightmare. You were curled up and your shoulders were heaving and I thought—I thought you were having a seizure."

Maybe *he* was having a seizure. Epilepsy would explain some of those drugs. . . .

"What happened?" Her eyes narrow, search my face.

"I saw someone die."

"How?"

"He overdosed," I say, and hesitate just a fraction of a second before adding, "On purpose."

Her hands round into fists in the sheets as her spine straightens. "So, that's three now."

I get out of bed, begin getting dressed. Technically, she's right, but there's something different about the boy I just saw. Or rather, *not* different. "This wasn't like the other night, with that girl. Or in England."

She's out of bed now too, the sheet wrapped around her body. Her arms are crossed. "Tell me."

I sit back down on the bed, staring out at the Manhattan

Bridge. "I could hear their thoughts," I begin. "The girl who jumped the tracks, her name was Beth. She played piano."

I struggle for words to explain what it feels like to inhabit someone else. To see what they see in their worst moments, to smell what they smell, and to live their experience—it's not a gift. It's a curse.

"What about Sam?" Mara asks.

I itch for distraction. Could do with a cigarette. I exhale slowly. "His last thoughts were '*Help me help me help me,*' over and over again, until his mind went black."

Her face loses its expression. She turns quickly and reaches for her shirt from last night, pulls on jeans.

"I couldn't help him, Mara. I wouldn't even know Beth's name if she hadn't thought it before she died."

She's quiet still, with her back to me.

"What?" I ask her.

She looks at me over her shoulder, fakes a smile. "Nothing."

"Liar."

She smiles again, a real one this time. "I take offence."

"Keep taking it," I say, and try forcing a smile but can't quite manage it. "I don't know what he was thinking. I felt the way I usually do when someone like us dies."

Mara doesn't flinch at that, and I love her more for it. "So, still no idea who he was, then?"

I search my memory for the still frames I sweep away after each death, those collages of misery. The pill bottles on the nightstand all have different names on them, different doctors, different addresses—

One of them matches the one scrawled on my arm. In imaginary fucking ink.

Fuck. *Fuck.*

"What?" Mara'd been watching me. Closely.

I regret saying the words before I even speak them, but it's too late to lie. "There's—I think I might know where he lived."

"Really?"

"He took pills—there's an address on one of the bottles." I slip my wallet into my back pocket, head for the doorway. "I'm going to go."

Mara slips something into her pocket. "No, *we're* going to go."

"All right, *we're* going to go," I say, but Mara hasn't moved.

"All of us."

"All of . . . whom?"

"You weren't the only one who saw Beth die."

"No . . ."

"We should tell everyone."

"Everyone in the subway that night? The police, the random—"

"You know who I mean. Daniel. Jamie."

I could talk to Daniel. He's sort of become the brother I never had, and never knew I actually wanted, but more than that, he's distanced from this—from me—in a way Mara isn't.

I can tell him about the suicides, and he might be able to help draw a connection without drawing a line through Mara.

Jamie, however . . . The issue of the professor scratches at my mind. "Why?"

"Because Daniel's my brother, and—"

"I mean, why Jamie?"

"He was there."

"On the platform, yes, we've established that—you want to tell Sophie as well?"

"God, Noah, *stop*. Jamie was *there* for everything. We were lab rats together with Stella, we had to break out of that fucking place together, we had to get to New York on our own together, with no money, and ended up exactly where your father wanted us. He was *there*."

And I was not. Guilt heats the back of my neck.

"And he's our friend, and the most loyal person I know. You want him to move in with us, for fuck's sake!"

Not because I trust him, necessarily. Possibly in part because I don't.

I give her a look, arrogant, condescending. "It can't have escaped your notice that he's wearing the pendant."

"So?"

"Haven't you ever wondered what was in *his* letter?"

Mara goes still.

"Jamie's never mentioned it? What the professor wrote to him?"

"Why would he?"

"He couldn't get his pendant on fast enough, as I remember it."

"What are you saying?"

The air feels bruised, and I press on it. "Our friend's thrown his lot in with someone who goes on about fate and destiny and made it quite plain that he'd like to use us as tools. Weapons, even, perhaps." That's a trigger of hers, and I pull it.

Her voice flattens out. "He doesn't want to use me as a weapon."

"No, he wants you to leave me instead."

"And we decided to ignore him."

"We did," I say. "But that doesn't mean *he* decided to ignore *us*." That thought tramples every other. "We're talking about a man who literally manipulated and lied to generations of my family and yours in order to *breed* us. He *said* it was our decision, our choice to make, whether we wanted to help him achieve his vision for a better world. We said no. Jamie said yes."

"Do you want to know what *Jamie* said after you went down on the platform?"

"I've a feeling you're going to tell me regardless."

"After he helped me get you into a cab—you don't remember that, do you? Leaning on Jamie because you could barely stand?"

I don't remember it, and I'm glad of it. It's shameful enough that it happened in the first place.

"He said he could kill whoever's doing this to you."

"No one's doing anything to me." And why was *murder* where his mind went, after a girl, a stranger, supposedly committed suicide?

"Really? So you're fine, then?"

"*I'm* alive. Beth and Sam aren't."

"Oh, okay, cool."

"Don't patronise me—it's unbecoming." Mara looks like she wants to hit me. I hope she does. "What makes you think what's happening to them has anything to do with me? You want to tell your brother and Jamie, fine. Tell them. But the boy who killed himself this morning, he wasn't like Sam, or Beth. They didn't want to die. He did."

"How do you know?"

I can't explain it, the difference between the suicides I've witnessed before. It's the difference between a kicked wasp's nest and a hanging beehive, between violence and free will. "He wanted to die, Mara. I wish he hadn't taken his own life, but it's done now, and I'm not going to violate his dignity by bringing a parade of strangers to his home, or wherever he is, to pick through his life."

"So, it's cool as long as it's just you? By yourself? Fuck that. It's all of us or none of us. Your choice."

"I choose not to choose."

"Then I choose all of us," Mara says. She crosses over to her mobile, to text Daniel and Jamie, presumably. And I let her. Because I love her anyway.

"He wouldn't love you if you weren't what you are."

Father's words, haunting me still, wherever I go.

16

EVEN IN PARADISE

W E'RE GATHERED HERE TODAY TO TALK about some shit," Mara says to Daniel and Jamie, having collected and deposited them in the sun-white living room.

"What shit?"

"Ours."

Jamie looks from me to Daniel to Mara. "I don't have any shit."

"You're full of shit, actually," Mara says brightly. "But this isn't about you." She pats Jamie on the head, and he pouts as he swats her hand.

"It's about the girl," I cut in, before they have another go at each other. "From the subway the other day."

The air changes, restless and charged. "What about her?" Jamie asks.

"She was one of us," Mara says. "Gifted."

Jamie doesn't seem surprised, but Daniel does. "How do you know?" he asks me. "The archives?"

That was not what I was expecting, and it must show, because he goes on, "There are names in there, files of other kids who were experimented on. Was she one of them?"

In the days since Sam's death, I hadn't even considered that possibility. Stupid. It was so obvious, I felt a bloody idiot for missing it.

"That's not how he knows," Mara says before I can stop her.

Daniel looks from her to me. "So that's not what was in the envelope last night?"

Now I'm the one who's lost. "What envelope?"

Mara's mouth drops open. "I completely forgot."

"What?" I ask as she rises from one of the sofas and picks up a plain envelope from a console table in the foyer. "The doorman gave me this to give to you last night, when I was walking everyone out."

She hands it to me, but Jamie starts talking before I can open it.

"So, let's recap," he says, standing not so subtly between Mara and myself. "The girl who jumped in front of the F train—her name was Beth."

I nod once.

"And she's like you guys, a Carrier," Daniel adds. He doesn't wait for my assent before he asks, "But how did you find out?"

"It's part of my ability." I'm still and watchful as I speak, hating the sound of my own voice. "When someone like us is afraid or in pain or whatever, I can see it."

"*See* it?"

"From inside them," Mara says. "He can see what they see from their point of view."

She's not quite right—it's only from their perspective when *they're* the ones causing the harm, but I'm not about to correct her. Not here, in front of everyone.

"Wow." Daniel lets out a breath. Jamie says nothing, looks as though none of this is a surprise. Which means Mara must have told him at some point. I'm sure the sense of betrayal will kick in eventually, but right now, I just want to escape.

Mara turns to me. "Are you going to tell them, or . . ."

"Oh, I'd hate to interrupt," I say.

Mara turns away from me, to Daniel and Jamie. "She's not the only one he saw. Someone committed suicide at David Shaw's funeral—"

"*What?*" Daniel's nearly out of his seat.

"I saw it too," Mara says.

Jamie's turn to look shocked. "Wait, not like Noah . . ."

Mara shakes her head. "I was there." A brief glance at me. "We left the service to—"

"Shit on his grave?"

"Actually," I say, "we left to fuck, but someone decided to hang himself in the bell tower, which rather interrupted the mood."

Everyone's gone quiet. I'm usually better at keeping my anger issues to myself, but. Not today, clearly.

After an extraordinarily awkward silence, Mara decides to keep at it. "Someone else committed suicide this morning."

"Jesus," Daniel says. "How many have there been?"

"A few," I say casually. "But not like this."

"Like what?"

This is why I wanted to talk to Daniel alone—without Mara, certainly without Jamie. To try and explain to him the difference between what Beth and Sam felt like and what the others felt like—the boy this morning, and the others I witnessed before Mara and I even met. I'd have had the chance to unpack that without being forced to discuss my own psychic disaster, which is precisely what'll happen next unless I change the subject, and quickly.

"The girl's thoughts, and Sam's, in England—I knew what they were before they died," I say, opening the envelope from the doorman. Probably just inheritance paperwork, but it gives me something to do with my hands instead of punching them through glass.

"That's never happened before?" Daniel asks as I sift out the papers, evading the question. One of them falls to the floor, and I bend to pick it up.

INTERNATIONAL BUSINESS
MAGNATE DAVID SHAW DIES AT 40

David S. Shaw, founder of the Euphrates International Corporation, died on September 5th. His family's spokesperson confirmed his death from the family estate in Yorkshire, England, offering no cause. Some media outlets in the United Kingdom reported that he died of a genetic condition.

A few short years after his graduation from Trinity College, Cambridge, Mr. Shaw started a small company that grew to become Euphrates International, which injected hundreds of millions of dollars into private and academic research laboratories for the funding of research in genetic modification.

In recent years, its dealings prompted an investigation by the U.S. Department of Justice. Mr. Shaw was born on ████████████ in London, England, to his parents, Lord Elliot Shaw and Lady Sylvia Shaw. He attended Eton before graduating from Trinity College at Cambridge University, with a degree in history. He lived with his wife and two children in their family home in England until Euphrates International moved their headquarters to the United States after controversial funding decisions prompted the opening of several ethics enquiries by Parliament.

His survivors include his second wife, Ruth, his son, Noah, and his daughter, Katherine. The family will be holding a private service at their estate in Rievaulx. In lieu of gifts, the family requests that donations be sent to the Shaw Foundation.

I look up at Mara. "What the fuck is this?"

She takes the clipping from me. It's from the *Times*.

"Your dad's obituary? I don't get it. . . ."

I withdraw the other piece of paper from the envelope. Also a clipping, but this one . . .

COPS POISONED!

New York, NY, 10:05 a.m.

"We are heartbroken to announce the death of Officer John Roland, twenty-eight, who died early this morning at 8:31 a.m.," Commissioner ███████████ of the NYPD announced at a press conference this morning. "Officer Roland was a two-year member of the NYPD and will be remembered for his sense of humor, his generosity of spirit, and his bravery."

Roland's death comes at the heels of eight other members of the department who have all died under suspicious circumstances that are being closely guarded by the NYPD. Under conditions of anonymity, an inspector consulted by the *Daily News* stated, "Their deaths are consistent with some sort of mass poisoning; they all succumbed within a finite period of time, and shared the same symptoms." The expert wouldn't elaborate on what those symptoms were, but a source close to the police has said that each of the officers complained of a bloody nose at some point before their deaths. Two sources confirmed to the Daily News that the ██████████ Precinct is being temporarily shut down for an inspection into whether an airborne toxin, like anthrax, may have been mailed to the department. Commissioner ████████ refused to answer whether they were considering terrorism as a motive at this point.

"This is an ongoing investigation and we can issue no further comment."

Officer Roland is survived by his parents, Mary and Robert Roland, of Providence, Rhode Island, and two younger siblings, Paul and Benjamin Roland.

Mara's eyes settle on the picture of the officer. She barely skims the rest of the piece before thrusting it back into my hands. Jamie snatches it from me directly, stares longer than Mara. Daniel has to urge him to part with it.

"What is this?" I ask no one in particular.

Daniel takes the envelope from me, turns it over. "Who sent these?"

"The doorman didn't say who left them," Mara says.

"But he gave them to *you*?"

"He called her Mrs. Shaw when she was walking us out," Jamie chimes in. "Passsssssword . . ." he singsongs under his breath.

"Why would someone send you this?" Daniel asks. "Who even knows you're here?"

Solid question. I didn't buy the flat under my own name, but anyone working for or with my father would probably have the means to find out where I'm living. So, not exactly a secret.

Mara takes the clippings from her brother. "Add that to the growing list of questions, like, why are we killing ourselves?"

We. The word stings like the bite of a whip. Why are *we* killing ourselves.

"Noah," Mara says, "where did you say the address was?"

"I didn't."

"What address?" Jamie asks. Three pairs of eyes watch me.

The words stuck in my throat, but it was too late to do anything but confess. "The boy who killed himself this morning—he did it with pills. The address was on one of the bottles. Two-thirteen Myrtle."

Mara looks at her brother, then at Jamie.

"Oh, I'm definitely coming," Jamie says.

Daniel looks at me for permission, and I appreciate the gesture. "Join us, won't you?" I ask.

He cracks a small grin. He takes out his phone and texts someone first, then looks up. "Ready?"

Mara's already by the front door, pulling her leather jacket from a hook. "How's Sophie?" she asks Daniel as the rest of us assemble.

"How do you know I was texting Sophie?"

"Because you're always texting Sophie." She opens the front door.

Goose is standing behind it, his duffel in hand.

"Hello, darlings. I'm home."

17

BRUTE NEIGHBOURS

S O, WHERE IS IT WE'RE GOING?"

"All in good time, mate," Jamie said, mocking his accent as he gestures for Goose to follow him. Then to me, "It'll be fine, old chap. I'll take care of everything."

I do not love the idea of Jamie mind-fucking my friend for the day, especially not on this ill-conceived excursion, but having Goose along for part of it might present an excuse for me to get on *alone* for the rest of it. I was the only one who saw what the boy saw. I could use that, perhaps, to pawn Goose off on someone else. And Jamie seems quite happy to oblige.

And so the five of us find ourselves standing on the corner

of Myrtle Avenue staring at a brownstone down the street that looks as if it's been dragged kicking and screaming into the twenty-first century. The front steps are cracked and buckling, and the door, which appears to have once been red, seems rotted through.

Goose looks bored. "What are we doing here, again?"

"Exploring Brooklyn real estate," Jamie says. "I'm not sure I want to live in the loft after all."

Mara and I exchange a look. Real or not real?

"And you are obviously a man of great wealth and taste," Jamie says in his normal voice, "So I invited you along."

Goose shrugs. He'll go along with most anything—one of his finer qualities. "What are we waiting for, then?

For the ambulance in front of one of the houses to leave, the house I suspect we've come to visit.

"Which house is it?" Goose asks.

Everyone looks at me, but Jamie's the one who speaks. "Two-thirteen. But we're waiting till the ambulance leaves."

Goosey looks rather put out. "That's absurd," he says, and starts walking in the direction of the house.

Daniel says to Jamie, "Shouldn't you . . . *do* something?"

"Goose. Stop," Jamie calls out—mind-fuck voice, this time. No response, no reaction. Possibly didn't hear him? He's quite a ways off. When I catch up with him, Goose is already at the ambulance, which is closing its doors.

"Good day, fine gentlewoman," Goose says to the EMT

about to get into the ambulance's passenger seat. "May I ask what happened over here?"

"Nothing I can tell you about," she says, tightening her straw blond ponytail. "Run along, boys," she says to us, shooing Goose away from her door.

The driver checks the rearview mirror. "Good to go."

"Have a lovely day, then," Goose says. "Excellent work." The EMT rolls her eyes as the ambulance drives off.

Mara, Daniel, and Jamie, however, are looking anxious, annoyed, frustrated in turn.

"What?" Goose asks.

"Nothing," I say, warning the others off. "They're just paranoid."

"'Bout what?" Goose is genuinely innocent—he has no idea what we're doing here. Which should've been fine, as Jamie's supposed to be handling this, but since he isn't handling it, and I'm not sure why and can't very well ask at the moment . . .

"Notice the two police cars parked down the street?" I say to Goose. "Some of us here have had a few run-ins with the law."

"Oh, who hasn't, really?" Goose says, clapping my shoulder. "When *we* were boys . . ."

Before Goose can finish his sentence, Mara ascends the steps and knocks on the door, silencing everyone. Then directs a glare my way.

So we're doing this.

Instead of an answer, however, the door to the garden apartment opens, and a moon-faced, doughy man pokes his pale, balding head out and examines us.

"Can I help you?" the man asks, his voice a bit scrapey.

The boy's father, perhaps? I was expecting . . . I suppose I'm not sure what I was expecting. The man looks rather . . . like a paedophile, really. He has this soft, moony, harmless look about him, and yet. His button-down shirt is tight around the middle, and he has the sort of worn-out, drawn, put-upon appearance, as if he's been a prisoner of war but doesn't quite remember the experience and would be embarrassed if anyone mentioned it.

The man squints at us. "You're like *them*, aren't you?"

I can feel everyone exchanging very tense glances as Goose asks, "Like whom?"

"Kid who died this morning. And the rest. All gone now." He breaks into a ridiculous, there's-something-not-quite-right-with-me smile.

Christ. Everyone's adrenaline's in overdrive—I try and quiet my mind enough to dissolve the noise into meaning. I can hear every heartbeat on the block, but ours are the loudest, the most frantic.

"Sir," I begin without actually knowing what I'm going to say, "I'm not sure what you mean. We came to visit some-one—"

The door creaks open. Waiting at the threshold is The Boy Who Watched.

"Rolly, I'll take it from here," he says.

And like that, moon-faced Rolly retreats into his apartment like a snail into its shell, and the boy's blue, unblinking eyes find mine. "Come on in," he says with a smile. Mara steps past me, through the doorway.

If I could go back to one moment in my life and undo it, that would be the one.

18

NUTSHELL OF CIVILITY

U P CLOSE HE SEEMS OUR AGE, WEARING A slightly too big dark blue T-shirt, with the symbols of each member of the Justice League on it. Though he stands with a slight slouch, he straightens when I walk past.

"Hi," the boy says to me—only me, I notice—and extends his hand. "I'm Leo."

"Noah."

Cloudy light spills through filmed windows in the long parlour of the town house; We face a banister painted a shade just off robin's-egg blue, and to our right, the parlour. Mint paint peels off the walls, and I'm thrown for a second—it's the colour of the room the boy killed himself in. He died here, and the address that somehow magically appeared on my skin and disappeared is *this* address. Every detail of this place matters— and everyone in it.

Though I don't see anyone else here but Leo. A line of dusty glasses on every flat surface, some rims stained with lipstick, announces that the house has not always been this empty. It's as though there's a ghost of a teenager draped on every surface; a tufted amber leather chaise with a slash in it, the ivory sofa and ottoman, the farm chairs at the dining table in the back. There's a chessboard resting on a faded Oriental rug, which seems to have been abandoned mid-game.

Leo, making his way to the back of the brownstone, asks, "Can I get anyone anything to drink?"

"I'm not sure we're staying long," I say, just as Goose says, "I think I do fancy one, thanks."

My idiot plan to bring him along to pawn off on Jamie is backfiring spectacularly, as Jamie's made no attempt to corral or even address the Goose Problem.

Like me, Jamie and Daniel have been warily eyeing what looks like the frozen scene of a hastily abandoned party. By contrast, Mara's stomping around like there's nothing weird about this at all. She even bends to move a piece on the chessboard, which is interesting, because she doesn't play chess. I don't think.

"Checkmate," she says, and she's right.

Leo glances at her over his shoulder, smiles. "I'm Leo. I didn't catch your name?"

"Mara," she says casually, and I hear Leo's heart stutter. He's stopped midway between the parlour and the kitchen, looking at Mara for a beat too long. Then the rest of us.

"I wasn't expecting all of you."

"You were expecting some of us though." Count on Daniel to say what I was thinking.

Leo's gaze flicks to Daniel, then back to me. In a slightly nasal, abrasive voice, "The Non can't stay."

The word clicks in place, like the safety off a gun. I knew Leo had to be a Carrier, but now I *know*.

"He's my brother," Mara says. "He stays, or none of us do."

"Then none of you do." He says it without pause or inflection, his face expressionless.

Mara walks over to him, and there's a responding chorus of quickening hearts because it's Mara, and who knows *what* she's going to do.

"It's fine," Daniel says. "It doesn't matter."

"Does, though," I say. To Leo: "You're the one who asked us here, I recall?"

"Did we?" *We?* He fixes me with that dark blue stare. "*Do* you recall?"

I grin at the challenge, say nothing, betray nothing, wait for my silence to unsettle him. It doesn't.

Things are spiralling—Jamie may not know the details, but

he's got things sorted well enough. And knows he's the only one who can even begin to try and fix it.

"Daniel's staying," he says to Leo. His words ripple the close air, plucking mental strings inside all of us, though the words are directed only at Leo.

He blinks slowly. An automatic smile creeps across his lips as he nods, compliant. The parlour is staticky with energy, my mind with the realisation that Jamie's mind-fuck is working on another Carrier. It's working on one of *us*.

"Well," Leo says, eyes flat, pupils blown, "if you're staying, don't just stand there." He turns around and glides to the kitchen, separated from the rest of the house by two shabbily painted French doors with transom windows above them.

That gets to all of us. "What the shit?" Mara whispers. Daniel slides his gaze to Jamie, who's trying for ice-cool and failing. His Adam's apple bobs in his throat. Pulses hammer and heartbeats gallop, and it sounds like there's an army in this house, not six teenagers.

This is what I know: Leo's a Carrier. He's singled Daniel out as the Other. He's not singled out Goose.

Not. Goose.

I turn to my Westminster friend. "All right, chap?"

"Never better."

"You know, this place isn't up to scratch." I glance at Jamie, who gets it. "Why don't you and Goose and Daniel go on with Mara to that café on Fulton, and we'll meet you there."

Goosey tilts his head. "You seem tense, mate."

"Hardly. Though, since you mention it, is there anything you'd like to share with the class?"

His mouth curves up, amused. "Can't think of a thing."

I don't know whether to stay and press, or leave and let it go.

The sound of indelicate footsteps descending the staircase barely merits my attention, but the voice attached to them snaps my head around. "He doesn't know," the voice says, a voice I haven't heard in months, not since Horizons. And there, standing at the foot of the staircase, is Stella.

19

OUR PREJUDICES

S HE'S DIFFERENT FROM WHAT I REMEMBER. HER
once-soft shape is filed down to edges, the spray of
freckles across her olive skin more livid. She does not
look well.

"Hi," Jamie says.

Stella's mouth is sewn shut. She's staring at Mara—
something flares between them. I know a bit about the
parting of the ways between Jamie, Mara, and Stella, but the
atmosphere seems nastier than it should be, considering Mara's
the reason Stella made it out of Horizons alive in the first place.

Leo returns, so it's us seven in the foyer, crowded in amongst old rucksacks and umbrellas. Leo bears a dusty bottle of wine and glasses.

"Stella," he says with an easy smile. "Allow me to introduce you to—"

"We've met," I say.

"Briefly," she adds through her pinched mouth.

Jamie puts his hand on his heart. "You wound me." He says to Leo, "We go way back."

"*Way* back," Mara speaks, for the first time in what feels like hours.

Goose slips sideways between us, back into the parlour. I follow, nicking a glass and the wine bottle from Leo's hand. Because this afternoon has just gotten far, far more interesting.

"From Florida?" Leo asks.

None of us has mentioned Florida.

Daniel's begun to sweat—his gaze bounces between Mara and Stella and Leo.

Jamie attempts a rescue. "Yep!" He follows Goose and me into the parlour. The rest trickle over as well. I settle onto the sofa, stretching out comfortably though my nerves are snapping with electricity. What the fuck is Stella doing here? How long has she *been* here?

Leo sits on the leather chaise, pats the seat next to him, "C'mere," he says to Stella, who's so tense she's more like a wood carving than a person. She obeys, though.

I hold the bottle up, casting a reflexive glance at the label. Ever the snob. "Shall I pour?"

"What doesn't Goose know?" Mara asks Stella. She doesn't speak though, not till Leo places a hand on her thigh. How very familiar of him.

"He's an amplifier," Stella says.

Goose's face is all-smile. "Are you all taking the piss?" Raises his eyebrows at me. "Is some American hazing ritual about to begin?"

"Those are the words coming out of your mouth," Stella says to him evenly. "But in your head, you're thinking, *The fuck is going on here? Why are we bothering with these people, and Noah, you wanker, you've really gone mental.*"

The smile on Goose's face vanishes, draining all colour with it, because Stella has just narrated his inner monologue.

Goose is here because of me, in Brooklyn because of me, in America because of me. This is my problem to solve, now. No one else's.

"Since you directly—or, indirectly, as it were—addressed me in your thoughts, I'll try to explain," I say to him.

"Oh, I cannot wait for this," Jamie says.

Goose's face is wiped blank, pretending at neutral. But I know him. He's more than unsettled, but would die before admitting it. And nothing I'm about to say is going to make it better—only worse.

"Simply put," I say, unable to help the curve at the corner of my mouth as I do, "Superheroes are real, and . . . we're some of them."

A raucous laugh explodes from Mara's throat. "Super*heroes*?"

Jamie slow-claps. "Five stars."

Stella turns to Goose. "I can hear people's thoughts," she says. "And Jamie can persuade anyone to do what he wants."

Jamie crosses his arms. "I feel like I've just been outed."

"You have been," Mara says.

Stella ignores them. "Noah can heal, himself and others."

Goose and Leo turn to Mara and Daniel.

"Daniel isn't Gifted," Stella says.

Leo's gaze lands on Mara like a fly before darting back to Stella. "And her?"

Stella looks even paler than when we first sat down. She's quiet, but her dark eyes are narrowed and blazing. She looks just as angry as Mara did upon seeing her, but it's mixed with something else—what, I can't tell.

"Noah?" Goose asks.

I ignore him, turn on Leo instead. "What is it, precisely, that you can do?"

"My Gift," Leo says, "my business."

Jamie slaps both of his knees. "Or! I could make you tell us. Since Stella didn't show us the same courtesy."

Which is when I realise that Stella's reading our thoughts. *Now.* She shouldn't be able to, not like this. None of us—myself excepted—have been able to use our abilities on each other before, not for more than a few seconds, at least.

In answer, Stella tips her head in Goose's direction. "He's why our Gifts are working on each other. It's him. He's doing it."

Goose shakes his head once. "I don't know what she's on about."

"How old are you?" Daniel asks him.

All eyes on Goose. "Eighteen."

"Have you noticed anything . . . different in the past couple of years? Any changes?"

"You mean, hair in places there hadn't been before, spots . . . ? The teachers covered most of that in year six."

"Ever get sick?" Jamie asks.

"Ill, you mean? Of course, who hasn't?"

"No, like, seriously sick."

"Mono at the end of upper fifth."

"Freshman year," I explain to everyone. Could Goose have manifested without knowing it? "How bad was it?"

"Wretched. They thought it might be meningitis for a while, the kind you don't heal from."

I watch Daniel file that away. He can come at Goose later, he knows, but Leo—could be a now-or-never situation. I want to ask about the suicide, but Daniel knows why I'm here. He'll either kick the ball my way or he won't, but I trust him on this. He can see the forest for the trees like no one else. Especially not me. Or Mara.

Daniel turns to Leo next. "How did you know about your Gift?" Using his lexicon, asking questions we need answered and acting familiar so he'll *feel* familiar. Fair play to you, Daniel.

Leo glances at Stella, and she nods. Cozy pair, those two. "You can make people do what you want them to do," he says to Jamie. "I can make people see what I want them to see."

The address. Fucking *finally*.

"Why were you there on the platform that night?" he asks me, skipping ahead. He wants to get right at it too.

"We'd just had dinner," Daniel answers instead, to Leo's annoyance. "And we were getting the train together."

"That's it?"

Daniel shrugs. "That's it."

Leo looks to Stella for confirmation. "He's telling the truth."

"But you," I say to him. "*You* were there. And unlike us, you were watching the girl who killed herself."

"We—" He catches himself. "We knew you'd be there."

"How?" Jamie takes a turn at the interrogation. Poorly, as he answers his own question: "Stella?"

"She heard your thoughts," Leo says.

"From how far away?" Daniel asks, cutting in. "Where were you?"

She hesitates. "I don't—"

"Your friend—Goose, is it?" Leo asks.

"As much as you'll get, it is."

"He's turning out to be quite useful."

Goosey turns to me. "And here I thought you invited me to the States to eat, drink, and be merry."

"For tomorrow we die?" Mara asks. A deeply uncomfortable silence ensues.

Daniel's the one to pick things back up. "But Gifts don't work on each other without an . . ." He looks to Stella.

"Amplifier."

Wonder where she got that from. Wonder if she and this lot have been studying up.

"So where were you?" Daniel asks Stella again, but turns to Mara before she can answer. "Did you see her that night?"

"No," she says quietly. "And I would've remembered."

"We had a fight," Leo answers for Stella—it's as though she's iced over, frozen. "She was already above ground when it happened." He turns to Jamie. "But you wanted to know if we'd ever been sick before, right?"

"Right . . ." Jamie says.

"It was just nightmares at first," Leo says, centring the attention back on himself. "Then hallucinations."

I'm not sure if Mara's pulse kicks up or if I'm imagining it.

"I was hospitalised—my fevers were out of control. But a lot of the time the doctors and nurses would treat me . . . differently. Like they were seeing things around me. Sometimes they wouldn't open the door to my room. I thought maybe they were seeing the same hallucinations I was, then wondered if I could make them see different ones. Project different images onto reality. Turns out, I can."

"When did this happen?" Daniel asks.

"Seventeen."

"Same as us," I offer.

"And the rest of you?" Leo turns to each of us. "How did you figure it out?"

Jamie shrugs. "Basically, the same. I'm a year younger than you guys, so, still working my shit out. But I'd say something to someone, I'd get sick, then they'd do it."

"And what about you, Mara?" asks Leo. Fuck. "What is it that you do?"

The air condenses in the room, thickening with silence. Stella says nothing. Something happened—something bigger than I'd thought. Stella's eyes skim right off Mara and land on the floor.

The tension's like having something growing in your chest, ready to claw its way out. And yet Mara seems the most relaxed of all of us.

"If I wish someone dead, my wish will come true."

Goose exhales, a smile appearing on his lips. "Wish I could do that."

"No," Mara says. "You don't."

My poor friend has no idea how to unpack that. "So,

just to be clear," he says, struggling, "you're basically saying you can kill any one of us, anytime you want?"

Mara doesn't answer. Her face is stone smooth.

"If I wanted to kill you, you'd be dead," Stella says. "That's what she's thinking."

Mara's smile gleams like the edge of a razor. "Guilty."

20

EACH OTHER'S MASQUERADE

STELLA LOOKS AFRAID AND POISONOUS AT ONCE. Mara looks satisfied. Daniel is watchful, Jamie thoughtful, and Goose is trying to pretend he's unruffled by the revelations of the last hour and failing.

And I, I don't know what I am. Mara talks a good game— she puffs up like a cat would to appear larger and more frightening than it actually is, and I usually find it just as hilarious because she looks so completely unmenacing, it's hard to remember that she actually is.

So the fact that she wasn't *talking* shit, but was thinking it? I can't say it isn't a bit unsettling.

Seems as good an opportunity as any to get to the point—*my* point, anyway.

"Are we going to talk about the person who killed himself in your home this morning?" I look around, but despite the paint colour, nothing else from that nightmare is familiar.

Leo stares for a blank moment, eyes watery and pale. "His room was down here. I'll show you."

I get up, and Mara follows without missing a beat. Jamie and Daniel are a bit slower, and Goose—

"Pardon? Did you say—"

I turn to my friend. "Goose. Mate. You're going to have to choose, very quickly, whether to shut up and stay or go home."

He closes his mouth, lifts his chin, and walks past. "Well?" he says, right behind Leo. "Come along, then."

The rest of us follow as Leo walks me back into my nightmare.

The windows are tipped in gold and red stained glass diamonds, kaleidoscoping the scuffed, abused hardwood floor. Even time hasn't quite managed to trample or fade the inlaid pattern in the wood that borders the room. The walls are the same colour, that faded mint green, the nightstand littered with the same smattering of partially filled glasses, some gathering more dust and mould than others. Then there are the bottles. The room smells like sick, but the bed's been stripped, mercifully.

"This wasn't Felix's room," Leo starts. "He came down here last night, after Felicity disappeared."

A laugh escapes Jamie's throat. "Wait, Felix? Felicity?"

Stella and Leo are quiet, and Jamie manages to rein himself in.

"How much do you know?" Leo asks me.

I glance at the stripped bed. "Pretend I know nothing."

A smile twists Leo's mouth. "I can't do that."

Stella looks back and forth between us and seems to make a decision. "Felix was our friend." She takes out her phone, scrolls a bit, then hands it to me. A picture of four of them— Stella, Leo, Felix, and Felicity. He has longish light brown hair and freckles, and looks slight beside the girl—she's taller than he, with curly ginger hair and an easy smile.

Stella turns to Daniel. "They're both eighteen. Both Gifted."

"Were," Jamie says, and Stella shuts down. "Don't you mean 'were'?"

Her eyes harden. "Yeah. I guess I do."

"I'm sorry," Goose says, "but shouldn't the police be here?" He thinks for a moment. "Wait, they *were* here. They just left and let you lot hang out?"

Leo directs his words at me. "Your friend—Jamie, is it? He's not the only one who can be persuasive."

Jamie pulls a face at Stella. "And here I thought I was special."

"*I* still think you're special," Mara says.

Mara, Jamie; it doesn't seem to bother them at all that they're standing in a room where someone ended his life.

Perhaps it's easier for them, having been through worse. A boy committing suicide must seem like nothing by comparison. I'm growing irritated at them for coming, at Mara especially for bringing them, at Leo for being coy about it, and at the entire bloody world.

"Why did you bring me here?" I ask Leo, and Mara's head snaps around because as I say it, I realise she doesn't know about the address he conjured for me to see. There'll be fallout with her later, which I can't even pretend to care about now.

Leo makes no move to speak, so I go on. "We know what you said—that Stella told you we were here, and you were curious about Goose's ability, I'm sure. But I saw you watching that girl on the platform before she jumped, before Felix killed himself. Who was she? Why were you watching her?"

Mara refocuses her attention on Leo, with effort. "Did you know her? Did you know she was going to kill herself?"

Leo pauses, and I notice something—he has no tells. No nervous tics. Slick, that one.

"We didn't know her," Stella says. "But like we said, we've . . . been able to find others with Gifts. We knew she had one." Her pulse is thready, heartbeat erratic. Stella's lying about something; about what, I haven't the slightest.

"We'll never know now, because she's dead," Leo says flatly.

"A lot of us have been turning up dead," Stella says.

"Turning up?" Jamie asks.

Stella's eyes dart away. Leo, undisturbed, says, "Committing suicide."

Mara exhales lightly, just loud enough for me to hear.

"Look at the house," Leo says. "Notice anything unusual?"

Stella unfolds her legs from beneath her, heads to the kitchen table in back. She comes back with a small pile of papers. Printouts.

News reports of missing teens. She places them on the scratched-up floor in a grid. Arcel Flores, a Filipina girl with a flashing smile, left her parents' two-bedroom in Queens to tutor a high school student in maths. Never came home. Jake Kelly, a lacrosse player with a dimpled chin, missed practice— his parents haven't seen him since.

There were six more. Six more names including—

Sam Milnes.

Mara goes rigid. "You knew them all?"

Stella won't address her directly. She puts down the last piece of paper.

Felicity Melrose, seventeen. Daughter of Chelsey and Peter Melrose of the Upper East Side. There are more details about her family, where she was last seen, but those don't interest me. I've never seen this girl before—not hurt, not in pain. She's just—missing.

Felix, however.

"How'd they do it?" I ask, though I know the answer already. "How'd they kill themselves?"

Stella and Leo exchange a look.

"You can't tell me because you don't know. They're missing, not dead—"

"As good as," Leo says, straightening his spine.

"Explain," I say, leaning against the wall.

Leo appears to be editing what he plans to say, which reminds me—

"Stella, are you *listening*?"

She turns practically white.

"To us. Our thoughts. Right now."

She shakes her head emphatically. "That's not what I'm doing," she says, though her gaze flicks briefly to Jamie, Mara. "I have to concentrate, hard, to do it. And I hate it, so I take drugs to blur out the voices. Otherwise, it's too much." She looks at Jamie. "You guys know that."

"Drugs?" Goose perks up. "What sort?"

"Prescription . . . ?"

"Actually," Daniel says. "No offence, Stella—"

"He's about to say something offensive," Jamie stage-whispers.

"I'd be more comfortable knowing you're not poking around in my brain either. I think that would go a long way toward trust, on both sides." Ever the mediator.

Stella looks to Leo, and when he nods, I can actually feel her relief. Doesn't escape my attention that she's been looking to Leo for quite a lot. Codependent or . . . something more? Something . . . else?

Stella retreats to the bathroom, returns with some pills. Shows them to Daniel. "Do they pass inspection?"

He raises his hands up in defence. "You don't have to show me. I know what you were going through last year. I know how badly you wanted a cure."

A cure. Mara mentioned that in passing, that it was Stella's main motivation for joining her and Jamie in their search for me. She'd hoped they'd find something that would stop the voices in her head. She'd hoped to find a way to be rid of her affliction.

A flush rises in Stella's cheeks. She's embarrassed. There's a furtive glance at Leo as well. Is she not supposed to want it? A cure? Fuck. I've missed so much.

She shakes out a couple of pills. We stand silently in the dead room, waiting, but they start to work quickly. Her heartbeat grows sluggish, her chest rises and falls slowly. It's possible she could still hear our thoughts, but when asked directly, she says no, and I believe her.

"Two days ago," she says slowly, "Felicity just disappeared. We were sleeping in our bedroom"—she nods to the stairs—"and when I woke up on Saturday morning, she was just . . . gone."

"Wait, she was *here*?" Daniel asks. "The paper says she lived with her parents—"

"She was Felix's girlfriend," Stella says. "He lived here, with us."

"Did the rest of them?" I ask Leo. "Live here with you?"

Leo doesn't answer immediately. Instead, Stella continues, "She told her parents she was staying with a friend Friday night, but then she just—"

A movement from Leo, slight, barely perceptible. But I notice, as does Stella.

"Obviously, Felix tried her cell phone, e-mail—Stella was listening, trying to find a trace of her but—"

"No," I say, annoyed and suspicious. "That doesn't track." I have the room now. "You followed Beth to the subway because you heard her thoughts, yeah? But you didn't know her ability." Which she was thinking about before she died, and which Stella would've known if she really did hear her.

Silence from both of them—something's off, but I don't press, because I don't want to admit to them that I heard Beth's thoughts myself.

"And us?" I ask instead, directing a piercing look at Stella. "You just happened to know we were in the city? Knew we'd be at the Second Avenue stop heading downtown?" I gesture to the papers of the other missing teenagers. "You said it yourself, Stella—it's hard to focus on one person in all the noise—and okay, yeah, I'll buy that Goose has an ability and is amplifying yours or whatever, but that doesn't explain why Felix would kill himself two days after his girlfriend went missing. So tell me," I say. "Stop fucking around and tell me. What is happening to these people? And how do you know about it?"

Stella's caught short by my aggression. Leo . . . isn't. He's considering, editing again.

"We know someone who . . . can identify people like us. Other Gifted."

And there it is. He doesn't go on, so Daniel tries to prompt him.

"And once identified, you bring them here?"

Leo shrugs. "Some people find us. Some people, we find. And we share what we know with the ones who stay here, practice with us—"

Jamie straightens up. "Practice? Practice what?"

"Using our Gifts." Leo has Jamie's full, hungry attention, which he knows, because he says, "I can show you, if you want,"

"Maybe later, thanks," I say, interrupting. "Right now we want to know everything you know about everyone who's missing."

"And everyone who's died," Daniel adds. Mara is notably silent.

Leo draws himself up. "Let me ask you this," he says to me. "How did *you* know her name was Beth?" All eyes on me. "You can find people as well, can't you?"

"It's not like that. I'm not hunting anyone," I retort.

"We're not hunting anyone either."

"Oh, so the people you find, they want to be found?" I ask. Even Daniel quiets at this, and I'm rapidly losing the plot. "Tell me how it works. Tell me how you knew Sam."

"Did *you* know Sam, Noah?" Leo's tone is suggestive, accusing.

"No," I say. But it takes effort to stay calm, dismissive.

"Why don't you tell *us* how it works?" Leo asks, "How you knew to come here?"

"I can see and feel what they see and feel when they're suffering, right before they die."

"But you didn't stop it," Leo says, picking my scabs.

"Because it's too late by then. I'm not *there* with them. I just see and feel. But this isn't the case for you. These are your friends, no?" I pick up the papers. "Some of them lived here, but they keep going missing—"

"They keep *dying*."

I round on Stella. "How do you know?"

Her eyes dart nervously. Before she can lie, Leo says smoothly, "One of us can . . . see connections. To other people with Gifts. And when one of us goes missing, the connection dies. They just—vanish. Wiped off the grid."

"And who's making these connections?"

"She doesn't *make* them, she sees them. Or feels them, I guess. And it's not for me to out her. If she wants you to know, she'll find you."

"So if they disappear," Daniel says, "How'd you know where to find Beth?"

"She says they flare up right before they die. I guess that part of her ability's familiar to you," Leo says to me.

"You could've stopped Beth from killing herself," I say, and then it's out there. The reason I'm so angry. They actually could've done something to help her, and they didn't—and without any guilt. I couldn't have, but feel responsible anyway.

"We didn't know."

"Bullshit," I say. "Stella could hear her thoughts."

"I couldn't. It was like there was something—cloaking them. She was . . . different, somehow."

"And Sam?" Mara asks, the first thing she's said since all this has come out.

"He was too far away," Leo says. "For *us* to do anything about."

Implying that there should've been a way for *me* to do something about it. I feel like hitting him. More than that.

But Jamie's actually the one to move on this, surprisingly. "How about Felix, then? He killed himself in your house!"

"He chose to," I say before catching myself. Leo's pale eyebrows rise slightly.

"Meaning what?" Jamie's focused on me now. "That the others *didn't* choose to kill themselves?"

"It's true," Stella says, saving me. "And anyway we weren't here when it happened."

"How convenient," Jamie says.

"It's not like he'd have chosen a time when he could've been rushed to the hospital and had his stomach pumped," I say without meaning to. Stella looks grateful, though I didn't say it for her benefit. I shouldn't have said it at all, as I've no interest in playing patient to Mara's or Jamie's armchair psychologist later—Mara's expression is shadowed, and Jamie's confusion has turned to suspicion. Daniel and Goose are both unruffled, knowing well enough to leave it alone. If Goose wasn't actually present for all the injuries I tried to explain away in school, he would've heard about them.

Leo takes advantage of my having thrown at least half the room off-balance. "Look," Leo goes on. "We all want this to stop happening, right?"

Daniel's the only one to nod.

"And we know what you guys went through," Leo goes on. "That place, Horizons. Looking for a cure. The experiments they were doing on you in Florida. The research you found."

Goose turns to me and mouths, "The fuck?"

Did they know who ordered it all, though? Was *that* what the envelope was about?

I inhale. "So you showed me your address, sent the clippings to let me know you knew all about me, and led me here to help you find the rest of these people before they die too?"

"What clippings?" Leo asks.

I can't tell if he's lying. Not even with Goose here, supposedly amplifying his heartbeat or whatever.

Seeing me thrown, Daniel takes the lead. "Someone sent Noah an envelope with his father's obituary and something about a poisoning in the NYPD."

"That's . . . random," Leo says. I notice Mara direct her attention to Stella—*all* of her attention.

Stella, still refusing to look Mara's way, says. "We didn't send that."

So, *who did?*

"Okay, question for another day," Daniel says. "We want to pool what we've got, stop this from happening to anyone else. Right?"

"Yes," Stella says. "That's what we were hoping." Leo nods once.

I'm trying to work him out. His breathing is even, heartbeat steady, but he doesn't seem . . . right.

All of us have gone quiet, so Daniel steps up again. "All right, there's a lot to . . . digest." He twists back to the windows, which are now giving off only the faintest beams of light. "It's late, and we should be getting back," he says to Goose, Jamie, Mara, and me. We nod like puppets. "But do you want to exchange numbers?" he asks Leo, who withdraws his mobile from a back pocket. Daniel gives it to him. Leo looks at me next.

Oh, why not.

As they lead us out of the house, Stella reaches out to Jamie, "It's good. Seeing you again."

A single nod. "Yeah. We'll catch up."

"I'd like that."

As Mara exits, Stella says nothing to her, nor Mara to

Stella, though she does offer the slightest of smiles to Jamie and Daniel. The five of us assemble at the bottom of the stoop, raising a final glance at Leo. Stella's already tucked herself back inside.

We walk back to the train, Jamie and Mara speaking in low voices, Daniel talking at Goose. I'm trailing slightly behind when my phone vibrates.

It's Stella. I need to talk to you. Without Mara. LMK before 8.

And then another text, right after:

p.s. Please don't tell her. Please.

21

NIGH INCURABLE

THE AFTERNOON SCROLLS THROUGH MY HEAD on a reel. I'm torn between irrepressible urgency and overwhelming—emptiness.

Seeing the names and faces of the Gifted—that's what Stella and Leo kept calling them, the word they preferred to use. But are we? Gifted? Seeing them cut skin, tuck pills under tongue, step into air. It's . . . I'm—

Triggered. Triggered is the word for it, much as I hate to admit. I keep trying to push it down, sweep it away, shut it down the way I always had when I'd seen the others hurt themselves or be hurt. But this—this *is* different.

This must be like what Mara felt when Jude was tormenting

her, pushing buttons she didn't know existed, pushing her till she lost control.

I'm losing control now. Jumping in to defend Felix's choice to die because he thought his girlfriend had. It feels like wolves are at *my* door, *my* house, circling.

I had a dream, after word reached me of my father's death. I saw myself standing beneath a tree, a shadow me, faded and incomplete. I watch myself tie a rope to a branch; there's no sound, no birds, no wind in the trees. I step onto a shadow and loop the rope around my neck. The ghosts of my family stand and watch, faces anaesthetised, wiped of expression. I meet my own eyes, and, without a word, my other self steps off.

The veins in my neck stand out lividly, my feet kick, but my hands don't reach up. It's a reflex, the last gasps of a dying body, of the meat that contains me, struggling for air, for life. It wants to keep going so badly. My feet stop kicking, my body hangs limp. I looked so peaceful, as if sleeping midair.

And then I heard the hiss of my father's voice in my ear, in my mind; *Coward.* I hesitated, just for a moment; I wanted to retort, to deny it, but I couldn't. Because I was.

That's what they call suicides. Cowardly. Selfish. But looking around at the little clumps of people on the train, part of me truly doesn't understand—how do they do it? How do they fill the minutes and hours and days and years of their lives? What's missing in me that I don't know how to fill mine? That I don't want to?

There's so much time, endless time, and I stand here in the

centre of it with my dick in my hand, completely clueless.

It's wrong, they say. Selfish, they say. Most people would do anything to get more time. They would kill me if they could steal mine.

I look at Mara—she's been through hell, and she did what she had to, to get out of it. She fought to stay here, and not for me. For her.

That was always Mara's purpose—to hold on to herself. From the very first, it's what she worried about most.

When we burned her grandmother's doll and found the pendant inside of it, the one that matched mine, and the one the professor had sent Jamie, we'd retreated to my room. She was shaking, ashen, and I was desperate to help her.

"Tell me what to do and I'll do it," I remember saying. *"Tell me what you want and it's yours."*

"I'm afraid I'm losing control," she had said.

"I won't let that happen."

"You can't stop it," Mara said back. *"All you can do is watch."*

I'd felt powerless for so long, I was resigned to it. All I *could* do was watch. And then she'd said:

"Tell me what you see. Because I don't know what's real and what isn't or what's new or different, and I can't trust myself, but I trust you. Or don't tell me, because I might not remember. Write it down, and then maybe someday, if I ever get better, let me read it. Otherwise, I'll change a little bit every day and never know who I was until I'm gone."

Mara was so wrong about herself, and so right about me. She was never in danger of losing herself. If anything, she *became* herself, and she never needed me or anyone to remind her.

I, on the other hand. I've always *wanted* to lose myself. She's all I've ever wanted to hold on to. So if I could die, if I lost Mara the way Felix lost Felicity? I would probably do what he did too.

I've failed to notice that we're off the train, at the clock tower, in the lift. Mara unlocks the door, and once we're in, Goose explodes.

"Okay. Someone seriously needs to tell me what the bloody fuck is happening. And by someone, mate, I mean you." He rounds on me.

"It's . . . complicated," I say to Goose.

"Yeah, twigged that," he says. "But, really, you couldn't be arsed to tell me about any of this before?"

"When?" I ask. "When would've been a good time to tell you about—"

"About your bloody *superpowers*? That girl back there, all of that—you're putting me on, somehow, right?" He looks from me to Jamie. Jamie shakes his head slowly.

Goose falls back onto the sofa, closes his eyes and rubs his temples. "Well then, you're going to catch me up, because despite that girl reading my mind and whatever else the fuck was happening back there, I'm not at all convinced you're not taking the piss."

I sigh. Only one way to convince him. Jamie's ability is

difficult to prove. Mara's—well. Self-explanatory. But mine. I glide to the kitchen, begin opening drawers. Then I find what I've been looking for—the knife block. The sound it makes when I slide the chef's knife out makes my blood quicken.

"No." Mara's voice is clear, defiant. Loud. "You're not doing that."

"You know," Jamie says, making his way to the kitchen, "I've always wanted to see this, actually."

"*No.*"

"Mara, it's the only way."

"It is *not*. You're not doing this."

I look past her to Goose, still in the living room, observing us with a sort of detached curiosity. I hold the knife in one hand and turn the other out, palm up in offering. "Just a small cut."

Jamie pouts. "*What?* Don't pussy out. Cut off a finger or something," he urges. "Does it grow back?"

"Never done it."

"No time like the present," Goose says, his voice edgy now.

"If you do it, it's over," Mara says. "We're over."

It takes a beat for that to land. Daniel, Jamie, and Goose are uncomfortably, awkwardly silent.

"I mean it, " Mara repeats. She's breathing quick and hard, so angry, so fast. "I'm leaving the loft, moving back in with my parents. We're done, completely."

"Mara." Daniel puts a hand on her shoulder—withdraws instantly, as if burned.

"*No.*"

"Mara, I'll heal," I say casually.

"That's not the point and you know it." She looks around at everyone, visibly holds herself back from saying something.

"Do I?" I push her without quite knowing why. I'm still holding the knife.

"Um, should we . . . give you guys a minute?" Daniel asks.

Mara looks at me, challenging. But I've decided. I want to do this, which is why Mara doesn't.

I'd done what she asked me to, all those months ago. I started keeping that journal for her, wrote about nothing *but* her, and then she went behind my back and read it, and we had our most splendid fight.

"You want to hear how I first learned about my ability? About being told that we were moving into yet another miserable home two days before we left by my father's secretary, because he couldn't be bothered to tell me himself? About feeling so numb to it and everything that I was sure I couldn't actually exist? That I must be made of nothing to feel so much nothing, that the pain the blade drew from my skin was the only thing that made me feel real?"

She looked like I'd struck her.

"You want to hear that I liked it?" I went on. *"Wanted more? Or do you want to hear that when I woke up the next day to find no*

trace of any cut, no hint of a forming scar, all I could feel was crush-
ing disappointment?"

"*You want* me to hurt you,*" she'd said.*

"*You can't."*

"*I could kill you."*

If I hadn't been so furious with myself, I might've laughed.
As if killing me would be the worst thing she could do to me.

I took a step toward her. "*Try.*"

Now she's threatening me again, but with something worse. So
I'm not quite sure what possesses me to take the knife and slide
it across my palm. The steel parts my flesh like soft butter, and
the blood instantly pours to the white floor, puddling, blooming.
Mara spins, deft as a deer, that gorgeous face marred by pain
and betrayal, and takes the stairs at a run, with footsteps hard
enough that I think she may shatter it.

"Dude," Jamie says, going pale, backing away.

Daniel rushes for a towel. "Pressure." He forces it against
my palm. I take it from him, let it fall. The blood hasn't stopped
rushing, hasn't slowed.

Goose even looks sick. "That's . . . mental. Jesus fuck."

Daniel again. "Noah, you need stitches."

A single shake of my head. "Watch."

We all do, all except Jamie, who has a blood thing, apparently.

"It's going to be fine," I say, but the words feel furred, each letter separate and fuzzy. Daniel forces the towel back into my hand, holds it there.

"Dude." Jamie. "Maybe we should go to the hos—"

"*Stop.*" I gather myself as Mara did, coalescing around a spark of white I feel in my chest. I close my eyes. "You wanted this. Both of you. *Don't pussy out now.*"

I watch the two of them watching me. Daniel watches the clock. Everyone's heartbeat is rabbit-quick and frightened. I ignore it, them, and listen to myself, a bundle of raggedy notes splintering at the edges. A mangled theme that won't stop scraping at me. If I blot out everyone else, concentrate on each note, I'll fix it.

My blood's soaked through the first towel, but with each breath, it slows, now only petaling the second. They all watch in curious, dazzled horror. But Goose watches with scepticism. I've never had to prove myself to anyone before this, and it makes me wonder for a moment—just a moment—whether I'll heal myself.

I peel off the towel, look down at the cut—still bleeding, pooling in my palm. But not to the floor. A surge of pride, and a gratifying—rush. Like I've let poison out, and for the moment, I'm clean.

We wait till the blood stops pooling, which, if I'm being honest, takes a bit longer than I thought it would.

"Well, there we are, I'm a cunt," Goose says.

"Not news." I get up to rinse my hand, and my body nearly

sways, surprising me, but I right it in time, before they notice. Run my hand under the faucet, and Goose, Daniel, and Jamie are all slack-jawed and staring. My anger's burned itself out, and I want to talk to Mara, talk her down, really, but the loft seems to breathe and stretch, the stairs seeming impossibly far.

"I'll be back in a bit," I say, and push off the counter.

Coward.

All in my head. Back straight, gait long—keep up or fuck off.

I find Mara in our bed, clothes on, curled on her side. Closet's open, and some clothes lie in a little nest at the bottom. One glance at her bag shows she'd started to pack.

"Going somewhere?"

She doesn't answer.

"Mara."

"Don't."

"Don't what?"

"Say my name."

"Shall I come back later?"

"You can do whatever you want. It's your house."

"I had to do it. Goose wouldn't've believed any other way—"

"Bullshit."

I stay where I am. "It isn't."

I can't hear her. Not her heartbeat, her pulse, nothing. The silence frosts the windows. All I can hear is the train trembling by on the Manhattan Bridge.

"You're really going to leave?"

She doesn't answer that, either.

It's like approaching a dangerous animal—show no fear. I cross to the bed and run my finger along her bare instep, and she kicks out at me and swears. For a moment she lies there, half shadowed by the ash grey sky, turning darker by the second. She leans up on her elbows and twists, lip under teeth. If looks could kill, I would be dead already

"You said you'd never cut yourself again."

"This wasn't like that—"

"You promised."

"Mara—"

"You lied to me."

"I didn't lie."

"You're lying now. To yourself."

I sit next to her on the bed. "Do you want to see it?" She looks down at my hand, curled into a fist. "It's not even bleeding anymore."

"That's not the point."

"Isn't it?"

Annoyed, frustrated. "Fine, that isn't the whole point." There she is, my Mara. "You weren't just proving yourself to Goose. You were . . . hurting yourself. On purpose. A chef's knife, a straight razor, your father's hunting knife. It doesn't matter how you do it. Or how you excuse it."

I risk a finger, tracing it down the line of her shoulder to the inside of her wrist. She's still quiet—all of her—but she doesn't protest.

"You're my preferred method of self harm." She tries to hide a tiny smile. If I didn't know her the way I do, I wouldn't catch it.

But I do know her. And I do catch it.

"I know I am," she says. "'You'll love him to ruins,' the professor said. 'Unless you let him go.'"

"Fuck's sake, Mara. Really? I'm *fine*."

"You're *not*, and if you say that again, I really will kill you, and you'll prove the professor right." Her heart's not in it though.

"All right," I say. "I'm not." Her body goes slack, and she curves back into the bed. "I'm—I don't know what to do with all this. Sam. Beth. Goose explains why I'm seeing, feeling *more*—he magnifies everything we've got. Which, by the way, means I'm even more safe around him. You have even less reason to worry."

Even as I say it, though, I realise the opposite must also be true. He must amplify her, too. I see the thought reflect in Mara's eyes.

"You think he's magnifying you, too."

"All for one, one for all."

I turn her face toward me. I open my fist. The cut is deep, still open, but not bleeding. "Look. No scar."

There is, though, and Mara knows it. The scars you can't see are the ones that hurt the most.

22

MAN'S CAPACITIES

As soon as I'm alone, I text Stella to say that I'll meet her tonight, and she almost instantly sends me a location. Jamie and Goose seem to have retreated to their rooms, and Daniel's gone back to his dorm, which saves me the trouble of having to lie about where I'm going when I leave. I write Mara a short note in case she emerges, then take the train to the park Stella mentioned. There's an old stone house at the entrance. Stella's waiting for me outside the gate.

"Thanks for coming," she says.

"Rather odd place to meet, isn't it?"

A slight, shivery shrug. "It's between your place and ours."

"Meeting in the middle," I say, looking about. "Obvious metaphor or just convenient?"

Her eyes crinkle at the corners.

"You're not worried about walking through parks at night by yourself?"

She arcs an eyebrow. "This is Park Slope. And it's basically a playground."

"Playgrounds without children are even eerier." A fall breeze rustles the trees, and a swing nearby creaks, making my point . . . until I see the dog that brushed it, squatting as his owner dutifully waits for him to finish his business.

"What did you tell Mara?" she asks, refocusing my attention. "About where you were going?"

"Nothing," I say. "She went to bed."

Stella's forehead scrunches. "So early?"

"We had a . . . disagreement."

"Trouble in paradise?" She examines me, and that's when I notice her noticing my wrapped-up hand.

I take the opportunity to look, really look, at Stella for the first time. She *is* different from the girl I knew at Horizons, which might as well've been years ago. It's not just that her hair's lost its shine, or that her face has hardened, her curves whittled down. There's something missing behind her eyes. Something lost.

"How'd you end up in New York?" I ask.

She blinks. "I was *in* New York. With Jamie and . . . Mara."

"Right, but as I understand it, you left?"

"I went home."

I wait for her to finish. Clearly, she has something she wants to get out, or she wouldn't've asked me here.

"Once it was obvious we weren't going to find a cure for our . . . Gifts . . . I just. I stayed for a while after that, but then after Mara . . ." Her voice trails off. "I was going to go back to Miami—I didn't know where else to go. But I left without anything—I had no money, no friends. I literally didn't know what to do. I ended up sitting for hours in Grand Central, just sitting there, when Leo just walked right up to me."

"What a coincidence."

She avoids my eyes. "It wasn't a coincidence. One of us can . . . find people like us. We told you that."

"You did, but failed to mention whom," I say, bored by the mystery already. Leo wouldn't give anything away, but perhaps Stella might.

"She doesn't live in the brownstone," she says. "It doesn't matter—the point is, Leo found me, told me I had a choice— he'd help me get home if I wanted to go, but also said I had a place with them if I ever wanted it."

"How generous."

She shrugs one shoulder.

"So you went home with a perfect stranger?"

At that, she laughs a little. "Safer than staying with my so-called friends."

"And your family?"

Her bitterness deepens. "Not everyone has a perfect home life."

"We have that in common."

"Anyway, Leo wouldn't have hurt me. I couldn't hear his thoughts, but I knew—he's not like anyone else I've ever met. He's special."

Aren't we all.

"Look, the town house is like a safe house for people like us. Anyone can go there, anytime, and they take care of each other. It's like—they're like a family, okay?"

They, not we.

"And they welcomed me in, and Leo helped me figure out what I'm capable of. And Felix, and Felicity and S—" she catches herself. Was she about to say Sam? I want to ask, but I don't want to throw her off. "They matter to me. I'm worried for them."

"We already said we'd help."

"*Daniel* said," she corrects. "You didn't."

"Is this why you asked me here in the middle of the night? Because honestly, you needn't have gone to the trouble—"

"I wanted to talk to you about Mara."

I'm on guard, but try not to show it. "What about her?"

Her eyes dart away. "You seemed . . . left out . . . at the house earlier."

Nerve struck. I pretend otherwise. "Excuse me?"

Stella meets my eyes. "What did she tell you about what happened after Horizons?"

"Why are you asking me this?"

"Because I heard what you were thinking!" Her voice echoes in the empty park, but it's the words that lift the hairs on the back of my neck.

She takes a deep breath. "You were right. I was listening to you."

"And what is it you think you understand?" My voice is low, quiet, but I'm furious.

"That Mara and Jamie went through something together that you weren't a part of."

She's pressing on bruises, and she knows it. I refuse to give her the satisfaction. "You didn't need to read my thoughts to know what's literally true."

"I know that she never told you what that something was."

"She never told me because I never asked."

Stella lifts her chin. "Because you don't actually *want* to know." She takes a step closer to me. "With your friend around? I can hear more than just the words you think before you say them out loud. I can hear what you're afraid to admit even to yourself."

My breath quickens as I grow angrier. "You were spying, in the most exploitive, violative way. Why should I believe anything you say?"

"Because you know I'm telling the truth."

"I can't believe I came out here for this."

A bitter smile. "I can. You came because you know something's wrong and despite acting like you don't give a shit, you give a shit more than anyone—about this, at least. You don't want anyone else to die. I may not be able to read your mind right now, but I know you can tell whether I'm lying or not. And you know I'm not."

"I know you *think* you're not. But just because you believe something doesn't make it true."

"And what do *you* believe, Noah? You think all of this is a coincidence? Everyone dying all of a sudden? Your father was the first, wasn't he?"

The words I was about to say die in my throat. Does she know about him? What he did? Who he was?

Instead of those questions, I ask, "So you did send the clippings."

She squints. "No. I didn't. But I did read the obituary."

There was nothing of consequence in the obituary. Which is what I'm about to say when Stella says, "It was a lie."

I keep my voice even. "Was it."

"He disappeared before he died."

How does she know? I want to ask, but I don't want to give anything away. "Why do you think that?"

"Are you saying it's not true?" she asks. "That he didn't disappear and then commit suicide—which happens to be how our friends are dying? How Sam died, at his funeral?"

A finger of ice trails my spine.

"What do you think Mara has to do with it?" I ask, but I'm feeling uneasier by the second, and my mind rebels against Stella's words, pressing on me to leave. "Look, whatever happened between you and Mara, you're clearly not over it, but I couldn't care less, so if that's all there is, I'll just be going—"

"Whatever happened between *me* and Mara?" She laughs without humour. "God, you really don't know her at all."

"Oh, but you do. Because you were so close?"

"Because I was *there*. When she murdered Dr. Kells—"

"And what's his name, right? Sorry, if you're trying to shock me, you're going to have to try harder."

"Do you know what Mara did to him?"

"Killed him," I say plainly. "Freed you, as I understand it."

Another icy smile. "Yeah. She killed him. But not before cutting out his eye. While he was *still* alive."

Got me there. I try not to show it, not to betray that her words cut me off midbreath.

"And she didn't just murder Dr. Kells. She *butchered* her."

"All of you were prisoners, test subjects. Mara got you out of there."

"She did, but not before locking herself in a room with Kells and cutting her into a thousand pieces."

"A bit dramatic—"

"With a scalpel. That she *still* has."

That's . . . indisputably disturbing.

She throws me a knowing look. "Oh, she left that part out?"

"Are you actually saying that you think Mara's responsible for people she doesn't even know committing suicide?"

Stella says nothing.

"What've you told Leo about her? Your friends?"

She lets out a puff of laughter. "That's what you're worried about? What I've told them about her?"

I'm feeling ill, light-headed, and not remotely about to admit that Stella is right about anything, any of this. Mara had no reason to want strangers dead—she wanted to find out about Sam as much, if not more, than I did. I stop playing defence, start playing offence.

"If Mara hadn't killed Kells, and Wayne, you'd probably still be there, or dead. And," I add, as Stella opens her mouth to speak, "despite all this, you still escaped with her and Jamie. And stayed with them for quite a while.

"I did stay. Until I couldn't anymore."

I already know I don't want to hear why. "You were fucked with, abused, tortured. Whatever any of you did or didn't after, you're not responsible for it."

She turns on me then, the force of her almost knocks me back. "We're responsible for *everything* we do. We always have a choice."

My words, once.

"And Mara chose wrong. *Every time.* There was this trucker—"

"Stop."

"A trucker picked us up. I had to go to the bathroom, so we stopped and got out and Mara came into the bathroom and I left and she came out covered—*soaked*—in blood and he was dead."

And? "That's not all of it, is it though?"

She pauses. Then, "What?"

"Come on. You don't expect me to believe she just killed someone for using the bathroom."

I hear, see, the blood rush to her cheeks. "He tried to—he was waiting for me."

There it is. "In the women's bathroom. At the rest stop."

Silence expands like a bubble around her.

"He raped you?" I ask.

A small shake of Stella's head, and I know. I wasn't there to witness it, but I know.

Mara's been through—hell. It's the only way to describe it, how this all started.

The boy, if he can be called that, barely human as he was, started out as her boyfriend before he became her tormentor. A night out with him and her friends had ended up with her trapped in an abandoned insane asylum, after he tried to force her, nearly raped her himself—that's how *her* ability first manifested. That's how the woman who raised him, a doctor bought and paid for by my father, forced it out of her. Mara thought she'd killed him and her friends that night, but he made it clear to her—and only her—that he was still alive, tormenting her with his existence, and no one believed her but me. I *was* there for that bit. Every second he lived tortured her. He took her freedom and crushed it, and then Kells did the same. Mara was violated, in every way, by people she was supposed to trust—her boyfriend. Her doctor. And she was committed for it—not even her family believed her, the people she trusted more than anyone in the world.

Her parents don't know. They thought they were helping, genuinely, and her mother would fall on her sword if she knew the truth. Mara knows that. She knows it's not their fault. And yet.

Mara also knows she didn't deserve what'd been done to her. But in Horizons, I saw this tiny cell of guilt—the thought that she accidentally killed her best friend—turn into shame when she believed she killed her friend to save herself. It grew every day, cancerous, threatening to eat her alive.

Maybe it finally did. I may not know everything about Mara—it seems I know less than I thought, but I know this—she would never let anyone be violated the way she'd been again. Stella might not get it, but I do.

"Mara came in. She killed him, and you got out."

"Yes, but—"

"She saved you."

"You weren't there!" Her words tear at the trees, sear the air. "You didn't see her face when she walked back to the truck.

You didn't see her expression when she decided to kill these two dumb college kids for practically nothing—"

What?

Tears begin to fall. "You don't know about the subway. The train tracks. Jamie and Mara haven't told you."

"Look, Stella—"

"It wouldn't matter to you that Jamie forced these two ass-holes onto the subway tracks to punish them for urinating on a homeless woman and calling him a—" She stops, and the word she doesn't say hangs there, sick and poisonous.

"They were racist, and horrible," Stella says, sniffs. "But they didn't deserve to die."

"Did they?"

"Did they what?"

"Die?"

Another head shake. "Jamie just wanted to scare them. But Mara"—she breaks into another laugh, chilled—"she was going to kill them. She kept them there, I don't know how— their noses began to bleed and—"

The droplet of blood from Sam's nose that ran over his lip, fell into the puddle beneath his swaying body.

A slight smear of blood on Beth's first knuckle . . . as if she'd wiped her nose just before jumping.

The weight of everything I realise I don't know about Mara, didn't want to know, is suddenly too much.

"They didn't die," Stella says, letting out the anger she has left. "But they would have. Jamie stopped her from killing them. Otherwise—" She stops, breathing hard, wipes her eye with her wrist. "You weren't there."

And there it is. That bruise that won't heal, the fracture still splintered. And she's pressing on it. Bending it. Waiting for me to break.

I'm so tired, suddenly. A wave of exhaustion crests, pulls me down with it. I want nothing more than to leave Stella there in the park and sleep. Forever.

"You're right, Stella," I say casually. "I wasn't there. And you weren't there when she sacrificed her own life for her brother's." Both brothers, in fact, but I leave that bit out. "So what are you trying to say, exactly? That she's a monster? Bringing death and destruction in her wake, wherever she goes?" The minute I say it is the minute I realise that that's what my father had been saying about her. How he tried to persuade me to kill her.

Stella lets out a shivery breath. Her eyes flutter closed. "What I'm saying is that she's not who you think she is. She's changed."

My head feels numb. I can't do this much longer. "And you haven't?"

"Of course, I changed too."

I nod. "You left Mara and Jamie—"

"And Daniel," she adds.

"But now here you are, fetched up in Brooklyn after abandoning them—"

"It wasn't like that—"

"But you're lecturing me about Mara, who's given more of herself for the people she loves than you will ever know."

The transformation is instant. Her face hardens, and she takes a step back, crunching dead leaves. "How much, Noah?"

"What?"

"How much of herself has Mara given up?"

When I don't answer, Stella says, "You don't know what she's given up either." She's the one to turn around first, to start walking away. But she tosses one look, one sentence, at me as she leaves.

"But you will."

23

TENDER MERCIES

WHEN SOMEONE IS HIDING A SECRET IN A house, something changes in the air. Unspoken words, half-finished smiles, eggshell steps—they distort reality, they muffle truth.

The person with the secret is changed by it—she smiles, but the corners of her mouth don't quite reach the height they used to. The corners of her eyes don't crinkle as deeply. The look in her eyes when she tells you she loves you—there's something behind it. You don't know what it is—what has she done?

Mara is many things, but a cliché isn't one of them. If she

does have a secret—and she does, I know that now, after that night with Stella, see it in everything she does—her secret isn't a person. It's a thing. A thing I can't know, because it would change us.

What Mara doesn't know is, it already has.

You can't keep a secret from the person you love and expect it not to change him, too. She doesn't trust me with something, which makes me distrust her, and that makes our hands miss each other when we pass something over the table. It makes my mouth just miss hers when I lean to kiss her lips and end up with cheek instead.

When you love someone, you're saying you trust them. You're handing them your heart and trusting them to protect it. To keep it safe.

Keeping a secret is like throwing that heart into the air and playing catch with it by yourself. But what you're really playing with is someone else's love, someone else's happiness. I've always wondered how people do it. I'm the farthest thing from unfailingly honest—in fact, I'm an extraordinary liar—but it's strange how different things seem when it's your own heart that's being tossed casually into the air. It's a dangerous game.

When I was a child, I read everything I found, anywhere I found it. The only thing that felt beautiful about my life was the way books let me escape it. I felt surrounded by nothing, and the boredom was thick enough to choke on. When you can choose to do anything, how do you choose? *Why?*

All my life I've heard the phrase *Do what makes you happy* tossed around—not at me, God knows. But generally, as a principle. But when nothing makes you happy, what do you do then?

This is the essential truth about me: Mara makes me happy. The *problem* of Mara makes me happy. I shouldn't say it, but it's true. I shouldn't think it, but I do. She's this endlessly complex, chaotic person, but there's a method to her madness, and I want to know it.

Can you ever really know another person? I thought I could. I thought I knew her, but now . . .

People who think they know me imagine me in control. When they see Mara and me together, when they think of us together, they see me as the lion tamer, and Mara the lioness. One crack of my whip, or a whisper, or a magic word, I'll tame her like all the rest.

I don't want to, is the thing.

But now, knowing what I *don't* know, I want to cage her. But I want to be in that cage with her, no whip, no magic, and lock the door behind us, lock the world out. And then:

I want her to split me open, to dig her fingers in and pry open my ribs, lick my heart and my blood and my bones. Pick open my bones and suck out the marrow. I want to be devoured by her. And she wants to devour me just as badly. It's in every look, every movement, every smile.

But her world is different now, and I don't know how,

because I missed it. My father took that from me, from us, and I didn't feel that missingness most of the time, but I feel it now. Mara works hard not to show it. She and Jamie or Daniel or all three will exchange a look, and I'll feel a kick of surprise in my chest. They were part of something that I hadn't been, forged something together that I was left out of. Excluded from. When I ask Mara about it, she skirts around it, says it doesn't matter.

But she's a liar too. It does.

24

HAVING DISCOVERED FIRE

URRENT MOOD: DAVID FOSTER WALLACE meets Amy Winehouse.

Mara was sleeping when I got home from meeting with Stella. I could've woken her, confronted her that night, and we could've fought about the secrets she's kept and the lies she's told.

But then, I would have to confess too.

Careful not to wake her, I climbed into bed beside her, but couldn't close my eyes. When she woke up the next morning, I acted like nothing was different. Though everything was.

How could I have it out with Mara when I've been the one avoiding the truth—whatever *that* is—this whole time?

And whatever is or isn't happening now, with the suicides, I'm certain, positive, that Mara isn't to blame.

So I've defaulted to doing what I do best: nothing. Jamie's been gaming, and Goose has been going out. Mara's started drawing again. She's been writing and drawing. I have no music in me.

Daniel's rather aggravated by the state of my affairs when he shows up at the loft days later. "We need to talk," he says. He's caught Jamie and me mid–*Duck Hunt*, shooting at the projector with an orange gun lifted out of the '80s and dropped into our flat. It makes an annoying-yet-satisfying plastic *click*.

"What about?" I ask as a pixelated bird falls to the pixelated grass. It's incredibly satisfying—I've become rather addicted.

"Your inheritance."

That turns even Jamie's head. Mara's in the shower, and Goose has decided to brave the Gowanus Whole Foods to procure provisions for a grand dinner party that exactly no one has asked him to throw.

"I want to explore the archives," Daniel says.

"I'm having the building demolished and turned into a community garden," I say without turning away from the game. "Next topic."

"Then you're either an idiot or selfish."

"That's a rather strong and unnuanced position," I say evenly, and aim the gun at the screen.

"Because it's that important. Can you put down the gun, please?"

"If I must," I say, laying it on my lap.

"Look, everything David Shaw did and had other people do is in there. All the research and tests and results—"

"Precisely," I say. "And you managed to break in and start going through it. How long until someone else does? Maybe someone else already has. We're obviously not the only Carriers in this city."

But Daniel's not keen on letting this go. "So what? Maybe there's something in there that would help create a cure—"

"Isn't that what Kells was trying to do?" I look at Jamie. "A little help, here?"

"Hard pass," Jamie says, turning back to the game.

Daniel leans his palms on the kitchen counter. "If there's a chance it'll help us find out how to keep whatever's happening to the others from happening to you guys, we can't afford to ignore it." I notice the shadows under his eyes, the strain around his mouth.

"You're worried about Mara," I say.

"Aren't *you*?" His voice is almost accusatory. Almost.

More than you know, friend. "Of course," I say. "But I don't think the shit my father did to her—to all of you and Jesus fuck knows whomever else—is going to help."

"So what's your plan?" Daniel turns up his hands. "Do you have one?"

"Plans are so formal," I say dismissively. "And they tend to go to hell where your sister's involved."

"You're just saying that because you don't have one."

"I've heard from Stella," I say, surprising myself. And Jamie, who leans closer to the TV to hide the fact that we now officially have his attention.

"My plan is that we should meet up with her and Leo and find out more about the others who lived with them. Work backward from there."

Daniel pauses for a moment. "Okay. While you're doing that, why don't you let me work from the files that might be on them?"

It's not that Daniel doesn't have a point. My father tortured, or paid others to torture, people to find out why I am the way I am—I'm sure he learned quite a lot about those of us who carry the gene that makes us "gifted." But if we use what he learned from that torture, that justifies it. Everything he did—to Mara, to Daniel, even—I won't. I won't do it. There has to be another way.

He blows out a sigh. "I don't get it, Noah. I don't get why you'd want to get rid of stuff that could help us. Help my *sister*."

"There's no cure," I say, and Daniel freezes. "I know you want there to be one, but there isn't."

"We don't know that for sure. *We* hardly know anything. You're wasting a huge opportunity, and it's stupid, and I know you're not stupid, so what is it? What are you afraid we'll find in there?"

Nerve struck. Never let it show. "Daniel," I say reasonably. "You're a vegetarian, yes?"

He shrugs. "Yeah."

I look down at his feet. "Do you wear leather shoes?"

"No."

"Is it because you don't like the taste of meat? You don't think leather shoes are comfortable?"

He rolls his eyes up to the ceiling. "One, we could end world hunger with the feed used to keep breeding animals for food. And two, the idea of contributing to an animal's suffering just so I can have a cheeseburger makes me sick."

"I feel the same way about my father's research. I don't want to use the product of so much suffering just so we can maybe, possibly, use the product of that suffering to achieve something else."

"Your metaphor doesn't work," Daniel says, crossing his arms. "But let's run with it anyway. I'd use medicine tested on animals if Mara was sick and I thought there was even a ten percent chance it would heal her." He leans back. "What would you do?"

"I'd heal her myself."

"And what if you were normal, Noah?"

There. There it is, in his voice.

"What if you were just a normal person and Mara was sick,

dying, and you couldn't heal her yourself but thought there might something out there, some way that you could?"

I get it, then. It's not just curiosity. Daniel is normal, but instead of the blessing that that is, *he* feels cursed. He feels helpless. Helpless and scared.

He looks to Jamie for backup, which, after Stella's revelations, I'm more certain than ever he won't get. Jamie was there, after all. And he's here, now, anyway.

Footsteps on the stairs, bare and uniquely Mara's. The three of us look up; her hair's wet and she's wearing an old faded T-shirt, once orange, now the colour of peach sherbet. Her toes, nails painted black, always, are visible through the glass. Her eyes meet mine, and everything else fades to dullness.

"I'll think about it," I say to Daniel, hoping that'll end the conversation. And that he and Jamie will miraculously leave.

"Think about what?" Mara cocks her head, a wolf catching a scent.

"I want Noah to grant me access to the archives," Daniel says.

"Wait, he won't?" Mara turns on me, unfairly tempting as she stands there in mismatched, damp clothes, her hair still wet. "Why not?"

Hope dies. "There's more paper, more files, more everything than we could sort through in a year," I say, resigning myself to the fact that this conversation is still happening. "So how will it even help us?"

"Because there's a system, and I figured it out," Daniel says, his voice tinted with *gotcha*, not pride. "Jamie and Mara and Stella—they looked where I told them to look."

Jamie finally speaks up. "True."

"So you don't have to worry about people breaking in and using stuff against us."

Daniel's hooked onto this idea and he's never letting this go. "All right. Listen. I haven't even had time to look through all of the paperwork my father's solicitors sent over." I realise that said paperwork is likely here, in the flat—in the same room as the trunks from the manor house. I could ask for their help going through them . . . but I'm not sure I want that, either. Did I even lock up my mother's things? Christ.

"I can help look," Daniel offers.

No going back now, alas. "Actually, I'd rather you didn't." That gets everyone's attention. "There's . . . family stuff." Mara's expression changes, and I need to choose my words more carefully than I have been. "Things of my mother's I had sent over. I want to be the one who sees it all first, all right?" I'm not above playing the dead mother card.

Daniel lifts his eyes to the ceiling, nodding. "Fine."

Because it works.

"All right, then," I say, reluctantly abandoning *Duck Hunt*. Jamie makes a sad face. "I'll go up and look for the correct paperwork," I say, improvising as I go. "I want to change the key code for the building and make sure there are safeguards in place so you're not followed, or anything like that. Want to take over for me?" I ask Daniel, indicating the gun.

"I'm gonna go to Sophie's. But I'm going to text you every day—multiple times a day—until you get it done. Bye, sister," he says to Mara. She lifts her hand in a limp wave, and Daniel walks out.

It takes Jamie less than a second to do the same. He stands, the plastic gun clattering to the floor.

Mara arcs an eyebrow. "Where are *you* going?"

Jamie looks from her to me. "Elsewhere. Rapidly," he says, already backing out of the living room.

"Because?"

"Because I'm abstaining from this particular argument. You kids have fun, though!" He whistles the *Hunger Games* theme as he climbs the stairs.

"Ass," Mara comments. Then, "What's going on with you?"

"I'm sure I don't know what you mean."

"I'm sure you do, but, fine, I'll play. One: Why don't you want us in the archives? Also, you didn't tell me you had your mother's stuff sent over from England."

"That's not a question."

"Seriously?" She looks murderous, and I have to work not to laugh.

"All right, in reverse order: I don't tell you everything, and because nothing good will come of anything my father was involved in."

"You're not him, you know," she says, her voice softening.

Sometimes I wonder if *she* can read thoughts. "I know."

"No, you don't. But, Noah, that research, it's not like the One Ring."

"Not where I thought you were going to go, but, all right." I take a step toward her, winding a curl of her hair around my finger, then tugging it. Two little lines appear between her brows, and she bites her lip. A few minutes ago I would've attacked her. But now . . .

"I should go and do what I promised Daniel I'd do." I move to leave, but she doesn't let me off that easily. She never does.

"You think that even if we try to use that stuff for good, it'll end up corrupting us somehow."

"And how exactly do you know what I think?"

"Because I know *you*." She searches my eyes. "And I know my brother. And I know you know my brother. You trust him with that stuff, but you don't trust yourself."

"What about you?" I ask, aiming my voice at her as I ascend the stairs. She slides away from it even before I ask my next question. "What if there's something in there that you could use against someone you think deserves it?"

A look, direct, unyielding. Honest. "I wouldn't do anything without asking you first. I promise."

The thing is, I'm not sure I believe her. Not anymore.

25

CONFIRMED DESPERATION

I CLOSE THE DOOR BEHIND ME WHEN I GET TO THE office. Just looking at the boxes from my father's solicitors and accountants brings not only his will, but the letter he included with it to mind.

Don't let her death be in vain.

Those *fucking* words. My father is dead, entombed an ocean away, but his efforts to twist my life into one after his own image live on. The professor alone, I could've ignored, and *have* ignored, but my father worked through him or he worked through my father or—

I kick over a banker's box of documents, and just barely resist the temptation to trash the room. Mara's downstairs, but I can feel her presence there; that watchfulness, those expectations.

The air is close and stale in here, tiny motes of dust visible in the shaft of light from the room's only window. It looks over onto the cobblestone street below. I desperately want to walk out, and just keep fucking walking.

Nothing good can come of anything my father wanted, and he wanted me here, looking through these boxes, somehow living up to the potential my mother literally died to give me, and all of it whittles away at any ambitions I might've had to find out more about Sam and Beth. I did want to help the helpless. *Fight for those who cannot fight for themselves*, as my mother put it. But were those *really* her words? Just as likely that her beliefs were manipulated by the professor as well.

If you don't fight, you will grow lazy and discontent under the guise of wanting peace, she wrote.

You will acquire money to acquire toys but the biggest ones will never be big enough.

You will fill your mind with trash because the truth is too ugly to look at.

And maybe, if you were another child, someone else's child, maybe that would be okay. But you aren't. You are mine. You are strong enough and smart enough and you are destined for greatness. You can change the world.

Brilliantly, perfectly vague, isn't it? *Destined for greatness. Change the world.* As if it isn't hard enough just to make myself want to *exist* in the world. I've seen the truth; I looked straight at it when my own father handed me a syringe, a knife, and a gun, and forced me to choose between killing the person I love most or killing the person *she* loved the most. I've never seen anything uglier than that. Why *should* I have to keep looking?

Maybe Mara and Daniel are right, and there's something worth finding amongst these boxes and trunks and whatever else my father's got stored up in his archives. But I've seen enough of the truth at this point to know the answers to the questions *we* want answers to won't be handed to us by anyone else. *We* have to *be* the answer. Ignore the past and just keep going.

My mobile vibrates in my back pocket. It's Daniel.

Update?

Horrid. I set the phone down on the desk and crouch amongst the trunks and boxes. My mother's, battered and beaten and ugly, taunts me silently a few feet away, and my father's paper empire has me surrounded. I can't leave the room without seeing Mara and I can't look at my phone without seeing Daniel's texts, so I rise up, open the desk drawer for the envelope of keys, and shake out a few at random. Let fate decide, if it exists.

One of them is a tiny, polished silver skeleton key, and there's only one trunk it seems like it would belong to, the walnut-wood, silver-edged one with all of those women's names engraved in silver. I move over to it and pick it up;

it's quite heavy, and without any obvious lock.

Opening it again, I look for a compartment inside, sifting through the letters sent to one E. S. by the various women he seems to have fucked, which at least makes me grin. The bottom is red velvet, like the rest of the lining, but—

The top of the trunk is a half cylinder. And hollow.

Maybe it's a piece of priceless history, who the fuck knows, but I take my house key to it and tear the fabric anyway. There's a silver keyhole beneath it.

My Dearest Wife,

I have found it. I cannot express my
joy in words—it is beyond measure. I am
eager to return home to you and the boys, but
I do not know when I will be well enough
to make the journey. Do not worry—I
am being expertly tended to and have been
given all manner of treatments—traditional
and . . . much less traditional. But I am
compelled to discuss a matter with you if—if,
against all odds, I fail to return.

There is a thing I must ask of you, a
thing I must beg of you. There is a girl—
she is orphaned and alone, but she has the
most exceptional Gifts—my darling, I want
to take her in as our ward. She would come
to London with me and live in our home and
be raised as our niece, despite—well, despite
her differences, which are not insignificant.

I regret having to ask this of you in a
letter. But I cannot bear to see her Gifts
wasted—I wish I could explain my reasons,

but I fear that our correspondence might be intercepted and I cannot risk it. But do know that though I want this very much, I would never make such a decision without your blessing. I eagerly await your reply.

Your Loving Husband,

S. S.

18. March

My Darling Husband,

I wish you were alive to see how the plain ward you have sent me has blossomed into the most exotic flower.

You begged me to treat her as if she were our niece, but the girl has become more like a daughter to me. She is as gifted as you promised, with more talent and accomplishments than I could have imagined. It took her mere days to learn to paint the most beautiful portraits. I wish you could see her, what she has become. Her dark hair is luxurious enough that she need only adorn it with a single flower. And though she is not gifted musically, she has the voice of a lark. When she enters a room, she draws everyone present like moths to her flame.

She is as demure and elegant and humble as she is accomplished, and she shows no signs of self-interest and has no ear for gossip; for that, I am afraid she lacks for friends. The latest crop of London society girls whisper and swoon over the slightest things; and I am most proud that she is not inclined toward that behaviour.

She is inclined to remarkable studiousness, however, and I know that you would delight in her curious mind, though I admit I find it a bit unusual. The tutor you've arranged for her is rather queer himself, as is the fact that she has a tutor rather than a governess, which as you surely knew is generally regarded as inappropriate, and yet I have been assured you desired that he, and only he, be charged with her education. I don't even know his name; Mr. Grimsby calls him the professor, and everyone seems to accept that.

The doors are always open during their sessions, of course, but somehow I can never quite hear what they're studying together, and though I have searched her room out of curiosity, she doesn't appear to have taken any notes. I shouldn't be so distrusting;

she has proven herself to be honest and kind and generous, mostly with me. I believe she knows I am lonely and indulges this poor old widow accordingly. When I remember that she is even more alone in the world than I, than anyone, in fact, my heart breaks for her all over again. But seeing her, the way the candlelight sets off the fire in her skin, the way she commands a drawing room conversation with just a few words—she is dear to me, Simon. A greater blessing than I could ever have imagined.

Your Faithful Wife,

Sarah

26

THE DEVIL GOES ON

HE SOUND OF MY MOBILE VIBRATING ON THE metal desk gives me a start. When I look up from the letter, the sky beyond the window is dark.

I stand to pick up my phone—hours have passed. Worse, there's another text from Daniel. I turn the phone off without reading it and nudge the lid of the trunk shut with my foot, leaving the letters, the keys, everything on the floor.

I desperately want it to be a coincidence that a nineteenth-century letter, written by one Sarah Shaw to one (apparently deceased?) Simon mentions "the professor." Surely there were many professors in Victorian or Georgian England or whenever the fuck they were written, the ink on the dates is smudged.

But it's him. All roads lead to him.

Enough. I've had enough.

I cross the room to leave, but as soon as my palm touches the knob, it twists and—

Mara's on the other side of it.

"Did you hear?"

"Hear . . . ?"

She seems a bit jittery. "Daniel said he texted you."

"He did," I say. "Asking for an update."

Her eyebrows draw together for a moment before she shakes her head. "Check again."

"I've turned it off," I say, rather bitchily. "Just tell me."

"Stella's missing," she says. "Apparently."

"What do you mean, missing?"

"Daniel said Leo texted him, and he thinks we should go over there. And that we should bring Goose." She rushes out, her footsteps echoing in my skull. I shake my head, rub my temples. My body feels heavy, as if I've been sleeping for days, and Mara's voice sets my teeth on edge.

"Come downstairs!"

I follow her slowly, not sure how to process this news, trying to will myself to stop ruminating and drag my mind back to the present. Jamie's voice carries from the first floor.

"What do you think?" I hear him ask Mara, but her reply is muffled. Walking downstairs feels as though I'm wading through mud, as if it's sucking at my trainers, making every step aggravatingly slow.

She and Jamie are standing together in the living room when I get there, while Goose is in the kitchen, slicing at something.

Not ready for Mara just yet, I turn to Goose instead. "What's all this?"

He separates two translucent slices of meat. "Prosciutto." He holds a paper-thin slice up in offer.

"Pass." The smell of it turns my stomach for some reason. I twist to look at Jamie and Mara. "Have you heard anything new?" I ask him.

Jamie glances at Mara before answering me. "What?" I press.

"She's not missing," Mara cuts in. She's standing on the balls of her feet, her body taut, brimming with energy.

"You seem quite confident," I say.

"I am."

Because she doesn't trust Stella, for obvious reasons?

Or because she knows where she is?

I don't even think I want to know, at this point.

"But we're going anyway," Mara says with a sigh. "Daniel's on his way there."

Daniel's waiting alone, standing at the cross streets by the house. The neighbourhood balances on the knife-edge of gentrification, and he looks rather relieved to see the four of us, assembled as instructed. We walk to the house together, no one saying much of anything because, I imagine, none of us is quite sure what's to be said. Daniel's the one Leo texted, so he's the one who knocks.

Rolly's head pokes out from the gate below the stairs, as out of place as a hard-boiled egg. His eyes sweep over us before he pops back inside just as Leo opens the door.

"Thanks for coming," he says. "We really appreciate it."

It's a damn sight harder to get a read on him today, as I'm not at all up to scratch.

"What's with that guy?" Mara mutters.

"Rolly?" Leo asks, waving us inside. "It's his house."

"You rent it?" Jamie asks.

"Not . . . quite."

Jamie and I exchange a look. "He doesn't let you live here rent free . . . ?"

"Like I said when we met, you're not the only one with a gift for persuasion," he says to Jamie.

"I'd like to meet the others," Jamie says.

"Help me find them before they kill themselves and maybe you will."

Off to a rather rough start. "So what happened?" I ask him, forcing myself to scrape this afternoon from my mind.

Leo sits down on the leather chaise, and the rest of us crouch/drape/lean on whatever other surfaces are available. I take the ottoman opposite him.

Leo bends forward, elbows on knees, and rubs his forehead. "Stella didn't come home the night before last."

Bloody hell. "That's all?" I ask, feeling annoyed and superior until I realise that the night Stella went missing is the night we last spoke.

"It's not like her," Leo says, eyebrows knitted, talking to himself. "She always comes home."

Home. I take in the brownstone again, the shabby, abandoned look of it.

"Thanks for coming," he'd said. *"We really appreciate it."*

Home to *whom*? Stella's missing, Felix is dead—who's *we*?

Mara almost seems as though she knows what I'm thinking. "Was this house always like this?"

Leo shakes his head. "A lot of people come and go." He pauses before saying, "Came and went, more accurately, I guess." His expression darkens, and if I hadn't been watching him so closely I'd have missed the way his eyes flit to Mara.

Fuck this guy. "Let's skip the bullshit, shall we?" I say. "Why did you want us to come?"

He raises his chin, turns to Mara. "Because I think you know where she is."

"You're mistaken," I say for her.

"Am I?" He's still talking to her. She doesn't respond. Doesn't defend herself. So of course, I do.

"I don't know what Stella might've told you—" I start.

"Everything," Leo says. "She told me everything." He looks at Jamie then. "Which makes me pretty wary. And she's not here to read your minds to tell us whether you're lying or not."

"Why would we lie?" Mara asks, but her voice sounds strange.

"Why would Stella leave you and be willing to go back home to a stepfather who abused her?"

My conversation with her bobs up in my memory like a dead fish.

"Leo found me, told me I had a choice—he'd help me get home if I wanted to go, but also said I had a place with them if I ever wanted it."

"So you went home with a perfect stranger?"

"Safer than staying with my so-called friends."

"And your family?"

"Not everyone has a perfect home life."

Fuck. *Fuck.*

But Mara's voice is even, not the least bit thrown. "Because she disagreed with a decision I made."

"To kill people." The words slither out of Leo's mouth.

Mara simply shrugs. All the jittery chattery energy she'd had in our flat is gone. She's completely calm.

"Right," Leo says derisively. "Forgive me if I'm kind of concerned that you might not have her best interests at heart."

Mara's face is stone smooth, expressionless. "I wouldn't kill Stella, if that's what you're asking."

I try and listen to Mara's heartbeat—it seems loud, clear, steady. She's not lying. I'm surprised—and disturbed—by my relief.

"We want to find out why this is happening as badly as you do," I say.

"Really?" He rounds on me. "How's that?"

Forget this afternoon. Forget the professor. Forget my father. "Because every time one of us commits suicide, I fucking *feel* it," I say, aiming my mind on *that*. "Their suffering and regret and fear. You think that's fun, do you?"

Leo pauses before asking, "Have you seen Felicity since—did you see her . . . ?"

I supply the word for him. "Die?" I say, and he nods. "No. Nor Stella. As I said, I can't find anyone for you."

"He's not a precog," Jamie cuts in, to my surprise. He's been playing at casual, hanging back, leaning against one of the French doors, but now I notice that he's hyperfocused on Leo, tense and attentive. "But you know one, don't you?" Jamie asks him.

Leo's face pinches a bit. "Yes and no. There was someone here who could do that, but they're gone now."

"Gone where?" I ask.

"Went looking for a cure, I think. Mentioned Europe."

"Then let's hear about the rest of your friends," I say, leaning back and stretching my legs as far as I can without kicking him. "And figure out which one of them might actually be able to help." If Leo wants to work, then let's get the fuck to work.

"My friends can't help us," he says, those watery blue eyes on mine. "But your father can."

27

ONLY WHAT THEY AIM AT

I NEARLY LAUGH AT MYSELF THEN. HERE I THOUGHT I was well shot of this shit.

Goose is the first to speak. "*Your* father?" He turns to Leo. "Noah Shaw's father?"

Leo seems to have a little speech already prepared. "Noah now owns a building that his father used to own. It was filled with files on everyone he had ever paid to have experimented on—"

Goose laughs. "*David* Shaw? Some sort of big bad super-villain mastermind? That's your theory?"

Jamie makes a cringey face. "It's . . . pretty much true, actually."

I snap back to attention. *"Jamie."*

"Dude, he already knows. Stella reads minds—whatever she knows about us, he knows."

He's right. I hate that he's right.

"The archives," Leo says. No one else speaks. "Stella told me about them."

"And?" I say, "is there a question in our future?"

"I want to see our files. I want you to take me there."

"Why don't you sit on Santa's lap and ask for a pony instead?" I suggest. "That would be more likely."

He straightens. "What do you have to hide?" He glances at Mara. "Something to do with her?"

I *do* laugh then. "I don't have to hide Mara. She's quite comfortable with her homicidal tendencies."

She nods slowly. "Quite."

Daniel rouses at the mere suggestion of Mara's involvement. "Stella was in the archives with us, yeah. But you didn't find out about David Shaw until she must've heard that rattling around one of our minds. So riddle me this: How have *you* guys been working to find your missing friends since the first one of them disappeared?"

Well done, mate.

"You must have done some kind of research," he goes on. "You wouldn't just wait for someone else to appear and rescue you or them?"

He's hit on something; Leo visibly shifts his approach to all this. To me.

"No, we didn't just wait for our friends to die. *We* actually tried to do something about it."

"What did you try?" Daniel asks, proving to be exactly the sort of chap I need right now. Daniel's the one who could change the world. If anyone were ever destined for greatness, it's him.

"I'll show you ours if you show me yours," Leo says to me.

"Let me think about that for a moment," I say. "No."

Daniel shoots me an unsubtle look this time.

"Look, we're here," I say. "Presumably, so is the shit you've collected. The archives—I don't even have the paperwork from the solicitors yet—"

"That didn't stop Stella," Leo says to me. "Or you," to Daniel.

"What they found there was meant to be found," I say. "They were left virtual instructions as to how to find it."

"That's not what Stella—"

"As was pointed out," I say, trying ever so hard not to kick anyone's teeth in, "my father orchestrated what happened to us." I gather up my ammunition, however bullshit it might be. "He was many things, including evil, but he wasn't stupid or careless. Codes would've been changed—the building might even be empty now, for all I know. I haven't been there myself."

As I say it, I realise it might even be true. Surely I could find whatever I might want to, *if* I want to, but who knows what hoops I might have to jump through to do it? I try not to let my satisfaction show.

"It *kind* of feels like you don't give a shit about finding Stella at all."

Jamie twists a dreadlock around his finger, pretending to examine it. "Actually, I'm not sure I buy that *you* care about finding Stella all that much."

Leo casts a dark look at Jamie. "Fuck you. I love her."

Jamie's right, though. There *is* something between Leo and Stella, I do believe that; but I'm not at all sure it's love. Not on Leo's end. The urgency *I* would feel if something like this were happening to Mara?

"If Mara were missing," I say, "and someone told me that cutting off my limbs might help me find her? I'd be fucking limbless, mate."

"I thought you actually wanted to stop this," Leo says to Daniel, changing strategy. He's frustrated and annoyed, but not panicked. Not *desperate*. "I texted you because you seemed like you'd care about people besides yourselves."

"You know," Jamie says, "when you're trying to persuade someone to do something, you usually have a better shot when you don't repeatedly insult them."

Leo takes a deep breath. Dramatic. "I'm sorry, I'm just— scared for her."

"How about this," I say, an idea forming. "Share what you've got, and I'll make arrangements for you, Daniel, and Mara to go to the archives together."

Daniel's mouth falls open a bit. Then he tries to hide it.

"That sounds like it'll end well for me." Leo sneers. "Going to an abandoned building with a Non and a murderer."

Mara throws her head back against the sofa, rolls her eyes. "Why would I be killing random strangers?"

"Eliminating the competition?"

She snorts.

"Mara has no competition." Jamie pats her head, and she closes her eyes and smiles, cat-like.

"Why would you even think that?" Daniel asks.

"The fewer of us there are, the less you have to worry about anyone getting in your way."

"Getting in her way of *what*?" Daniel asks.

"She's your sister," Leo says. "I don't expect you to understand."

It doesn't escape my notice that Leo hasn't answered the question.

Daniel shakes his head. "If you don't trust me, why text me? Why waste our time?"

Leo hesitates. "Because your friends trust you, and if you told them to come, I knew they would."

He *was* right about that. But, confession: I'm not here for information about Stella. Leo's basically admitted he doesn't have any, and I'm not entirely convinced she's even truly missing. I realise that I'd have likely left already if it weren't for Sam and Beth.

This—whatever this is—started with them. Hearing their thoughts, which, in hindsight, I've got Goose to blame for, but they gave me an insight I'd never have had, otherwise.

Sam didn't want to die, but he killed himself anyway.

Beth didn't want to die, but she killed herself anyway.

And then Stella reappears in our lives, only to disappear days later?

There's a difference between taking pills in a bed, planning never to wake up, and climbing a centuries-old tower and hanging yourself while another man is being buried. A difference between throwing yourself in front of a train in front of strangers, and locking yourself in the bathroom to let your life drain out with the bathwater. The public display of anguish, and the isolated, private expression of it. How you choose to die can reflect how you chose to live.

Whoever found Sam, Beth, the others, and however she did it, Leo relayed that they went missing; their connection to her was cut. And then they reappeared when they were about to die. They were at war, I think—between needing, for some as yet unknowable reason, to end their lives, and their desperation to be stopped.

Sam wanted help. Beth wanted help. They killed themselves in public because they wanted people to *know*.

And not just people generally, in Sam's case: I think he wanted *me* to know. He ended his life on the day of my father's funeral, at my father's childhood home. What if he knew about me? If he wasn't just begging for help when he died, but was begging for *my* help?

Sam didn't just throw himself in my family's path, or mine—he crossed Leo's path as well—through one of Leo's Gifted friends, likely. The one who finds the others—on her own, or perhaps for him.

If you listened only to Stella and heard her version of her misadventures with Mara, it would be easy to lay blame and death at Mara's feet. Easy for Leo to seize on her perspective and believe it paints a whole picture instead of just a fragment. Easy for him to look at me, knowing who my father was and what he's done, and believe that's the key to unlocking this misery, instead of looking, *truly* looking, at the lives of each of his friends.

I've excavated far too much of my own past looking for answers for Mara, and I love her. Leo's not going to take the easy way out, if I can help it.

"If you really love Stella," I say, "then you're going to have to unpack your trust issues another time, because the only way you're going to the archives is if you go with Mara and Daniel, full stop."

"Why not you?" Leo asks.

"Because I believe it's pointless." True, and never more so

than today. "And that there are better ways to go about finding missing people."

"Like?"

"Jamie can persuade most people to do most things. The more eyes we can get looking for our friend, your *girlfriend*, the better chance of someone actually seeing her. Felicity as well."

"Don't you think I thought of that?"

"I don't really think about you at all, to be quite honest."

"The more eyes looking for them, the higher the chance of eyes on us," Leo says. "Who we are. How we're different."

"Isn't that part of what you do?" Jamie asks. "Cast illusions?"

Leo inhales. "How am I supposed to do that if I'm in the archives?"

Bollocks, and I'm calling him on it. "You do realise you're wasting time we could be spending trying to find the girl you claim to love?"

"He's right," Daniel says. "We can all do this together. We *should* be doing it together."

"Kumbaya styles," Jamie says.

Leo folds his arms. "Yeah, you seem like the Kumbaya sort."

I'm surprised at the fact that Mara speaks next. "If Stella actually did tell you the truth about us, she would've also told you that we're loyal."

"We're in the same place, mate," I force myself to say. "These abilities—we're going through shite other people don't know enough to have nightmares about, even. We don't need to know who you and your other friends are to care about you not being fucked with."

"All for one, one for all?" Leo asks. He knows I'm full of shit. Must do.

"Something like that."

"Then why don't you seem like you're worried about turning up dead yourselves?"

This, at least, I *can* answer honestly. "Because some of us have experienced things worse than death. Hope you don't have to find that out for yourself."

28

MEMORABLE COLLISION

MY LITTLE PROPOSITION SEEMS TO HAVE worked, however, for Leo leads us up the stairs into a large red room with a cracked nonworking fireplace and one long, massive desk along the wall—a counter, more like. The rest of the place might be falling apart, but the Mac is massive and new. What holds my attention though, is the map.

The thing spans an entire wall of the room, crisscrossed with differently coloured threads and pins. I move toward it, but Leo closes the drapes, shaking dust into the air and making Jamie sneeze. And casting the map in shadow.

The monitor blinks, swinging my attention toward it.

Leo gestures us all to the screen, opens an app and types in a URL.

"You're using Tor?" Jamie.

"Wouldn't you?"

"Touché," Jamie acknowledges.

Mara raises a hand. "Um, Tor?"

"The dark web," Daniel says.

"Because let's make everything sound as sinister as possible," Jamie says.

"Some of it is," I say. "Snuff films on there, aren't there?"

Jamie nods. "Afraid so."

"Lots of porn though, I imagine?" Goose says.

"If one can think of it, there's a porn of it," I say.

Mara half smiles. "Oh?"

"It is known," Jamie agrees.

Leo clicks an app that looks like a globe. "So this is the Tor browser," he says when it opens. "Like Google, but completely anonymous. If we're going to work together on this, you should probably all download it."

Goose looks rather sceptical. "Won't that land us on some Big Brother American Patriot Act government watch list of some sort?"

"We . . . crossed that bridge a while ago," Mara says.

Jamie turns his palms up as if to say, *What can you do?*

"Well, I haven't crossed it," Goose says.

"Don't whinge," I say as a page appears on our screen as if

from 1997, a message board, with the words "special snow-flakes" written in Comic Sans.

The messages vary in their weirdness. One post is titled "How do I make myself psychotic?"; another one "gifted cats?" Jamie sweeps by Leo and clicks on it before he can stop him—dozens of cat GIFs appear, mostly of kittens falling off things, others of kittens riding things. Scottish folds are quite popular.

A shadow darkens Leo's face. "Um, can I have that back?"

"Sorry," Jamie says. "I just really like cats."

Mara puts her hand on his shoulder. "Who doesn't."

Leo types a URL into the browser: 61f73d/4ffl1c73d

"Wow," Jamie says. "Takes me back to my MUD days."

"MUD?" I ask.

"Multi-user dungeon."

My mouth silently rounds the word "Oh."

Jamie looks at Mara, "You deserve better."

Haven't got the time or the interest to decode whatever Jamie's on about. "So what are we looking at?" I ask Leo. I hadn't known it was possible to be impatient and bored simultaneously. Leo clicks on a screenshot of a local news site in Charleston, South Carolina.

SUICIDE CULT CLAIMS FIVE

South Carolina: Police discovered the bodies of five students in a basement on Montagu Street on Monday, victims of an apparent suicide pact.

They included two students in their senior year at Ashley Hall,

and one student from Summerville High, also in his senior year.
Two freshmen at the College of Charleston were also among the
dead.
No further details are available at this time.

Below the screenshot is a post from someone calling themselves truther821:

"This never happened. I was one of Marissa's best friends. She
never would've killed herself. She was GIFTED, like us. Cover-
up maybe???"

I try and match up what I know to be true with that post, and . . . it doesn't. I'd have seen them die if they were like us, no?

Leo scrolls down. On and on they go, posts from teenagers, purportedly Gifted, in several states—in several countries, in fact, though I don't call attention to that detail—posts about teenagers going missing or committing suicide in the past three months.

"They're not all legit, obviously," Leo says, reading my mind. "But they're getting more frequent. All feature someone eighteen years old or close to it, all with prior diagnoses of mental health disorders, or so the media claims." Leo sucks in a breath. "I also know that some of the posts are about people we *knew*, and some are written by *Nons*."

"You keep using that word . . . ," Jamie starts.

"Non-Gifted. Friends of theirs, or family I guess. Anyway, word's getting out, is the point."

But how could it? He claims to have known some of these people—past tense. But again, I've seen only three deaths thus far.

We're all silent, until Leo says, "And in the interest of not wasting any more time, I also know that this doctor—Kells?—wasn't just experimenting on you. She was injecting other kids with something, trying to induce abilities in them." He walks over to one of the plastic card tables and holds up a file. "I imagine the name Jude rings a bell?"

29

A MELANCHOLY ACCIDENT

I DON'T LOOK AT MARA AND JAMIE, BUT I'VE NO doubt they've got *FUUUUUCCKKK* written all over their faces, because, well. That's the expression I'm trying to keep from mine.

"Stella told us about what happened to her. What the guy, Jude, did, to her, to you—" He nods in Mara's direction. "She told us about the gene—1821? That gets switched on in some of us and not in others, and she told us how Kells set out to try and create someone like you." Leo looks at me.

"All true," I say, ever so calm. "But how, precisely, does that help find Stella, exactly?"

"We don't know who was experimented on and who wasn't."

I offer a general-purpose smile. "Neither do we."

He falls back into the chair, rolls up his sleeve to scratch his arm, exposing the edge of a tattoo.

"What's that?" Mara asks.

He rolls the sleeve up the rest of the way. On his biceps, curling over his shoulder, is a black image of a sword, curved, sprouting feathers on each side, as if the sword is the spine of it.

I seize on it immediately. "Where'd you get that?"

"The tattoo? Pen and Ink—"

"No. The idea for it."

He shrugs like it's nothing. "They're symbols of justice—the feather and the sword."

All roads lead to him. My blood is electric, and there's an acrid taste in my mouth. "Who told you about it?" I ask Leo.

"Why?"

I round my hands into fists to keep myself still, even. In control. "I'm not going to ask you again."

"Look, most of us here? We don't really have what you'd call a happy home life, okay? Some of us don't have homes at all. Or families. Some have one dead parent, one abusive one. Others come from places, backgrounds, where they're shunned for who they are—not in the Gifted sense, but in every other sense. For being gay. For being Latina or black or Asian. For liking the wrong music, the wrong clothes, for being depressed, for being anxious, or angry, or scared. For being who we are.

Anyone who walks through those doors knows that they're not going to be persecuted or harassed or told they're broken. They come here because they want what we want—to use the Gifts we have to make the world a better place."

Familiar words, those.

"And most of us tattoo ourselves as a reminder to use our Gifts for good."

More familiar by the second.

"And it's become kind of a symbol of who we are—a family. This house?" He gestures to the room. "*This* is our home now. And I'm the only one left in it."

I can't get a read on him—my sodding brain is split between here and now and this afternoon and before, but Mara, dear girl, takes over for me.

"Who designed it?" Mara asks him. "The tattoo?"

"I don't know," Leo says.

"How do you not know?" Jamie asks, which shocks me a bit, honestly.

"Because I wasn't the first person to have it. Isaac—one of our friends—was. He told me what it meant to him, and that meant something to me."

"And where is Isaac now?" I ask.

A half shrug from Leo. "He's a bit older, graduated from high school a couple of years ago. I think he's travelling in Asia, now? India maybe? I don't know—does it matter?"

To me it does. Because the feather, the sword—the design

might be different, but the symbol—that's the professor's.

And *this* is what he does. He wrote to Mara:

My particular Gift allows me to draft a vision for that better world—but my curse is that I lack the tools to build it.

My Gift is useless on its own. And so I have found others to help me.

Uses others to help him, more like. Finds them and uses them, the way he found Mara, me, my parents, Jamie and Stella and now Leo. And every second I devote to thinking about him helps him, gives him what he wants.

So I scrape one of the folding chairs in the opposite direction, toward the map, and give Leo one command.

"Talk."

There are over thirty Carriers who have crossed paths with Leo in person, he says, twenty he was able to get to New York, at a point. Some came because they wanted to get rid of their abilities, others because they wanted to strengthen them. Leo was the second sort. Stella, of course, belonged to the first. Mostly, they reported the same stories: Their lives started to go tits up as early as sixteen, for some, which, Jamie notes, given that not everyone develops at the same rate, makes sense ("Fuck puberty."). By seventeen, many, if not all, were diagnosed with some sort of *Diagnostic and Statistical Manual* mental disorder. Which, as I know quite personally, means fuck all. But Leo and his friends—Stella and Felix and Felicity, at least—they began to catalogue them. Names, birthdays, hometowns, abilities.

Some could manipulate dreams, induce sleep, wipe memories. Others could cloak the abilities of others (different from cancelling them out, apparently), and something Leo said made it seem like they knew someone who could predict events.

"We all wondered why this was happening to us," Leo says. "But no one we came across had any idea how they got their Gift." No memories of having been experimented on, though many had been in treatment for their particular diagnoses or involuntarily or voluntarily committed at various points.

So, wanting answers and finding none, they took to the Internet. As one does.

Leo walks over to a different table, stacked haphazardly with file folders, pictures, medical charts. "Here's some of what we found that we thought might . . . mean something. I don't know." He rubs the bridge of his nose. "It seems ridiculous now, but what were we supposed to do? We didn't even know where to start."

Jamie's eyes narrow. "Well, wait. You actually said you started by trying to strengthen your Gifts, right?"

Leo catches himself. "Some of us."

"Like you."

He nods once.

Daniel walks over to the pile. "So who collected this?"

"We all did. You know Stella," he says to Jamie. "She

didn't want to be able to do . . . what she could do."

"Yeah, the cure thing was her idea." Jamie moves over to the table. "She's the one who—whoa."

"What?" I'm at his side immediately, but I don't—

"These are from Horizons," Mara says, looking between our shoulders. Then, to Leo: "Stella gave you these?"

I watch him mentally edit, which for me, confirms it: Stella took the files from the archives. Files that anyone who's ever been here could've looked at, copied, to be used on us or against us. Either way.

And now she's missing.

"Can we copy this stuff?" Daniel seems to be the only one with the presence of mind to deal with the clusterfuck this presents. Leo reluctantly assents, and everyone's got their mobiles out, snapping away at files, the map, all of it. Before we leave Leo's, someone promises to be in touch about the little archives party—not me. I'm thinking about arson, explosions, flooding—burying it all forever.

"So!" Mara says, closing the door of the flat behind us. "Stella stole from us."

Jamie, on his way to the kitchen, says, "Technically, she stole from Noah." He reaches up, grabs a glass from the cabinet. "Technically, we all did when we brought the Kells crap to my aunt's house—"

Now I'm barely clinging on. "You *what?*"

"We couldn't exactly go back there every day and use the place like a library," Jamie says.

I'm wordless, iced over, frozen with the knowledge that this toxic, radioactive mess has already been leaching out into the world.

"It shouldn't exist," I say. "None of it should."

"But it does," Daniel interrupts. "And Leo might be right— there could be something in here that we didn't catch before."

"You've seen it all before, no?"

"We weren't asking the same questions then," he says as Mara hands over her mobile. I follow, as does Jamie, and Daniel begins to scroll through each of our pictures, quick as anything. In just over a minute, he freezes, and my phone in his hand seems to grow in density, weighing him down like a stone. His lips part, eyes glaze over in shock, so much that his heartbeat becomes arrhythmic.

"What?" I ask, switching over to his other side, worried he might faint, and also desperate to know what's got him so unnerved.

"*Daniel,*" Mara says, and her voice brings him out of it, prompts a swallow. His eyes meet hers, still dazed, unfocused. "What?"

"Sophie," he says, handing the phone to me without looking at it.

"Your girlfriend?" Jamie asks, checking my face, Mara's, for confirmation. "What about her?"

Daniel takes the phone back from me, swipes the screen to zoom in. Holds it up. "This is her handwriting." He turns to Mara. "On your file."

FALSE SKIN

"OH MY GOD," SOPHIE SAYS, HER EYES WIDENING as she takes in the flat. "*This* is your apartment?" she asks. "It's incredible."

It was decided that Goose's little dinner party would be the setting for Sophie's interrogation. Daniel was under strict orders to act perfectly normal, as if his girlfriend of the past year hadn't been hiding the fact that she's an X-Teen. Mara was under strict orders not to kill her, accidentally or otherwise.

"Thanks," I say, taking her trench. "Getting bad out there?" The English and weather; there's nothing we excel at discussing more.

The rain dribbles along the clock faces and the darkening

sky, and the smells of braising lamb, searing scallops, and roasting vegetables ripen the air. When I bring out the wines, I begin to wish this actually is only a dinner party.

"No vegetarians round the table, I trust?" Goose asks.

Jamie tips his head at me. "Shaw only eats pussy—"

"Fuck off."

"Daniel's a vegetarian," Sophie says, and looks at him. "I've been thinking about it too, actually."

"How's Juilliard?" Mara cuts her off. Awkward pause ensues.

"Um, hard?" She blushes. "I mean, it's incredible just getting in, but now I'm practicing with students who are so much more talented."

Elbows on the table, Mara leans forward and says, "You have to be super *gifted* to be admitted in the first place, though, don't you?"

Bloody hell.

A slow nod from Sophie as she continues to feign ignorance, and acts appropriately thrown by Mara's targeted passive-aggression. Which won't remain passive for much longer. "I've never had to work so hard at anything in my life."

"You're being modest," Daniel says, his arm around her, giving her an awkward squeeze.

This is going to be savage.

"What about you?" Sophie asks Mara, elbows off the table, hands in her lap. "You guys are—" Her face blanks for a second. "You're at . . . NYU?"

Mara bends over like a snapped branch, and I hear the slight crunch of paper in her fist. For half a second I think about stopping her, letting the charade go on, dodging the scrunch until we've settled in a bit more. But then . . . it's Mara. She's going to do what she does.

She slides a printout of the smoking gun across the table to Sophie. Sophie doesn't look at it—she looks to Daniel with a nervous smile. "What's this?"

"How long have you known?" Mara's voice slices the air.

"Known . . . what?" She still hasn't looked at the printout. Good show. Perhaps all of us have underestimated Sophie Hall.

"Known that you were Gifted?" Mara asks her, and Daniel turns away to try and hide how fucking miserable he's been since he found out.

"Well," Sophie says politely, and turns to me. "I've been playing since I was four. . . ."

Mara bends down once again, then slides another sheet of paper toward Sophie. And another. All printouts of pictures of Horizons files with Sophie's handwritten notes, among others', all over them.

She finally sheds her smile and looks around at us. "What are these?"

Daniel, sitting next to her, lifts one up. "Your handwriting. On my sister's file from Horizons."

But Sophie's expression is placid, impressively innocent.

Daniel turns to her. "What the fuck?" he says.

Jaws drop. I don't reckon I've ever heard Daniel say the word "fuck" before.

There's a pause before Sophie folds in on herself, like a limp puppet.

"How long have you known?" He presses, barely containing himself.

When she looks up, there are tears in her eyes, wet streaks running down her face. "I knew when I was sixteen."

"How?" Daniel asks.

"I have . . . a sense about people. It's like—it's like I can see these connections, invisible strings, almost, that aren't there, with points of light attached to them—and they look—they look like they're tied to me. I get this weird feeling, almost like butterflies in my fingertips, when I meet someone who's . . ."

"Gifted," Jamie intercedes.

She swallows and nods.

Daniel rubs his hands over his mouth. "You knew the first time I introduced you to my sister that she was different." His voice wavers but it isn't weak.

Sophie swallows hard now, forcing back tears. "When she came to school. The first day. I felt it."

"Before we even met," Daniel says flatly.

A tiny nod.

"Well," Daniel says, trying for angry but the ache of sadness throbs in his voice. "So that's why you asked me out."

This is going rather off course. . . . I try to catch Mara's gaze, but her eyes cut Sophie to pieces.

Sophie looks genuinely horrified. "No. Daniel, *no*."

His breath is rattling in his chest. "You find other Carriers—Leo explained it to us already. That's what you do. So you found Mara, and then figured out that the best way to get to her was to go through me."

She shakes her head fiercely. "It wasn't like that—"

"It was exactly like that!" His face is transparent with betrayal and anger. "You knew about Jude. You knew he was alive and torturing Mara—you could sense him. And you just let me go on thinking she was sick? That she just needed help, when she was actually being tortured."

"You're the one who told Leo we were here," Mara cuts in. "*You're* the one who found us. Leo's been lying for you this whole time."

"I wanted to tell you before that," Sophie pleads. "I hated lying."

"Then why did you?" Daniel looks as though he might be sick. The food sits curdling, puddling on the table. "You've been lying to me for as long as I've known you."

"But not as long as you've known Leo," Mara says, her head tilting at an angle. "Right?"

Sophie sniffles, nods. "I met him at a Juilliard audition. He's a cellist."

"Nobody cares," Jamie adds.

"Were you telling him everything that was going on with us?" Daniel says—it's hard to know whether he means "us" in the couple sense or the group sense. Sophie's shaking her head vehemently, pleading with him, but if I were him, I don't know whether I could trust her again. Steady heartbeat notwithstanding.

"We just stayed in touch when he left Florida," she says, which visibly perks Jamie up. Was he from there? Just visiting? Or recruiting, as it were? "Last year, while we were all at Croyden," Sophie goes on, visibly trying to compose herself. "He was telling me about stuff that was going on in New York—people he was meeting, wondering if I could sense them from long distances or if it had to be in person. He told me how he and a bunch of others were practicing, trying to exercise our Gifts . . . they're a muscle, he explained, and training makes them stronger."

"Did you tell him we were coming?" I ask. "To New York?"

"Yes." She looks down, her blond lashes grazing her cheeks.

Goose leans in. "What, you sensed us when we landed at JFK?"

"No," she says, rather impatiently. "*Daniel* told me you were coming. Or that Mara was coming, anyway. With you." She turns her aqua blue eyes on me.

Splendid. I'm keen to move on, myself. "You were at the subway with us when the girl died." I can hear everyone hold a breath. "You knew she was Gifted—Goose was there, he'd have been amplifying your ability. You knew she was going to die."

Her lips part, but no sound comes out.

"Her name was Beth," I say to her just as she begins shaking her head. "You could've saved her life."

"We didn't know what she was going to do—Stella wasn't with us that night—"

"That's not how we heard it."

"They didn't want to out me, okay? But it's true, Stella can hear thoughts when she knows what to listen for, but she didn't know what to listen for, and anyway she wasn't there! She and Leo lied to protect me. But even if she had been there, this hasn't happened enough for any of us to even know what to expect beyond the obvious."

"Which is?"

Her voice tightens with frustration. "For me, I just knew—it's like, imagine all of us walking around with a candle. And then the light snuffs out. It just started . . . happening. People going missing. So we started tracking it."

"The map?" I ask.

She nods.

"You created it?"

"Yes . . . and no. It's not like I can just sense people all over the world. But being around you"—she turns to Goose—"it changes things."

As it does for us all, it seems. My thoughts slide to Goose

and Mara, but I mentally run like fuck from that. "How'd you put that map together?" I ask.

"The normal way, mostly. People came and went from the brownstone—but pretty much whoever came to the safe house would stay when they got there. Everyone told us where they were from, what they could do—we started piecing together whatever we could."

"But you were in Florida," Mara says at the same time. "At school."

"Around the time I met Leo, he formed a sort of chat client, so we could all stay in touch. I started talking to Stella a lot. She helped me."

Daniel's eyes meet Sophie's for the first time. "All those times you said you had a concert last year, out of state. You were actually coming here, to meet up with Leo and whomever, weren't you?"

She sucks in her lower lip ever so slightly. I can see the moment when she hovers between lying and telling the truth. She decides to tell the truth. "That's what I told my parents, so they'd keep paying for me to visit last year."

This is shit. I'm so sorry for him, but nothing I can do at present. "Fine. Now that you have that map, and know what you know, can you sense us, still, even when we're not right in front of you?"

She nods.

"From how far away?"

A slight shrug. "I don't honestly know. Goose—that's not your real name, is it?"

"Yes. I'm the fourth generation Goose in my family," he says with a marvellous straight face.

Sophie blinks, but goes gamely on. "Well, you amplify— everybody. Everything. Do you have to focus on it or—"

"This isn't about him," Mara says. "It's about you."

"It *should* be about Stella," Sophie says, her voice quiet but threaded with self-righteousness. "And Felicity, who's still alive."

"It is," Jamie says, without any hint of his usual charm or humour. He's furious.

"Then why aren't you asking me about them?"

"Why aren't you telling us about them?" Mara's exterior is calm, watchful.

"Because I don't know anything! That's the whole point— we can't do this by ourselves. We all have to work together—"

"But you're the hunter—sorry, forgive me—the, what do you call yourself?" Mara asks her.

"What do you call *yourself?*"

Casual shrug. "Murderess, butcher—"

"Quit it," Daniel says to Mara. She tucks her fangs behind her lips, for now.

"Like I said." Sophie turns to me, having decided that I'm the Reasonable One, "when I'm on my own, I only know some- one's Gifted when I meet them. When Felicity and the others went missing, they fell off the map. Literally. There's nothing I can do."

I can't help but sympathise with that last bit, not that I'm about to admit it. And I don't know that I want the answer to the question I'm about to ask, but I ask anyway. "Who was the first?"

A beat before she answers. "Beth's the first one *I* saw, but Sam—I think Sam was the first."

"Why?"

"I didn't know him personally—a friend of Leo's, her name's Eva—he was *her* friend. I never actually met him, and he died in England. *You* were there. With Goose."

And Mara.

I close my eyes, and when I open them, everyone—Daniel, Jamie, Goose, Sophie—has a trickle of blood running from their noses. Mara appears to be smiling. Christ, I need a sleep. I blink hard, rub my eyes, and the image vanishes, thank fuck.

"Eva told Leo when Sam killed himself, and said he went missing just before that. That's when he thought we should try to keep track."

"Not working out very well though, is it," Daniel says.

Her eyes are cast down at her plate. "No." She lifts her gaze up to Goose. "But you're helping, even though you don't know it. I'm starting to recognise what it feels like, when someone goes missing."

"What about Felix?" Jamie asks. "If his connection timed out, or whatever, you'd think he'd be the one you'd notice?"

"Felix never went missing. He wasn't . . . like the others."

"Just an old-fashioned suicide." Mara says what I'm thinking, what Sophie's just confirmed. There *is* a difference between the deaths, between the willing and the murdered.

"Look, we're scared, okay? For our friends, for ourselves." A pleading look at Daniel here, who looks pained but doesn't bite.

Mara, however: "I'd like to know why you were taking notes on my Horizons file."

At least Sophie has the good grace to pretend to seem ashamed. Or perhaps she actually is. I'm not sure I care. "We thought it might help to learn everything we could about what that doctor did to you guys."

"You could've just asked," Jamie says, unsmiling.

"Right." Sophie makes a noise. "Like you would've believed me if I told you what I could."

"Leo believed you. So did the rest of your friends," Daniel interrupts. "You deliberately hid it. From me, from my sister—"

"From me as well," I say.

She meets my gaze. "I didn't know you were Gifted."

"How's that?" I ask.

"No connection."

"Not a metaphor, I'm guessing."

"No. I can't sense you. It's like you're not even in the room."

Goose looks disturbed. "You're not going to off yourself, are you, mate?"

"No," I say just as Sophie does.

"I've *never* sensed him," she continues. "It's not like he's gone missing all of a sudden. Speaking of which, whatever's happening? There haven't been enough . . . deaths . . . to see a pattern yet. I don't know how long it'll be before Felicity dies, or Stella—"

"How do you know they *will* die?" Daniel asks.

"Because Sam died."

"A pattern of one isn't exactly a pattern."

She shakes her head. "Felix knew when Felicity was gone."

"Because *you* told him you couldn't find her, and he lost hope," I say, drawing Mara's attention.

She lets out a shaky breath. "No, Felix was an empath. He could feel, and change, people's emotions. And when Beth went missing, and killed herself—he knew it was happening to Felicity, too."

"I don't know, seems like he gave up kind of quick," Jamie says.

"He didn't want to live in a world without her," I say. Daniel looks up—my defence of Felix is an unintentional defence of Sophie, so I circle back to offence, where it's safer. "So what's your plan, Sophie?"

"*My* plan?"

"You must've thought about it," Mara says. "Or were you planning to lie to us forever?"

"You've read my file as well, I imagine," I say.

She shakes her head. "You don't have one."

Jamie's forehead scrunches. "Sure he does. I've seen it."

Sophie shrugs. "Maybe Stella never took it out of Horizons, then."

"But she stole mine," Mara says—to herself, I think. A slight smile appears on her lips. "Of course she did."

"Tell me something," Jamie cuts in. "Did you know about me too? In Croyden? Because we've both been there since elementary school—"

"I didn't know that there was something going on with *me* until I was sixteen, and you're two years younger than me. When I met Leo and he told me I wasn't crazy, I never thought there was anything special about you—"

"Thanks."

"We passed each other all the time, and nothing, until one day—"

"Something," he finishes, leaning back against the chair.

At that, Daniel stands up. "I can't. I can't do this anymore." He rises from the table, and Sophie scrambles to follow. The chair scrapes against the floor as she pushes it away from the table.

"I'll take the train back with you," she says.

"Pass." He goes to get his coat, but Mara crosses the room and says something to him I can't hear—Sophie's talking at him, Jamie's asking Sophie for her address, and Goose is going for the whiskey.

"Called you a car, dude," Jamie says to Daniel before he

walks out the door. Jamie looks down at his mobile. "It's just down the street. It'll be here by the time you're downstairs." Daniel pauses for a moment, then says to Sophie, "You'd better head out. Before it leaves without you."

She looks confused. "You're not coming?"

"Not tonight."

That visibly shakes her. "I love you," she finally says, quiet and honest and sad.

Daniel doesn't reply, but Mara opens the door and holds it open. Once Sophie's walked into the hall, Daniel says, "You don't lie to people you love."

If only that were true.

"Daniel, you should spend the night," Mara says as he stands by the now-closed door.

"I want to be by myself," he says flatly. "I'm just waiting until I know she's gone."

"You can be alone here," Mara insists.

"Stop."

"You should," I say. "It's late. We have the room. We'll let you alone."

He wants to argue, but he's wrung out. "Where?" he asks, glancing upstairs.

"Second floor, make a left after the first bank of rooms. It's completely quiet—"

"I don't want quiet."

"There's a telly," Goose says. We all turn to him. "What? There's one in all the rooms."

"Not ours," Mara mouths to me.

Because we have better ways of spending our time, I'm a bit tempted to say, but, not quite the moment, is it?

"Fine," Daniel shrugs off his jacket, loops it over his arm. "I'll see you guys . . . whenever."

"Take care, buddy," Jamie says.

"Night, brother," Mara calls up as he disappears. No response.

Jamie and Goose awkwardly disperse, leaving Mara and me alone.

A dark look up through dark lashes. "I'm going to bed." She doesn't look tired. I think I hear her heart charged up, her pulse pounding in her veins.

"I'll be a bit," I say. "I want to clear up."

She nods, then, letting out a long-held breath, says, "I could kill her for what she did to Daniel."

An edge of a grin. "Literally or figuratively?"

She kisses me lightly on the mouth, then darts up the stairs and calls out, "Haven't decided yet."

With Mara, there's no way to tell whether she means it.

31

BY MY EXPERIMENT

Unable to sleep, I clear the untouched mess left in the wake of the inquisition on my own and am in the kitchen burning toast and making tea when Mara descends the stairs at dawn, desultory. The sun fades in through the windows, pale and weak.

"Morning," I say.

"God is dead."

"Coffee?"

"Fuck you."

"Again?"

She folds her arms on the counter and lets her head fall

over them, issuing a muffled, "I hate everything."

I ignore the toast and the prospect of tea (and sex, let's be honest) and stand beside her. Stroke back her hair, prompting a turn of her head that leaves one cheek and eye exposed. She's so hurt I ache.

"What can I do?"

"I don't know. He's been crazy about her since our first day at Croyden. And now he thinks she only started talking to him because of me. To find out more about *me*."

"That doesn't mean she doesn't love him now."

Mara rounds on me. "She lied—"

"Don't we all?"

"Why are you defending her?"

A good question. I do find myself sympathising with Sophie a bit. Something she said last night—seeing Beth in the subway, her light appearing on Sophie's mental map again just in time for her to snuff it out herself. I know what that's like.

There's much about Leo and his little operation, which we now know includes Sophie, that I find suspect—but so far I can't find an excuse to lay the blame for Sam's and Beth's deaths at their feet. And so far they're the only ones with real connections to the Gifted who've gone missing. Not us.

What's different about *us*?

"Look," I say, needing to appease Mara before I can get away to think on it. "Daniel was betrayed by someone he loves. It's savage. But here's the thing: Part of that betrayal isn't heartbreak—it's because she had her eyes on you. It's because he loves *you* that he's hurting so much. He feels like he should've seen it coming."

An assumption, surely; one I make because it's how *I* feel about her, though there's no one more capable of protecting Mara than Mara. But I know Daniel as well.

"He feels like he failed you," I say.

Incredulous, she says, "How could he think that?"

"Because he feels responsible for you."

"But he knows me, he knows what I can do—"

"He's your big brother. No matter how strong you are, he'll always worry about you." A stirring of guilt, because I'm not there, haven't been there, for my own sister. Haven't even been thinking about how she's faring in the roiling, shark-infested sea of adolescence and mourning the loss of her doting father.

Mara's face falls again. "I know. I hate what she did to him."

I let Mara have that, but, confession, I don't. Hate her, that is. Sophie lied by omission, true, and she may well have been spying on us for Leo et al., of course. But I haven't got the sense that it was malicious. Wary, yes. Curious, surely. But we've been acting the same toward them, in truth.

Despite differences in specifics, they want what (most of us) want: answers. The truth. They care about one another the way we do.

And then, I've an idea. "I think you, Jamie, and Goose should meet with Leo today."

"What?" Mara rears back a bit. *"Now?"*

"Now that we know what we know from Sophie, I think we've got to come around to the fact that Stella's genuinely missing. It's been a long fucking night, and I've thought about it. Two of us have killed ourselves already—Sam hung himself, Beth jumped in front of a train." Mara dips her head, knowing what's coming, that I'm right, before I say it. "We should work with the others. Match the pieces we have with whatever they've got. You and Jamie and Goose, despite his appearance to the contrary, are brilliant."

"So why don't we figure it out on our own?"

"Because we had no idea who they *were.* They might have some documents and tapes and reports and shite, but we don't *know* the people this has been happening to, Stella excepted. Sophie and Leo do. It's *their* friends committing suicide so far, but there's a grand design somewhere, and a clock counting down, and we've no idea when, or for whom. If we want to find a connection, we need to look, *really* look, at the people connected, and so far, that's them."

Mara wilts into a curl of sulk.

"What? You don't want to go?" *You don't want to help Stella* is the question I don't ask.

"It's not that. I'm just—I hate leaving Daniel alone."

"He needs it."

Mara reaches out, tugs at the hem of my shirt. "Why don't you come with us?" she asks.

I wind a finger around her hair, concealing the tiniest hint of resentment and self-loathing in my voice. "I want to look through the things the solicitors sent over. From England," I lie. Sort of.

"And you want to be alone."

"No," I say. "It's just that you sorting through old architectural plans and whatever else is likely to be less productive than you sorting through what Leo and Sophie collected. No one knows more about what really happened at Horizons than you," I say. "And Jamie."

Jamie descends the stairs first. "Off to find the droids we're looking for, I hear."

"You'll keep yourself entertained, I trust?" asks Goose, right behind him.

"Always," I say as they pocket their mobiles and shrug into jackets. The sun arrows through the glass clocks, slicing the apartment's shadow with white.

Mara tosses one watchful look over her shoulder, so I half smile at her. "Don't be too long," I say, just loudly enough for her to hear it.

She turns away, but not before I glimpse her eyes rolling and a grin on her face. I shut the door behind them.

And head straight for Daniel.

32

MEN OF STRAW

I KNOCK ON HIS DOOR, NOT POLITELY. I TRY THE door and it's locked. "Daniel!" I shout. "It's an emergency! I need your—"

He opens the door, eyes bloodshot but wide. "What is it? What happened?"

"Time to wake up."

His face puddles into confusion. "What—"

"Nothing happened. Everything's fine."

"Then what the hell—"

"I need your help."

"You're going to have to live with disappointment," he says, and begins to close the door.

I stop it with my hand. "Sorry, but no. Get dressed. You've got class."

"I'm skipping."

"Daniel, Daniel. Remember who you are."

Nothing. His eyelids droop, his arms cross against his chest. "I just want to be alone, okay?"

He sounds pathetic, and it does pull at the single heartstring in my chest, but.

Petulant, he adds, "You said I'd be left alone."

"I say a lot of things. And anyway we did leave you alone last night. Time's up. Get dressed."

His nostrils flare, and for a second I see the family resemblance that's normally hidden between him and Mara. "Where are we going?"

"I think you know."

I'd never wanted to see the place before, and now that I stand here, looking up at it, nondescript and shuttered in a toxically ugly part of Brooklyn, I feel justified. There are windows stretching up for stories, boarded shut, crudely. Father always was good at hiding.

"You're serious?" Daniel asks, staring at the building.

"Deadly," I say. I lift the metal shutter; it groans in protestation, and I feel my way for the lock. The rusted red door opens, and I slide my hand over the wall for the light switch.

The lights slam on at once, the sudden artificial brightness a bit shocking. "I don't think we're going to find anything in here that's going to help prevent whatever's going on," I say, looking up at the towering shelves, "but you do. And I trust you with whatever might or might not be in here."

Daniel's quiet, staring ahead at the aisles that go on forever.

"So this is what's happening today," I go on. "Mara, Jamie, and Goose are at the brownstone with Leo—"

"And Sophie, probably," Daniel mumbles.

I shrug a shoulder, as if it doesn't matter. "Perhaps. No one's texted yet, and I don't much care, honestly. But listen—there was a map that I just barely got a glimpse of—I have a near-photographic memory, but the room was dark and I couldn't make everything out. Now that we're all on the same team—"

Daniel's eyes drop, and he looks away.

"The same let's-not-allow-innocent-people-to-die team," I inhale, trying not to sound frustrated. "You've always thought the answer to the suicide question was here. So Mara and Jamie and Goose are *there*, collecting names of the other Carriers, places they came from, their abilities, and most importantly, getting you pictures of that map. And you're going to cross-reference them with the shit in here."

Daniel barks out a laugh. "You have no idea how it works."

"All right, how does it work?"

"Kells gave the kids she experimented on false names, so they couldn't be traced in case anyone did find this place. I assume that was your father's suggestion," Daniel says. Sounds like it.

"So trying to match up names, find files—the idea of cross-referencing them is"—he looks up at the scale of the building—"It's impossible."

"Even with that map?"

"Maybe, maybe not." He bites his lower lip. "There's a system. That's how I found Kells's own files and everything I thought we'd need, which we brought to Jamie's aunt's house and which Stella apparently went back and stole." He exhales. "But we were looking for different stuff then—the stuff that led to Jude and Mara and all that. We might—if I knew where these other Gifted kids were born, maybe, well—obviously, actually—there were probably other so-called treatment facilities. I mean, has anyone even asked where Leo is from?"

My thoughts exactly. A corner of my mouth lifts. "This is why you're doing this." Pause. "And no one else."

His eyebrows scrunch together. "What do you mean?"

"I mean, I'm granting you access. You and only you."

"So when you told Leo you were going to let him come here with me and Mara, what you actually meant was—"

"The exact opposite."

He doesn't seem surprised, but he is a bit frustrated. "I need at least someone to bounce stuff off of, help me go through things. Divide and conquer, you know?"

I wave that off. "You're not giving yourself enough credit, mate."

But Mara and Daniel wear what they're feeling, and I

know what Daniel's about to say before he says it.

"You're talking about Mara," he says. You don't want *Mara* to know that I'm here."

Carefully, I say, "I don't want anyone to know, *including* Mara."

"Why not?"

I let out a tight sigh. "You know why not."

At this, he bristles. "No, I don't. You love her, but you don't trust her?"

I see immediately where that train of thought's headed, given Sophie's betrayal, and stop it before it gets there. "That's not it at all. Look, when it comes to me, her, and most importantly, anything that has to do with my father and our history? Mara isn't a girlfriend I'm keeping secrets from. She's . . ." I search for the right word, one that'll trigger the response I need without risking a response I can't manage. "Unpredictable," I say finally. Every word matters right now. "You know what Mara can do," I say, rather than *You know what Mara's capable of.*

An interminable pause before Daniel shrugs one shoulder. Enough for me to go on.

"Have you ever seen her do it?" I ask, swerving hard to avoid specifics.

Daniel does the same. "You mean, face-to-face?"

"Face-to-face, or on camera, or anything like that? With her mind or with her hands?"

Wrong words, those. I can physically see Daniel's attitude change. "She killed people, and I use the term 'people' loosely, in *self-defence*." Loyal to a fault, the Dyer family. He loves her so much. Therein lies the rub.

For me as well. The word "love" doesn't begin to capture what I feel for her. But I do see her in a way that he can't—that no one else can. We've seen each other raw, stripped down to our essences, for better and worse. I recognise her, and she recognises me. I love her for the person she *is*, not the person I think she is, or want her to be, because I don't *want* her to be anything else.

Daniel's love is different. He *can't* see her that way. In fact, I'm sure Mara's gone to great lengths to avoid sharing that private, secret pleasure she takes in her ability to destroy.

"You don't think she also wants this to stop?" He looks incredulous. "You think she wants people dead?"

I don't know what she wants, I don't say. I don't know whom she wants dead, is the truth.

"She's not a serial killer," Daniel says. "She's not a mass murderer."

They are statements, not questions, and I'm not even sure Daniel believes them. His heart is racing, I notice uneasily.

The thoughts that arise bubble up from my conversation with Stella. If Mara does have something to do with it, it can't be intentional—it doesn't fit *her* pattern. "Whatever she does, she does because she believes it's justified," I say, trying to ease his mind a bit. And mine. "And I do trust her."

"I sense a 'but' in the future of that sentence. . . ."

I shake my head. "There isn't one. I love her. I'd do anything to protect her. And this is how to protect her. There *is* something about Mara that separates her from people like Stella, and Leo, Sophie—"

Daniel's expression darkens. "Right. Sophie."

"And Felix and Felicity, and even Jamie."

"And you," Daniel says, voicing what I avoided.

"Right. Me as well. You heard what Sophie said. She can't sense me for some reason." Maybe I should feel paranoid, or unnerved, but mostly I feel numb.

"But she can sense Mara." He swallows. "You think she might—be at risk in some way?"

Not in the way Daniel's thinking. But perhaps I can use it, his fear for her, so I nod.

He thinks about that for a moment, then takes a few steps forward, running his hands over some of the labels on the boxes nearest us. "I've been thinking that the common factor might not necessarily be a person but a trait."

Yes. Brilliant. "What sort?"

"You've seen the list, right?"

"Which?"

He walks farther, footsteps echoing on the cement. "Dr. Kells created this list that she showed to Mara and Jamie and Stella, too, I'm guessing. There were two versions, actually—one that said you were alive, one that said you were dead."

Ah. That list.

"Both listed all of your names, along with a bunch of others, Jude's included, and had this designation after it," he says. He peers over into the next aisle. "'Original,' 'suspected original,' or 'artificially manifested or induced.'"

"You think that's got something to do with all this?"

"Maybe," Daniel says. "I mean, part of what was brilliant about what Kells did was giving the twins she worked on aliases."

This I'd heard about only in the briefest of summaries—my own fault. Mara didn't talk about it, so I didn't ask.

"Go on," I urge Daniel as broadly as I can. I'm not sure I want him to know just how much I *don't* know.

"The infants she fostered—I only found records here under their aliases, corresponding with the alphabet. It was all coded, and they died at different ages, from different symptoms, but there were at least seven, not including Jude and Claire, and someone, somewhere, would know about it if they were all from the same locations."

"But they weren't."

Daniel shakes his head. "From all over the country. As diverse a roster as she could manage, probably. And she was on your father's payroll then, so he'd have helped cover tracks."

No wonder he'd moved us to the States, ultimately. "It's a big country."

"It's a big world," Daniel says. "Like I said, looking for names in here won't get us far, but if we think more broadly— countries or cities of origin, birth dates, maybe, somewhere buried in what will probably look like a bunch of useless boilerplate corporate crap, we might find records for at least some of the people who've . . ."

"Gone missing," I finish for him.

"I thought of looking up Stella's stuff in here, actually, once she popped up here in the city. That was one of my first thoughts when I came to you." His eyes rake over the height of the shelves, resting at the top.

"Why didn't you just say so when you first asked me?"

He pushes his glasses up on the bridge of his nose—a nervous tic of his. "Mara and Stella and Jamie have an . . . unusual dynamic," he says finally.

"You didn't want Mara to hear about your plans either," I say, feeling rather self-righteous for a moment until Daniel shakes his head.

"Actually, it was Jamie I was thinking of."

Well, well. "Why's that?"

"So, I always thought it was odd that Stella was designated as a 'suspected original.' Not 'original,' like you and Mara, not 'artificially manifested,' like Jude. Once, when Mara wasn't around, I asked Jamie about it." He turns to face me. "Actually, it was when you guys all got those letters, remember?"

Would that I could forget.

"Anyway, we'd been talking about the Superman versus Spider-Man thing, born versus made theory, and I brought up the theory that maybe they didn't know Stella's genetic history when that list was made, and maybe that was how they were typing you guys."

Typing. I wonder for a moment if Daniel knows about the archetypes we supposedly represent—where my parents got the idea that I was destined to be some great Hero, and my father's conviction about Mara being the Shadow, destroyer of worlds or some shite. That all came from the professor, a subject I'm desperate to avoid.

"Anyway, Jamie mentioned that he was also a 'suspected original,' and I knew he was adopted; I kind of wanted to push the issue but, you know, still be . . . sensitive? Anyway, he went to get the mail when that came up. Stella got a letter too," Daniel says. "Remember?"

Now that he mentions it, I do, but just barely. Daniel had thanked me for saving his life from my own father, and I was trying to close my eyes to the world, just then. But I nod anyway.

"I felt kind of left out. I didn't ask to read Mara's because she'd just been through . . . stuff. All of you guys had been, so I kind of wandered off to give you space. When I saw Jamie next, he was wearing that pendant you used to wear, and was acting totally different. I tried to pick up the conversation we'd been having before, but he shut it down."

Not surprising.

"But I asked him what he thought we should do with Stella's letter, given that she'd left. I thought we should throw it out, maintain her privacy. You know what he said? *'We'll be seeing her again.'*

"That's . . ." I struggle for the word.

"Weird?" Daniel's nodding his head. "Yeah. Back then I thought it was just something to say, like, *Oh, Stella's around, not lost and gone forever*, that sort of thing—but now?"

"Now it's weird," I echo.

"And did you see Jamie seize on it when Leo mentioned that those guys all practiced their abilities together?"

"What if everything that's happening is someone flexing their little Gift?" I think out loud.

Daniel's brow furrows. "It could even be unintentional."

"Could be." Doubt it is. I doubt equally that Jamie's the one responsible, but that he might be connected to whomever is seems more plausible by the moment.

"What do you make of Leo's tattoo?" Daniel asks me, and I go still. "Don't think I didn't notice you seizing on that at the brownstone."

It takes a conscious effort to remain blank.

"Leo's tattoo. Jamie's pendant——"

And mine. And Mara's.

"Which he got from Lukumi or Armin Lenaurd or whoever he is, who wrote the letters you all got. I thought you liked me because I was smart."

"More for your dashing good looks," I say. "But fair play to you. Make anything of it?"

"Where did you get your pendant from?" he asks.

I play the only card I have. "My mother," I say. "I found it in her things after she died."

"Oh," Daniel says, shifting his weight.

This was the moment. I could tell Daniel my sordid family history and my pathetic little sob stories, tell him about the letter my mother wrote me, the letter the professor wrote Mara, and on and on until he knew everything. About me. About us.

But Mara hadn't told him. She kept her letter to herself.

You will grow in strength and conviction, and apart from you, Noah will too, the professor had written to her. *You will love Noah Shaw to ruins, unless you let him go.*

That's why she'd kept it from her brother all this time. She'd let me read it, though. It was our grand fight, the one we repeated in a hundred incarnations over the hundreds of thousands of hours we've spent together. Whether she should leave me, for my sake.

I have seen his death a thousand ways in a thousand dreams over a thousand nights, and the only one who can prevent it is you.

I refused to accept that then, and I refuse now. The stakes for Daniel are different, needless to say.

"Do you think the professor's still a player?" I ask, as if it hadn't occurred to me before now. If I hadn't just mentioned my dead mother, he'd likely call me on it.

His eyes narrow just slightly behind the lenses of his dark frames as he nods. "He could be a candidate for chess master this time around. . . ." His voice trails off awkwardly, having invoked both of my dead parents in short order.

I do wonder, though, what he would think if I told him everything. "What would that entail?" I ask. Hypotheticals are safe ground for him. For both of us.

"I mean, Jamie mentioned 'precogs' when we met with Leo, and the guy's always seemed to be one step ahead of us in the past. . . ."

"But how would that even work?" I say. "He knows everything that's ever going to happen? Free will doesn't exist?"

"It . . . would present a lot of philosophical problems," Daniel says, nodding.

"You're a man of science. What do you believe?" I ask, genuinely curious.

He smiles now, back on familiar territory. "Admittedly, your ability and Mara's and Jamie's and so on strain the boundaries of logic, but there's at least a framework for them. Limitations. You're carriers of a gene that's turned on by environmental and biological factors. Cancer works that way, so, it's precedented at least. Through some, I don't know, maybe subatomic mechanism, that gene enables you to affect matter in different ways. Lukumi was also the author of *New Theories in Genetics*," he says, shrugging. "It seemed absurd when Mara first showed it to me, but then, well, you know the rest."

I do. "So, do you believe in free will, or predestination?"

"Free will," he says decisively.

I know things that Daniel doesn't, and I've seen things he hasn't, but I believe the same. I have to. Or else, what's the point?

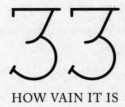

HOW VAIN IT IS

WE LEAVE THE ARCHIVES SHORTLY AFTER, having satisfied Daniel's curiosity and letting him reach his own conclusions about what to do next.

"Get invited back to the brownstone, find points of origin for all the Carriers Leo knows, cross-reference for subsidiaries of your father's company that might've operated there or nearby, and then use that to come back here and see if there's a Kells-ish person in the mental health field who's treated more than one of them, who might be at the hub of a particular wheel. Start small, branch out."

"Brilliant," I say. The metal shutter screeches as I pull it down over the door. "We start tonight."

"Have your flatmates send their pictures over to me, and I'll start on the map. And you . . ." He waits expectantly.

"Will talk to Jamie."

"And Goose," he adds.

"And Goose," I parrot, before we part ways.

When he first brought it up, he'd asked what Goose's moral compass was like, and I said I didn't know, that the last time I really spent with him, he could scarcely shave. "Why?" I'd asked him.

"Because," Daniel said, running his hands through his hair, "I hate this expression, but there's no denying he's a game changer. If . . . what's happening . . . is connected to Mara . . . somehow . . ."

What went unsaid is that he could turn Mara into a weapon of mass destruction, if she wanted to be.

I watched Daniel as he spoke the words, knew he was thinking that she wouldn't want to be.

I'm not as sure.

I'm anxious to get back to the flat, and not just to see Mara. My shield's been up for too long today, and it's bloody exhausting.

No one else is there when I arrive, though. I should be relieved; instead, I'm a bit overwhelmed by the emptiness of it. Even when it's just Mara and I, her presence is enough to fill it.

I pace to the bar, pour myself a shot of whiskey. Down it, then another. My inability to get properly, thoroughly wasted only makes me feel worse.

My footsteps echo on the stairs, and I ignore the chilled air and the swift movements of clouds beyond the glass that make me dizzy for some reason. When I reach the office, I close the door behind me.

Daniel's wheel metaphor has been spinning in my mind. I can't seem to break it or stop it, so I let it spin and end up standing in front of the trunk full of my mother's things. Hardly surprising, considering I spent the day in my father's archives. I would bore even the worst therapist.

I rummage through her books and things, not finding anything of particular interest until a small red journal peeks out from under *The Once and Future King*. There's a ribbon threaded through the pages edged in gilt.

A day may yet come when I stop being my own worst enemy, but that day is not today. I open my mother's journal and begin to read.

26 June

Jesus fuck, I've just met David's parents for the first time, and I think I might be happier if I were to drown in the Thames—or to jump from one of the turrets of their beloved manor house—than marry into that wretched family.

His harpy of a mother greeted me with a look of disdain to compliment her nearly invisible smile, then his father, not an altogether horrid man, peppered me with questions about hunting and shooting, both of which I abhor, which David knows, and I could practically hear him grinding his teeth during tea, worrying what his common beloved might say and do to offend the Lord and Lady.

It isn't just his family. I wish it were, honestly. David is just so... dull. Not dull-witted, obviously. Never second at anything, not collections or mods or finals—his gang of mates is always scrunching on him about it, out of jealousy, likely. He's the only one at the pub on Suicide Sunday, not worrying in the slight-est whether he'll pass or fail his classes. And he is objectively gorgeous, one has to give him that. It's the brandy after dinner shite, the "summering" in Cornwall, Yorkshire, for the "season"—by which he means hunting season, though we've talked (shouted) about that, and he's sworn to stop, which will send Lady Sylvia into a fit. He _is_ trying, and I know he's trying for _me_, which almost makes it worse.

He's desperately in love with me. I can feel it when we're together, a heat coming off him, the hunger in his stare, and it happened so fast, and so easily. He is a boy–not a man, not yet–used to getting what he wants, and he's decided he wants me. _I_ did that. I can't fault anyone but myself.

The professor's told me it's my Gift, to create desire (and kill it, I imagine, though he's never been explicit about that–he's so bloody dodgy when it comes to my own questions). But honestly, I think I've always had some sense that I was different, and special, even before I met him, before he told me. By all rights, an abandoned baby, a girl without a family, should've been an undesirable little charity case! To be raised by nuns probably! Never mind that I attended Cheltenham, or that my parents were splendid–the fact that even my _adoptive_ parents died seems to scandalise Lady Sylvia (what doesn't?). She pretended not to know, but David told me she did, that she was in a flap about them having died in a "brutal and violent" car crash (are fatal car crashes ever _not_ brutal?). But really it's that neither Mum nor Dad really had any family to speak of, besides a few distant cousins I've never met. It's _that_ sin, that I'm a girl from nowhere with almost nothing, that they can't abide.

It was a bit of a shock at first–I thought I'd charm the knickers off the pair of them, but they were oddly immune to whatever it is that makes me irresistible to everyone else. I think if my parents were still alive, they'd fight David less.

Part of me wishes I'd died with them. Wants to die without them here.

I know it would be selfish, and a waste, blah blah, but Dear Reader Who Does Not Exist Because This Is My Diary So Fuck Right Off, if it weren't for the professor, I think, I might've done it already—God knows there's a ready supply of drugs, even (especially) at Kings. I've no problem with blood; I know how to slit my wrists the right way, and if not that, I could always mimic the night climbers and dive right off the tower. (There are still no railings—has it really not occurred to anyone to try? Really?)

So you see, Diary Dearest, this is the train of thought that won't stop, the train that runs in my head at night, even after I fall asleep. I'd never tell David, but I think he suspects some melancholy beneath the surface, some vulnerability he's just aching to soothe. He wants to fix me, poor thing.

I don't know if I can bring myself to love him.

That's the truth. It's ugly, I know it, and despite his (many) flaws, it just generally seems a crime to marry not for love, but for purpose, even though I know it won't be forever. Is that even worse? Marrying him, conceiving his child, knowing that someday I'll die for it?

I've talked to Mara about it—she's changed her mind, I think. Says she's dreamt about my death "a thousand ways over a thousand nights" and that there's no timeline in which I'll have his child and live. It's odd—I never wanted to be a mother before, but now that I know who my child will be, what he or she will do, become—I'm anxious. Ready. She says

I might regret it, my choice, once I have that child in my arms. That being needed so desperately by something so innocent and good and pure, something I created, will change my heart and might change my mind, and by then it will be too late. I'm already in this.

As the professor says, every gift has its cost.

34

HIGHER LAWS

IT IS TRULY FUCKING JARRING, READING MY MOTHER'S
journal. Perhaps the one bit of good parenting my father
can be credited with is that he never let me know it existed.
Maybe he even read that bit himself.

I don't notice how much time's passed till stompingly loud
footsteps rattle the staircase and someone knocks on the door.

I snap the journal shut, along with the trunk. I open the
door to find Jamie on the other side of it, and my promise to
Daniel comes to mind, but at the moment I just need air.

"Didn't mean to interrupt," he says cautiously.

I brush past him. "Then why did you?"

"Your phone's been buzzing with texts from Mara—"

"What?" I round on him. "She's not with you?"

Jamie looks at me warily. "No . . ." He draws out the word. "That's what the texts are about. She wanted to stay."

"Why?"

"Maybe she *texted* you why. . . ."

"Is there something in particular you'd like to say to me, Jamie?"

"Not in your current state, no."

I close my eyes and take a deep breath. "Sorry. I'm a prick."

He smiles brightly. "You *are*. It's nice to hear you admit it." He airily walks past me and down the stairs. I follow.

"So what happened today?" I force the words out.

"With the Brownstoners, you mean."

"Cute," I say as he swings toward the pool table. Not green, this one; a dark teal setting off the copper rails.

He arranges the set. "*Fancy* a game?"

"You mock me."

"Your friend Goosey's rubbing off on me." Jamie swipes one of the cues from the rack. "I wouldn't mind if he actually rubbed one off on me."

"Indeed?"

"Indeed," Jamie says. He offers a cue. "Am I his type?"

Type. I literally can't escape this.

"I've never known Goose to abstain from indulging in pleasure of any sort," I say.

Jamie crouches into position. "Excellent news."

"Pray tell."

He calls the first shot. "Mostly what we expected—shit I've seen before. They've got the Doctor Kells: The Early Years stuff, her twin experiments, crap from Horizons like my generous psychological profile, yours, Mara's, The List." The cue ball spins and sinks the striped 6.

"The List?" I wonder how ignorant I can pretend to be. Daniel's a known quantity to me, but the relationship between Mara and Jamie—I can't be sure. Especially not after this afternoon.

"The Kells list."

"Right. I've never actually seen it."

Jamie looks up, sets his cue up right. "Shut up." A lift of my eyebrows. "You've never seen that?"

"Am I going to have to bribe you with sexual favours in order for you to tell me about it?"

"Don't you wish, *love*. But I know *all* the places you've been."

"Did you take a photo?"

Jamie shakes his head. "But Mara took one."

I race to check my mobile—there are indeed a thousand texts from her. Some pictures, some just blocks and blocks of text. She's coming round to Leo, it seems. Even Sophie. And is sharing literally every detail with me. Well and good. I scroll through for images as I skim her texts. Finally, I see it—initials, our last names—

I walk back to the pool table, staring at my phone. "This it?"

Jamie takes it, swipes to zoom in. "Yup," he says, popping the *p*.

Double-Blind

S. Benicia, manifested (G1821 carrier, origin unknown); side effects(?): anorexia, bulimia, self-harm. Responsive to administered pharmaceuticals. Contraindications suspected but unknown.

T. Burrows, non-carrier, deceased.

M. Cannon, non-carrier, sedated.

M. Dyer, manifesting (G1821 carrier, original); side effects: co-occurring PTSD, hallucinations, self-harm, poss. schizophrenia/paranoid subtype. Responsive to midazolam. Contraindications: suspected n.e.s.s.?

J. Roth, manifesting (G1821 carrier, suspected original), induced; side effects: poss. borderline personality disorder, poss. mood disorder. Contraindications suspected but unknown.

A. Kendall: non-carrier, deceased.

J. L.: artificially manifested, Lenaurd protocol, early induction; side effects: multiple personality disorder (unresponsive), antisocial personality disorder (unresponsive); migraines, extreme aggression (unresponsive). No known contraindications.

C. L.: artificially manifested, Lenaurd protocol, early

induction, deceased.

P. Reynard: non-carrier, deceased.

N. Shaw: manifested (G1821 carrier, original); side effects(?): self-harm, poss. oppositional defiant disorder (unresponsive), conduct disorder? (unresponsive); tested: class a barbiturates (unresponsive), class b (unresponsive), class c (unresponsive); unresponsive to all classes; (test m.a.d.), deceased.

Generalized side effects: nausea, elevated temp., insomnia, night terrors

I stare long enough for Jamie to snap his fingers in my face. "You kosher?"

"Dandy," I say, though my voice faded at the edges. I feel dizzy, light-headed—I can count on one hand the times I've felt ill, and all were in the presence of Mara. But she's nowhere near here.

"Jamie," I say, placing the phone down, more for something solid to hold on to than anything else. "It mentions the Lenaurd protocol." I lower myself over the cue and call, "Three, side pocket."

A shadow passes over his face as I sink the ball. "Yes. . . ."

"As in, Armin, Abel, et cetera."

"Yes. . . ."

"As in, the man who created the blueprint for the shit-box FKA Jude."

"Yes."

"When was the last time you saw him?" And, done.

Jamie's breath catches, but he recovers quickly. "Why?"

"I think he might be why Stella's missing," I say plainly.

Jamie shoots at a ball, and it bounces off. "Then you should probably ask him about it."

"Perhaps I would, if I knew where to find him. Unsurprisingly, you haven't answered my question."

"I'm not Lukumi's keeper."

"Is that even what you call him?"

"Actually, no, but I liked the wordplay."

"Grand." I roll my eyes. "How old is he?"

"Dude, can we not?"

"Why's it such a mystery?" I *saunter* to the other end of the table, because I'm not *that* interested, just asking out of bored curiosity, obviously.

"Doesn't have to be," he says, feigning indifference, but even without Goose, I hear that rise in pulse, that tell-tale heartbeat. "We all got letters and something with them. You don't wear yours, but you know where it is, don't you?"

"I do," I say. Mara keeps them in a tiny sewn pouch that she slips into every pocket or carryall. They're with her, always, but I don't have to look at mine to know every etching, each curve and line by heart—ours are mirror images of each other's, not meant to form one whole. I glance at Jamie—the silver blinks through the collar of his shirt as he leans over the table, but I can't quite get a glimpse of how his was cast. I can't see which side is the feather and which is the sword.

"So put it on and ask him your questions yourself."

"Is that what you do?" I press. "Have you asked him why your friend's gone missing? Why we're killing ourselves?"

Jamie makes as if to line up his pool cue, but he's restless and edgy now. He stands straight. "It's not like that."

"Of course not," I say. "I don't understand—he's supposedly the Architect of some Better World but can't achieve it without using us as tools—"

"I'm nobody's tool."

There it is, a thread I can pull. "You are though," I say. "You report to him, don't you?"

He sighs, leans his cue next to one of the clocks, and hitches up on the table's edge, his legs long enough now that he can barely swing them.

"Your letter," I say, and watch the shadow pass over Jamie's face. "Whatever you read made you commit, at that moment, to the mission of a man who's been manipulating us for months—years. God, decades even. Before we were even born, in my case." Still he was silent. "Maybe in yours as well," I finish, hoping to provoke an answer. To get that much from him, at least.

"Like you said, he's trying to make the world a better place."

"How? Has he told you that? Has he told you exactly how?

Jamie's quiet, which is all the answer I need.

"That letter doesn't define who you are. Or what you do. That's your choice. Only yours."

"You're right, it is."

"Not your parents'."

There's steel in his eyes, now. "You don't know anything about my parents."

"You're right," I say. "And I barely know anything about you, except that Mara loves you, and she doesn't love lightly. But three people've died, and someone you know is missing, and you're in a position to ask someone who claims to have all the answers, but you won't?"

Jamie is silent, but he doesn't avoid my gaze. He's not rattled.

"What happened to thinking for yourself?"

At this, Jamie just rolls his eyes. "Classic splitting."

"Pardon?"

"Didn't all those years in therapy cover this? Splitting: Everything's black-and-white with you. I'm interested in what the professor's doing, so to you that means I've given up my autonomy. It's all or nothing. Good or evil."

I lean against the wall, languorous, casual. "Is that right? Explain Mara, then."

I watch him think for a moment. "She's your tragic flaw, I guess." His lips curve into a smile. "Every hero has one."

"Don't tell me you believe my father's bullshit. Please don't tell me that."

Apathetic shrug. "It's not your father, Noah. It's just—who you are. Not lawful good, but chaotic good."

"Do you plan to make sense anytime soon?"

His eyes turn to the clock face behind me, and he stares at some spot in the middle distance. "Daniel's lawful good."

"Still have no idea what the shit you're talking about."

"Alignment. Dungeons & Dragons? Wait, don't tell me." Jamie holds up a finger. "You've never played it. *Quelle surprise.*" He tugs one of his dreadlocks, stares at it. "How does Mara even talk to you? You're barely nerd-compatible."

"We make it work," I say archly.

Jamie holds up a hand, a look of horror on his face. "Say no more. Please. Okay, lawful good is basically, you believe in the morals of the world you live in, and you live by those morals always—or you try your best to, at least."

"Daniel," I say.

"Precisely."

"But chaotic good is different. The player is less rigid about the ways he tries to achieve what are still ultimately good goals— good in the eyes of the world of the game. Still with me?"

"Clinging on, thanks for checking in, though."

"NP," he says, leaning farther back on the table.

"So what does that make you?" I ask.

"Chaotic neutral," he says without hesitation. "When the player has their own moral code, and has the flexibility to achieve his goals according to his code."

Mara. "Or hers."

Tips his head, acknowledging. "Or hers." He goes on, "You never know which way he's going to go, which other players he's going to become allies with, or enemies with."

I'm reminded of Daniel's earlier wariness, but I just . . . don't feel it myself. "So what you're saying is"—injecting sarcasm into the words—"you're a *wild* card."

He shrugs a shoulder. "You could say that."

"Rebelling against the mores of society. So, this is how you think of Mara as well?"

"Totally."

"Chaotic neutral," I repeat. Another way of saying "dissonant," which does fit.

"Yep." But he pauses, long enough for the silence to stretch from pensive to awkward. "We don't have the same code though."

His voice sounds bruised. There's a weakness there—to exploit. And so:

"You killed Anna Greenly, I hear."

He blinks at the name, reacting as though he's never heard it before. But then, "Yeah. Guess I did."

Me, neutral. "Do you feel guilty?"

He hops off the table, picks up the cue. "Not really." I can't see his face now, which is no doubt intentional.

"Because of your code?"

"No. . . ." He draws out the word, arranges the pool cue

between his fingers. "First of all, I wouldn't have killed her if I'd known that, like, just telling someone to drive off a cliff meant that they'd basically do the equivalent. Not all of us are perfectly in control of our Gifts all of the time." He aims for a ball and pockets it. "But I'm not sorry she's dead."

Oh?

Tilting his head at the table, he says, "The bullies never remember, but the bullied never forget."

I've known Jamie for nearly three years now. I'd seen how he'd been treated, by Anna, others. But I want him to keep talking. I need to keep learning. "What if she would've changed someday?"

At that, he scoffs. "Nobody changes. We are who we are until we die."

I raise an eyebrow. "Well, that's not dramatic at all."

He inhales, circling the table after I sink the ball. "People grow up into slightly more complex versions of their infant-slash-childhood-slash-adolescent selves, but that usually means they get worse with age. More apathetic. Less passion-ate. Bored." He glances up. "Numb." Another ball, another pocket.

He's the one pressing on *my* bruise now, except it's worse than that—it's a raw wound. I can't seem to help but rise to the bait. "So according to your philosophy, I'm the Hero, and there's nothing that'll change that."

"Nope." He laughs, a mixture of genuine mirth and sarcasm.

"You walk into a room preceded by the scent of sandalwood and unicorns or whatever. Your skin sparkles in the sunlight."

"Why, Jamie," I said. "If I didn't know better, I'd think you were bitter."

"Not bitter, just annoyed. There's a difference."

"Do tell."

"Because it's so fucking obvious!" He spins, throws his back against the wall. "Privileged white kid—now officially an orphan—with a troubled past—destined to save the world. Come the fuck on, man. You've read that book a thousand times."

"I have," I say tonelessly.

"And surely you must look in the mirror," he says, mimicking my accent now. Poorly. "Your strong jaw, your perfectly mussed-up hair, the lean but somehow still muscular body, the height—you're practically Captain America."

"Except English."

"Even worse!"

"True. But surely, mate," I say, exaggerating my own accent, playing right back, "you've seen yourself in the mirror? You know how you look, how people look at you—men and women both. I mean, I'd fuck you, if you asked politely."

"Hard pass," Jamie says, but he's unstoppable now. "Okay, I'm not wearing my Greek chorus T-shirt, but I'll play anyway: You're so focused on avoiding your family shit, on not becoming your father, or what your father said you would be, that you're totally unwilling to look for answers in the only places that matter."

The air in the room changes. It's feverish, electric.

"And it's not because you don't want to help Stella, or the others, because you do. Why do you think I haven't really given you shit about it?"

"Because *you* don't care?"

He breaks into a grin. "Sure, deflect by being an asshole."

He's right. Jamie's many things, but not callous. He almost left when Stella did. Because Mara would've killed people who didn't deserve it, so Stella claimed.

"That's shit," I say, conceding. "Sorry."

Jamie shrugs. "You heard what your father said: You're the Hero. You so *don't want* to be the Hero that you're letting your dad write the only other part you *can* play from beyond the grave."

"Which is . . . ?"

"The Fool," Jamie says.

Another archetype. The hair rises on the back of my neck. I try to hide it by taking a shot. "What about the others?" I ask as the ball bounces off the edge.

"Before you deflect, consider the reverse psychology in handing you the keys to his kingdom, knowing how much you fucking loathe the king. Basically guarantees you'll never actually explore the kingdom, doesn't it?"

"Wow, Jamie. That's some next-level insight there."

"Thanks. I try."

"Five, corner pocket," I say, and then proceed to miss. "Assuming you're right, what precisely do you think is buried in said kingdom that I'm trying subconsciously to avoid?"

He rolls the cue between his palms. "Something about Mara, I'd guess. Probably something that means you can't be together."

"Nothing means we can't be together," I say, and the words are hardly out of my mouth before a Cheshire grin appears on Jamie's lips.

"See? That's your endgame. And hers. Alas, you're the hero, she's the villain—the star-crossed lovers, fated to be apart."

"You honestly think *Mara's* behind this?" I ask. He doesn't call her a Shadow, at least, though that makes it harder to know if he's speaking abstractly, in tropes, or if he actually believes whatever nonsense my father was spouting.

"No, I'm saying that we all have roles—the ones we think we're playing, the ones other people think we're playing, and the ones we're actually playing. But the game's been set up long before any of us appeared on the board." He makes his next shot.

"So I'm *fated* to play whatever part's been assigned to me?" I ask, unable to hide my disgust. "You truly believe that?"

"Your dad wasn't wrong about everything, Noah. We've all got legacies. Own your shit."

I once told Mara, "*Own yourself.*" God, I am the Fool.

"So what about Stella?" I ask as I line up my cue, miss yet again. "What's her alignment?"

"Stella." He drags out the sound of her name. "If you asked me before shit got real, I'd have said lawful good."

"But now?"

"I don't know. Before she vanished, I got a different read off her. Chaotic good, I think. Haven't quite figured it out yet. Eight ball, corner pocket," he says, positioning his stroke.

"Let me know when you do?"

He makes the shot. Game over.

"Well done," I say, letting my cue fall against the others, turning away from him and the conversation as quickly as possible. I hear Jamie's voice behind me as I head upstairs with my mobile.

"Only play the games you can win."

35

DESPERATE THINGS

MY FOOTSTEPS ECHO DULLY ON THE STAIRS as I head up past the second floor, and the third, straight to the roof. The sun's dying, being swallowed up by the screaming spires of New York's skyline and the thick twilight that's already begun to fall. I check for new texts—none—but I do scroll through the images Mara sent. Some scratch at a vague memory I once had, but can't reach now. It's more than unsettling—I've never had to pore over books or notes or paintings or anything to remember every detail. I turn over my palm, the one I cut to show Goose. The slash in it is closed, but the wound is still red, angry. My mind turns back to the list.

Suspected original
Artificially induced
Lenaurd protocol

The last two, a twisted attempt to create the kinds of abilities that we have naturally, which resulted in Jude. His sister, Claire, must've been a failed . . . experiment, or whatever we are. But *we're* not all the same, as Daniel pointed out. If one believes what my father did, then Mara and I are different because we're two sides of a coin. But the others on the list, Jamie and Stella excepted, are all dead now.

Possibly Stella, too, even. I'm leaning over the glass-enclosed roof deck, the vertigo nearly sickening. The sight of the street so far below is viscerally appealing.

And then, remembering my mother's journal—even suicidal ideation appears to be genetic, in my case. My legacy, as it were. I'd stolen a pack of cigarettes Goose kept in the kitchen and withdrew one to light it. Haven't done in a while, and the smoke filling my lungs is almost—comforting.

"Bum a fag, mate?"

The voice is obvious, but the phrasing sounds so wrong to me now. Too much time here. "Thought you preferred rolling your own?" I say to Goose as he glides up to the railing and looks out at the city with me.

"I did," he says. "I do. Haven't got any papers left though, and you've stolen my spare pack, so. Let's have it."

I pass it to him, and he shakes one out, gesturing for my lighter, then cupping his hands around the flame. He sucks in a lungful of smoke. "Fuck, that's satisfying."

"Is Mara downstairs?" I ask. He draws his light eyebrows together, then shakes his head.

"She didn't come back with you?" My heart quickens.

"No, we got hungry, they had no food in the house, wanted to hit up a pub, I stayed for a bit but the place wasn't quite up to scratch, so, I came back."

I check my mobile. Nothing new from Mara. I text her.

He takes a long drag. "Think I saw a rat in their kitchen."

"You've been spoilt." I exhale smoke through my nose.

"Horribly. Got out just in time."

I check my phone again at the exact instant it vibrates. Not Mara, though. Jamie.

Dude, you're gonna wanna come downstairs

He added a grimace emoji at the end of the sentence, instead of a full stop.

I flick my cigarette over the side of the tower.

Goose grins. "What, no smoking in the house?"

"Mara hates it."

"Americans. Such Puritans."

"Aren't they just?" I say as we descend to the living room to see Mara sprawled out on one of the sofas.

My heart stops for an instant until I hear her laughter. I glance up at Jamie. "Don't look at me. She was sober when I left." He escapes faster than is humanly possible.

I take Mara by the forearm, lift her up to standing. Dreamy smile on her face, she swoons backward into my arms.

"You're cute," she says. Fuck's sake. I look at Goose; he shrugs innocently. Mara's limp and smiling, still, her lids at half-mast.

"What's wrong with you?" I ask.

"Nothing you can't fix," she says, voice sliding into sultry.

"I'll leave you to it, then?" Goose backs away, but not before I ask, "Did *you* take anything?"

"Really, mate?"

"Indulge me."

A head shake. "They did mention something about getting high though."

"And you *left* her?"

Eye roll. "It wasn't anything to do with drugs, it was about their, Gifts, or whatever. They said using them can get them high sometimes."

Sublime. "Are you mental? That's even worse."

"Do you really keep her on that tight of a leash, mate?" Goose hardly knows Mara, of course, and while I completely, completely understand why he wouldn't believe the implications, right now my overwhelming impulse is to shake him.

"Fuck right off."

"Happily. Enjoy your evening, old chap."

Mara waves good-bye, still back-bent in my arms. I swing her forward onto the sofa.

"Ow!"

"What?"

She pouts. "I bit my tongue. Kiss it better?"

"Tempting, but, no. What did you do tonight, darling?"

"I learned how to practice using . . ."

"Practice using . . . heroin? Coke?"

"Using. My. Gift."

"Are you aware of what your supposed Gift is?"

"Yes," she says, dragging out the word, turning her eyes on me.

I don't know how seriously to take this, as she's clearly out of it, and Goose is practically clueless. "So, what? You thought you'd engage in a spot of casual murder this evening?"

Her eyes narrow. "No," she says, and her voice sharpens a bit. "I didn't kill anyone."

"Then what did you do? And what, precisely, did Leo and Sophie do while you were at it?"

A slow, one-shouldered shrug. "They helped me. Showed me how they started practicing to make their Gifts stronger."

"And you think that's a good idea for you. *Really*." I look at this slip of a girl and wonder, fleetingly and for the first time, if I help her undress tonight, will there be someone else's blood on her skin? Or just on her hands?

"I think it's good to learn how to control it," she says.

"Surely." She's still drunk with whatever energy's coursing through her—I don't know that I'm making out the tenor of it. I hear one rhapsodic note wavering above the rest. But it *is* wavering. If it's Mara, it'll wear off soon enough. And while she's like this, I wonder . . .

Daniel and I have both shied away from the slightest implication that Mara could be responsible for what's happened to the others, so it didn't occur to me to bring up my conversation with Stella with him.

But now, here, alone with Mara like this—her tongue might be loose enough to trust.

"Where's your scalpel?" I ask.

Her spine straightens at the word. "What?"

"Where is it?"

Her shoulders lift into a shrug. "I don't have one, why would I—"

This time, I do hear her sound change. Liar, liar. "Is it on you?"

That wicked smile. "Maybe."

"Well," I say, "Isn't this a dangerous game."

Mara's eyes take on that cat-slant. "I'm not playing."

I take her by the wrist, lift her up to standing. She's sober enough that she doesn't sway. Much.

"Put your hands on the wall," I say, and tip my head toward it.

She arches an eyebrow.

"Go on, then."

She crosses the living area carefully, but makes it to the

wall. She splays her palms against the flat white paint, and I stop inches from her body.

"Spread your legs."

She laughs, full throated, sounding more and more like herself, which means I'm running out of time before she kicks back in and outsmarts me. "Is this foreplay?"

"If you're lucky," I say, and crouch down to her ankles. I run my hands up beneath the cuffed hem of her torn jeans, then over them in a neat line up to her hips. Nothing. I shift and trace my fingers along the inseam—she shivers just before I reach where she wants them most. I switch to her stomach, running them up over her shirt just before I reach her breasts, then under. My head is tilted down to hers, a few strands of my own hair mingling with her dark waves, my rough jaw meeting her smooth cheekbone. It's our only point of contact—our bodies aren't touching at all—but the charge is explosive, the air searing white, edging out every other thought that isn't *her*. I stop because I need to find that scalpel, if it exists, and if I don't look now—

She feels me hesitate, turns, gives me a look; a dare. "What?"

My eyes drop to her chest. I catch her smile.

"Looking for something?" Can't tell if she's mocking or serious, still high or dead sober.

"Do you have something for me to find?" I ask.

She takes my hand, weaves her fingers through mine, and

leads me upstairs. The city's lit beyond the glass, but the moon is full and outlines her curves in shadow and light. I close the door behind us, and she pushes me up against it with the full force of her.

Her mouth is on mine, her hands on my waist and in my hair—there isn't one false move, one wrong note. Every movement, every touch, every kiss is where I want it and how I want it, like she's inside of my head, unspooling my thoughts and following along. I begin to lift the hem of her shirt, and she traces her lips along my neck, tilts her head up, and whispers, "I'm going to shower." Bites my earlobe with those sharp little teeth. "Come with?"

It might've been the teeth, or her flawless execution of my fantasy, but I tug on her tank, lowering it. "Wait," I say. The half grin on her mouth falters. I press myself against her, push her back against the bed.

"I'm really dirty—"

"I know," I say.

"No, seriously—"

We edge up to the bed until she's standing up against the mattress. Looks up at me through a fringe of dark lashes, her gorgeous face half hidden in a tumble of hair.

"Turn around."

I wonder if she'll refuse. She doesn't. She tucks away a smile though, intimate, full of mischief.

"Bend over," I say.

She obeys, to my surprise, bending at the waist over the edge of the bed, stretching her feline outline in front of me. I slip my hands up beneath her shirt, then lower. Dip them into the loose waistband of her jeans, then lower. My breath hitches at the sensation of cold steel slicing through my fingertip. My hand curls around the scalpel tucked into the elastic of her underwear. God knows how she's managed not to stab herself—or me—before now.

I hear the smile in her voice, smudged by her cheek pressed against the bed. "How did that get in there?"

"Yes. How?"

She turns over, still bent at the waist, chest rising and falling as she bites her lip.

"Why do you have this?" I ask, like I'm asking why she chose to wear those jeans today.

"It makes me feel safe," she says plainly.

I turn it over carefully, wondering if this is, as Stella said, what she used to cut down her enemies. I turn over Mara's lie as well.

It's a trophy. I can't deny it, not even to myself.

"Hey." She stands, and since I haven't moved, she's up against me, her knee between my legs. She tilts her head up to kiss me, and with one hand, reaches for the scalpel, which is now behind my back.

I press my palm against her breastbone and step back, needing the distance, needing a breath. Mara backs up, bounces lightly onto the bed.

"Noah," she says, and the sound of her voice seizes my heart even now. She blinks slowly, her eyelashes dusting her cheekbones. She looks like art, a living sculpture. And then she speaks.

"Come to bed," she says silkily.

I bend down to her ear, feel her smile against my cheek. "Sleep it off, sweetheart."

Then I leave the room, leaving a trail of blood behind me.

Oh God, Simon. My hands shake, my words—I can scarcely bring myself to write this, though it's been a fortnight already. But I must. You would want to know; and I believe you do know my thoughts as I write them. Perhaps it will give me some measure of peace.

The night began so beautifully. Her wedding was glorious—her dress like no other. She looked so rare and exotic and exquisite, her husband could not take his eyes from her, and neither could anyone else. I thought to-night, having invited everyone who matters from society, they would finally understand: The colour of her skin does not make her any less. If anything, the way the spun gold in her white dress reflects the bronze of her skin, they should have seen that she was more. So much more. More beautiful, more elegant, more intelligent, more accomplished—more. The blondes and brunettes in their common dresses with their common conversation and common skills were no match for my daughter—I have come to think of her that way, husband. My daughter. The one I always wanted and never had.

The authorities showed up near dawn. They were shown into the sitting room, their hats and coats still on, dripping, puddling rainwater onto the floor.

When you died, they allowed Mrs. Dover to take their hats and coats, and they sat with me while I cried.

This night, they did not let me sit.

Mrs. Dover woke me, knocking quite loudly on my door, opening it before I could answer. She stood there as I awakened, carrying her candle. I felt as though I'd been caught in tar, my dreams still staining my mind with blood.

"What is it?" I asked, my voice husky with sleep.

"I'm sorry, my lady, you must come downstairs at once."

The panic I felt, Simon! "Is it the boys? Elliot, Simon, are they—"

"They're sleeping, they're well," Mrs. Dover assured me. It's—the police, my lady. They refuse to tell me their business.

They refused Albert as well. They demand your presence immediately. Come now, let's get you dressed, all right?"

I didn't answer, but I stood, trembling, and allowed her to slip on whatever clothing she could over my dressing gown; my fingers were frozen. I felt a terror I couldn't yet grasp, but I felt it.

Mrs. Dover led me down the stairs, arm in arm, as if I were feeble. When we reached the brightly lit sitting room, my eyes skimmed their faces, some of which seemed to mirror mine, which terrified me further.

"Lady Shaw," one of them began. "There's been"—he struggled for the appropriate word—"there's been a murder."

My hand covered my mouth. Mara. My Mara.

"Is it my—" I almost said "daughter." "Is it my niece?" She was Mrs. Christensen now.

The inspector met my gaze directly. "Her husband, Mr. Christensen, I'm afraid. The servants heard nothing, but one reported passing their bedroom earlier than usual, unable to sleep, and said that though she heard nothing, she felt compelled to check on them. When she knocked on their door and received no answer, she took it upon herself to fetch the master key, and unlocked it. Her screams woke the house."

"Mr. Christensen was found in their bed. Mrs. Christensen was not," a different inspector said.

"I don't understand," I insisted. "Was she taken? Kidnapped? Could her husband simply be ill or—"

"There was blood. On the bed."

"Well, naturally," I said, losing all sense of propriety. "It was their wedding night!"

"No, my lady." The inspector looked down, embarrassed. "There was much of it. And none in him."

"We must find my niece at once!" I insisted. "She's in danger!"

"One of the other servants reported seeing her in her travelling cloak leaving the house at about that hour. We are searching for her now, rest assured."

But I could not rest, not that night

nor any thereafter. I will not mourn her, cannot believe that she has died. I cling to the desperate hope that she had been stolen, somehow, but was alive, and we would be reunited someday in life.

But there are whisperings, Simon. That she fled in the night with a demon. That she was a demon, one we had foolishly welcomed into our home and let settle into our family to feed on our kindness and generosity and love like a tick, until she'd grown full, and found someone else to feed on.

I cannot believe it. I must not. But God forgive me, husband, I dream it. A vision covered in blood in her dressing gown, staring down at her new husband—it haunts me every night.

I am cursed.

36

DEPLORABLE SUCCESS

I AWAKEN WITH A SCREAM PERCHED IN MY THROAT.
Flames licking at boxes, melting metal shelving. I
glance down—I'm not holding the journal any longer.
It's morphed into a bottle of lighter fluid, and my hand is
no longer my own. It belongs to a girl, her fingernails painted
blue, wearing a delicate ring on her middle finger made of
twisted gold. Her lungs are full of smoke.

Please I don't want to die please I don't want to.

I fall through a hole in the floor of my mind, landing hard in
my own reality; back in the flat, back in the office. But my body
still feels what hers does—my lungs shudder, trying to expel

smoke that isn't there. I stumble to the door to get everyone up, but it opens before I make it there. Mara and Jamie are in the doorway, together.

"Something's happening to one of us," I tell them, thirsting for oxygen. "It's happening again. I don't know if it's Stella but —"

"It's not Stella," Jamie says.

"I need to stop talking," I say, trying to catch my breath. "Search her mind—but I wanted you to know—" A coughing fit grips my body. "It's happening," Mara says, and takes my hand, tugs me down the hall. It takes every cell, every neuron firing to make sure I don't fall down the stairs. I've got my back up against the wall when I reach the bottom, and when I catch my breath, I manage to ask, "How do you know it isn't Stella?"

"Because she's on the news."

In the living room Goose is hunched forward, elbows on knees, watching a video of her on CNN, the massive screen split with an anchor speaking over Stella's voice. I can't hear what either of them is saying because the noises in my skull are too loud.

The girl in my mind is stepping on broken glass in her boots.

The girl on the television is in a dark room, her face glowing in the light her mobile gives off.

The girl next to me, my girl, has her hands in my hair and is whispering my name as I try to hold on to it, hold on to Mara's voice. Get control, enough so I can look for a sign, something to tell me where the burning girl is and who she is, though I think I already know.

On the underside of her wrist is a small heart tattoo, the letter *F* inside of it. She turns it up as she reaches for something, I can't see what—the flames are too bright, searing her retinas. It's like she's standing in an oven; I watch as her hand reaches out for something, and hot metal brands her skin instead. The fire roars, the smell of burning plastic, fabric, and paper, so much paper, and something under it, something dizzying, chemical—

Glass explodes; the shards fall like glitter, showering her body, a thousand stinging pieces piercing skin that is already blistering. Felicity stares up at the ceiling, and I know—

"She's in the archives," I say out loud, and I know Mara and Jamie and Goose hear me, though I can't hear them, not anymore.

The explosion rings in my ears, swallowing my consciousness, but I know one thing: She is alive when she begins to burn.

37

AN INTERNAL INDUSTRY

I DREAM OF FIRE, BUT WHEN I AWAKEN MY CLOTHES are soaked through.

"She's dead," I say to no one. The white ceiling towers above me, hundreds of kilometres away. I'm not even entirely sure I'm on Earth until I hear Daniel's voice.

"We know," he says, and any horror I felt is drowned by the relief I experience knowing that he's here, alive.

I sit up anxiously, remembering what Mara and Jamie said before Felicity burned. "Stella—"

I get a brief glimpse of Daniel's face, deeply uncomfortable, looking away.

"Where's Mara?" I ask, trying to sit up, but Daniel stops me.

"She was just here," Daniel says. "Bathroom, maybe?"

"What happened to Stella?" I ask.

He exhales slowly. "She made, is *making*, a video. Right now. Nobody knows where she is, but she's—she's talking," he says, his voice lowered. "She hasn't outed you guys . . . yet . . . but she's talking about the fire, and Felicity, and whatever's happening to her right now."

"And what is that?"

"What's been happening to the other Carriers, the ones who've gone missing. Or that's what she's been saying."

"She's been at it for a bit." Goose's voice, from somewhere beyond my field of vision. When I twist my head, everything blurs.

"Since when?" I ask, trying to collect myself, or at least hide that I'm so wrecked. I hate the thought of them seeing me like this. Even Mara. It's unbearable.

"Since you started having your fit, mate," Goose finishes, then claps me on my shoulder as he sits beside me. My teeth rattle in my skull. "Glad to have you back."

"Show me," I say immediately, first to Daniel, then to Goose. He points at the telly, but the anchors are dissecting what Stella's saying, playing parts of it over again. "I need to watch it straight through."

"I've been recording it," Jamie says. "Sophie and Leo are on their way over."

Daniel's expression changes, perhaps at the mention of

Sophie. But he's given over to it, I suppose, given the circumstances.

"Should I play it?" Jamie asks from the kitchen. I turn carefully around. This time is better. I'm getting better.

Goose mutes the news, and Jamie lopes over with his laptop, swinging his long legs over the sofa. He sets the screen on the side table nearest to me. Stella's video's got more than fifty thousand hits already.

"When did this go up?"

"Not even half an hour ago," Jamie says. "It was cross-posted on social media first, then finally the news picked it up, because obviously."

"Obviously . . . ?"

"You'll see." He presses Play.

All I see is Stella's face, her skin tinted bluish from the screen. She's staring straight into the lens.

"It's happening again," she starts, and there's an unsettling smile on her mouth. "It's Felicity. I didn't really think I'd be next until I realised I was driving. And this was next to me, in the passenger seat." She picks up a gun.

"Jesus fuck." I breathe.

"Yeah," Jamie says. "Keep watching."

The camera lens is so small the gun fills it—you can't really see anything around her, nothing to give off any hint of where she is. Her face appears in the frame, and she smiles again.

"I guess you wanted me to do *this*?" She puts the muzzle

in her mouth, one eye looking at the lens, her lips still curved into a smile, showing teeth. She pulls the gun out.

"I actually. Bought. A gun. In Vermont, apparently—you can get one at sixteen there, did you know? I don't know how *I* know, but I do. You must know too." Her eyes narrow, and she leans toward the lens, her pupils dark and blown. "I can feel you in here. Pushing me. I think you've been inside me for a while, but I never really noticed, even after I saw you again. I mean, you have to be careful, you know? Don't wanna get caught now, after everything you've done. Right?"

She's vague enough that she could be talking about any-one, *to* anyone, but I know. Even though she hasn't said Mara's name yet, I know.

Her face goes slack. "She's still alive. Burning. He's not going to save her in time." She lets out a bitter laugh. "I knew he wouldn't." She blinks, looks down at something, then back at the lens. "I think you could, though, if you opened your mind to it. To them. But she'd never let you. She wants you broken. She likes broken things. Loves that she's the one breaking you."

She picks up something else—she must have her mobile resting against something, because the lens goes dark, but we can still hear her.

"I bought these, too." In the next frame, you can see a hunting knife and a bottle of something, as well as needles. "I can feel you in here, but *I'm* still *me*. My time's not up yet.

I mean, I know there's nothing I can do at this point"—she shrugs casually—"I was made this way, to not be able to fight you. But I figure, at least I can choose how I die?" Her face vanishes, and the shot pans over the knife, the needles and a syringe, the gun and a box of ammunition, lingering on each for a shaky moment. "But nothing here's really speaking to me." She inhales deeply. "The gun feels like *you*. The needles . . . definitely not you. You hate needles. You used to hate blood, remember?" She throws back her head, laughing. Her throat moves, fills the shot. "You've changed a lot." Her expression hardens, her eyes distant again. "We all did. But you the most."

There's a knock on the front door, and Jamie pauses the video just as I shake my head. "Goose, let them in. Daniel, how long does it go on?"

"I think it's still going," he says, glancing back up at the TV. Jamie checks his mobile before getting up as well.

I lower my voice. "You know what Stella's saying," I say to Daniel. "Do you think Mara . . . ?" My voice trails off. I can't even make myself say it, not even to him. I twist around— Jamie's still by the door, with Sophie and Leo and Goose. Where is Mara?

Daniel shakes his head. "This points at her, yeah. But I don't think it is."

"Why?"

"Listen to how Stella's describing it—this isn't murder.

This is—someone's in their heads, influencing them to do it. *Coercing* them." He glances back at the door. Jamie's on his way back over, along with Goose and Sophie and Leo. "Did you do what you said you would?"

I nod.

"And?" he asks.

"Gang's all here," Jamie says, standing beside Goose, Leo, and Sophie.

I remember last night. The scalpel Mara hid. The secrets she's kept. I swallow my words, put my fist out to stop the train of thought that's barrelling toward me. I catch Daniel's eye and shake my head. He would rather believe it's got something to do with Jamie. But this isn't Jamie.

Sophie's seated on another sofa, and Goose has taken the armchair. Leo's standing, watching the silent news.

"I'm sorry," I begin, looking at him. "About Felicity." No response.

"The news picked up the explosion," Sophie says. "Her parents . . ." Her cheeks and nose are red. She's been crying.

Daniel turns to me. "That building is in your name," he says quietly. "You're going to start getting calls."

"I haven't heard anything." I check my pockets. My mobile isn't with me. Must've left it upstairs.

"You should check your phone," Daniel says. "People are probably trying to reach you."

I'm not sure how much I care, but I rise anyway. "Keep

watching," I tell them, though only Daniel and Sophie seem to be listening to me. "See if there's anything that gives away where Stella is. Sophie, you haven't seen her, have you?"

She shakes her head. "She's missing, for me. Still. She didn't . . . flare. If that's what you're asking."

It is. "So there's still time."

"Uh, mates?" Goose has unmuted the television. "You should hear this."

Stella had been missing from the frame, but she's picked up her mobile again, or whatever she's using to record herself.

"I want you to see it," Stella says to the lens. "To watch me do it, not from inside my head but what it looks like on the outside, too. I've got all this stuff here, but it's not . . ." She shakes her head. "It's not what I want. Not that I want this at all, but since I don't have a choice—since you're bullying me into suicide, basically, at least I can still choose to go out the way I want. I still have some choices left."

The echoes from my conversations with Daniel, with Jamie, with Mara—it's as though she'd been listening.

"That's why I'm recording it all. Everything. I know you think you're the most loyal person alive, that I already betrayed you by leaving you—you realise I could name you, you know, right? All of you? I know you're watching this. I want all of you to see me do it, but . . . this isn't . . . right. It's not . . . personal enough." Stella looks somewhere else, then back at the lens. "I want *your* eyes looking at *my* eyes when she kills me.

I want you to see what she's really capable of," she says, and a cold finger trails the back of my neck, because I know she's speaking to me. "You won't believe it any other way."

Then Stella reaches toward the lens, and the screen fades to black.

38

THE CHIEF END OF MAN

"Looks like you got your wish."

It takes me half a second to register that it's Leo speaking. He's still staring at the television screen.

"Pardon?" I ask, because no one else speaks up.

"The archives are gone, just like you wanted," he says plainly. "Whoever killed her made sure she'd throw you a bone on her way out."

It doesn't escape me that he uses the pronoun "she." Unconsciously, I look for Mara again. "That's not fair," I say, unsure if I'm saying it in my own defence, or hers.

"Not *fair*?"

"Guys." Daniel stands up, between Leo and me. "This is

the exact definition of 'unhelpful.' Leo, I am truly, terribly sorry about Felicity, but we might still be able to help Stella. Sophie, is there anything at all, any way you can tell if she's . . . around?" He's grasping at straws, and Sophie's the nearest.

"It's not like she's wearing a GPS collar," Sophie says flatly.

Daniel closes his eyes. He's not one to shout, but if there were ever a day to start . . .

"I'm going to check if anyone's called," I tell him, hoping to redirect him for the moment. He meets my eyes. Nods.

I avoid giving Leo the satisfaction of my attention as I pass, and climb the stairs. Not that I'd know what to say to anyone if they were to call, which version of the truth to hand over, and let them pick at. I consider shutting my mobile off when I find it, until I remember that Stella has my number and might call or text.

My pace quickens—she might've called already. The office door is cracked open. I push it the rest of the way to find Mara sitting on the floor.

She's sitting cross-legged, holding the journal I'd just read from in one hand, while in the other, a letter, old, unfolded. The small silvered trunk is still open.

She looks up at me through a fringe of black lashes. Her expression isn't guilty, or ashamed, or even angry. It's nothing.

Mara speaks first. "You didn't tell me."

I don't know which letter she's holding, I've no idea what pages she's read, but it doesn't matter. It's enough that she didn't ask, and feels entitled enough to accuse me of hiding things from her.

"We don't have time for this," I force myself to say. She stares at me like I'm speaking another language, and I'm reminded of the way she looked when she got up from bed one night and threw out her grandmother's doll, with no memory of it in the morning. Maybe Daniel's right, and it is involuntary, and she's got no control of it.

I crouch, taking the letter and journal from her hand. Making contact with her skin. "Felicity's dead," I say. "And Stella . . ."

The name brings her to life. "I saw."

I examine her face, search her eyes, but she looks like herself. Sounds like herself. "You didn't see her big finish," I say finally.

Mara blinks, once. "She didn't—"

"No. Not yet. But she was talking to us. In the . . . film . . . she made."

"Did she name me?"

I'd used the word "us." Mara wanted to know if Stella named *her*.

"If she's going to, she hasn't yet," I say, standing up. It could mean something or nothing, and maybe Daniel will know. I grab my mobile. Indeed, there are over twenty missed calls. Most recently from Ms. Gao, one from Ruth, none from Katie. Maybe she doesn't know, hasn't heard.

Or doesn't care.

Stella hasn't called or texted either. "Come," I say to Mara, reaching for her hand. "You can watch the whole thing downstairs. Jamie's recorded it."

"She went viral," Mara says, shaking her head, still sitting on the floor. "Everyone will be looking for her. And she has more time, Felicity didn't die until—"

"Stella doesn't want more time," I say, and the words spark something. "She's resentful, of all of us. But you the most. She thinks you're pulling her strings, and she'd rather cut them herself."

I know the words are true because I understand what's behind them. Stella's fought, hard, to change who she is, what she can do. She tried to use her ability for good, to channel it, but it brought her nothing but the sounds of misery and destruction. I understand wanting silence, after that.

But you don't go public if you want silence. You go public if you want to make noise.

OF MOTIVES

I WALK INTO THE MIDDLE OF AN ARGUMENT downstairs. The news at high volume in the background, Goose glued to it. Sophie's face is tearstained; Daniel looks nauseated. Jamie is circling the flat, trying to disguise his pacing. "Who is doing this though?" he asks.

"It doesn't matter *who*," Daniel says. "We should be trying to work out *why*."

Sophie's eyes are drawn to mine, mid-stair. "Well, whatever motive's behind this, it's the same one that apparently aligned with destroying Noah's dad's research."

"It wasn't his father's research," Daniel says. "It was

research his father paid for, to save Noah's life."

"That makes no sense whatsoever."

"That was how he justified it to himself, and you weren't there, Sophie."

"And as I understand it, you were unconscious."

"Stop it," Mara says, standing at the foot of the stairs. It's not just Sophie and Daniel who are silenced—it's everyone.

"My brother's right," she says. "It doesn't matter who's doing this to Stella, at this point—she knows she isn't dead yet, but she thinks she's in the slaughtering pen."

"And that you're the butcher," Leo says to her.

"That's what she thinks," Mara acknowledges. "I'm not. But it doesn't matter. What matters is why *she's* doing it. She doesn't want to die, right?" Mara looks at me first and then at Leo.

"Not that she's ever said." He looks surprised to have even been asked. "*I* don't understand why she's doing this."

"Because she wants some control back," Mara says, looking to me for affirmation. "She knows it's just a matter of time before whoever is doing this makes her kill herself. You heard her in the video."

"She thinks it's inevitable," Jamie cuts in. "Like telling someone they've got a degenerative brain disease so they might as well sacrifice themselves to a volcano to save a nation of people."

Goose looks at him, then at me. "And here I thought I had no idea what was going on before."

"Never mind," Jamie says. "I'm just saying Mara's right. Stella's still in control right now—to some extent. Something made her drive to Vermont to buy a gun and put it in her mouth," Jamie says. "I don't think she'd do that, even as a joke."

"The police, everyone's going to be looking for the same things we are," Mara says. "Anything that identifies . . . *any-thing* . . . from where that video was taken. It looked like a cell phone—that's probably where they'll start?"

"We've been over that already, while you were doing whatever. This is New York," Leo says. "And she has an iPhone. Can cell towers place you that specifically? Enough to find where she took the video?"

"She left her phone there," I speak up, and everyone looks to me. "That's what I'd do, if I wanted to lead people in the wrong direction."

"But why the wrong direction?" Leo asks, his voice nearly pleading. "She said—*you* said—that you *knew* they didn't want to die."

I try and edit myself before I speak. Take a leaf from his book. "Because for her, she's made a decision. She intends to honour it."

"What if no one's looking for her?" Sophie asks. "What if they think she's just some crazy girl on the Internet—"

"They're questioning her mental health and trying to identify her, definitely," Daniel says. "Find out who she is and whether she's still alive."

"Not just that," I say. "She mentioned Felicity by name in her video. And the number of missed calls on my mobile about confirms that people know about the fire—"

"Explosion," Goose corrects. "They called it an explosion on the news."

"Right, the journos've picked it up. She's now a person of interest in whatever investigation'll go on about that."

"By that right, so are you, mate."

That was what Daniel had been trying to say, before, why he'd thought of my phone.

Jamie's the one who speaks up, though. "We should get out of here before they come looking for you, Noah. I mean, I can hand-wave a lot, but it'll be easier if—"

"They're not going to *arrest* me," I say.

"They can hold you for less than twenty-four hours for whatever they want," Mara says. "Without arresting you."

"'Murica," Jamie mutters.

"Felicity was murdered in a property you own," Daniel says.

"She committed suicide," I say. "And with my father's lawyers—they wouldn't dare." I glance at Mara, only just beginning to fully grasp the extent and reach of the privilege I've enjoyed.

"They won't send a SWAT team here," she says. "Probably just a couple of detectives."

"Are you actually worried about yourself when Stella just announced to the world that she's going to commit suicide imminently?" Leo asks me. Rage simmers beneath his placid, amphibious expression. Where was all this feeling when she went missing?

"I'm concerned that if I'm detained, I won't be able to help in any way." I don't even give him the satisfaction of meeting his gaze. Instead, I pocket my mobile and my keys, one of which belongs to a car I've never driven and didn't ask for but was bought for me anyway, by the assistant. No time like the present. "Shall we drive?"

"Drive . . . where?" Sophie asks.

"Anywhere but here, until we figure out where she is," I say.

Daniel meets my steps to the door. "Works for me," he says. Then, lower, "I was the last one in the archives. The police are going to want to talk to me."

"No, they won't. We left together."

"I went back."

It takes effort to appear as though he hasn't said anything.

"It doesn't matter," I say quickly. "You had my permission. And as Jamie said, he can hand-wave any questions—"

"Where do you think she is?" Mara asks me. She's slipping into a jacket just as Sophie and Leo join us.

"We have to try to think the way she's thinking."

"But she's not thinking, is the point," Leo cuts in. "If she were thinking, she wouldn't be doing this."

"She *is* thinking," I insist. "She's just thinking the way—the way someone who's given up hope would think." A pattern I'm familiar with.

"How can we predict that?" Sophie turns to me, then Leo. "How am I supposed to find her before . . ." Her voice trails off before she finishes her sentence, but she doesn't have to.

"People who think about dying think about what they'll miss about this world, if they're to leave it. So what does Stella love most?" I ask Leo.

"Um, I thought . . . I mean . . . I think . . . she loves me?" he finally says.

Nice try, mate. "No, what does she *love*?"

"Her friends, family," Sophie says.

I avoid looking at Jamie and Mara—seeing their scepticism won't help.

"You're not listening. Other than the standard shit people say on dating profiles," I say to Leo.

"How would you know what people say on dating profiles?" Goose asks.

Mara twists around. "Really?"

"Just asking."

"If you were to take away something from Stella," I say, searching for the right words, "what thing that if you took it away, you'd be taking part of her away too?"

Leo and Sophie look at each other. The silence is worse

than uncomfortable. No one in this room seems to have known Stella at all.

"She loved the water," Jamie says suddenly. "Loves," he corrects himself. "She loves the water."

"She was on the swim team in high school," Mara says to me. "I remember her saying something about that at . . ."

Horizons.

"What did she say in her video?" I ask Jamie. "Let me see your phone; play it back."

"The whole thing?"

"Just the last bit." He hands me his phone. It's especially eerie now, hearing her voice, knowing what she's planning to do.

I want all of you to see me do it. . . .

I want your own eyes looking at my eyes when she kills me. . . .

"It'll be public, like the others," I say. "Though not exactly the same." Not a hanging, not jumping in front of the train. Whatever part of Stella still has autonomy is aware of the others. She wants her choice to stand out.

"The river?" Jamie looks at Mara, then Daniel.

"Which one?"

"Mates," Goose says, "I think it might be too late for us to get out of here. I just saw two helicopters. . . ."

But I'm already moving through the flat toward the east clock face, to the glass that separates us from the Manhattan Bridge. It rises out of the East River like a prehistoric beast, its pylons rusty with age, almost appearing to ripple with muscle. The main span is like a spine, the suspension cables, ribs. It stands between islands, stretching its neck, its tail, carrying thousands of people, even now. And I know that Stella is one of them.

. . . *your own eyes looking at my eyes when she kills me*

She doesn't just want an audience; she wants *our* audience. My audience. She wants me to witness. She would choose to end her life in a way I can't help but see, from almost every direction.

I press my palm to the glass. "She's on the bridge."

I WILL BREATHE

WE WALK SILENTLY AND A BIT scattered—Jamie's first in our little queue; I follow with Daniel, Leo, and Sophie. Mara and Goose are behind us. We approach at Jay and Sands streets and we're not stopped. The police might not know what's happening, if she's even here. She's picked a good hour for it.

"She might not even be here." Daniel gives voice to my thoughts. Having him beside me is steadying, stops me from thinking about Mara in the study—or office, rather. My father had a study.

I blink in the soft, dusty light. Below us, somewhere, is the carousel, encased in glass like a jewel box. Around us is graffiti, harsh and livid. The sun is trying to rise, like a chick trying to break free from its egg. But it's not dawn yet.

It feels as though we've been walking for ages when I spot the first officer. He's turned to the side, hands in his pockets, staring at something but I can't tell what, from this angle. He's still—unnaturally still—as we approach him. He doesn't turn his head, his eyes don't move at all, not even to blink.

Jamie looks back at us. "What new devilry is this?"

"Not devilry," Leo says. He and Sophie exchange a look. "I'm trying something."

Goose shouts from behind us. "Has it got anything to do with why I feel ill all of a sudden?"

Leo stops. "I'm working on something. An illusion. For the cops and us."

"Might've been nice to have a warning," Goose says, looking peaked.

"I didn't know if it would work," he says. "I still don't know."

"Sophie, how many people are here?"

"I'm only seeing us."

I hang back, to let Goose catch up. "What're you feeling, mate?"

"Bloody awful."

"More specifically?"

"Like I've just given ten pints of blood . . . from my brain."

Daniel tenses. "If Leo's using you to create whatever . . . illusion . . . he's creating, on however many people . . . there's not going to be much Goose can do for anyone else."

Still, next to him, the percussive sound of thousands of heartbeats batters my skull. The bridge trembles as the trains run, but I don't hear any cars. Maybe the police have caught on to what's happening and stopped traffic?

Ahead of us, Jamie's stopped. When we reach him, I see why.

Stella's climbed the fence. She's clinging to it, facing the walkway, not the water. She's been waiting for us.

She's not the only one here. There are police above, paramedics as well, and one of them's suspended between the upper level of the bridge and this one. But like that first officer, they too are frozen.

"I'm glad you came," Stella says, drawing my eyes. "Wasn't sure you'd bother to find me."

Jamie's nostrils flare. "Of course we—"

"I'm talking to Noah," Stella says. "I knew you'd find me, if you could. But you don't have his *Gifts*." She spits out the word. "What a bullshit word."

"Are you doing this because of me?" I ask, point-blank.

She laughs. "Don't flatter yourself." She looks at Leo, then, and her eyes tear up. "Neat trick," she says.

"I wanted us to be able to talk without them getting in the way."

"If they *were* in the way, maybe they could actually help . . ." Daniel mumbles.

I shake my head, knowing that Stella heard him—his thoughts, if not his actual words. "If they were in the way, Stella would jump. Isn't that right?"

She smiles. "I like the water." She twists her head to the left, as much as she can while she's gripping on to the fence. "I kind of always wondered what it would be like to jump."

"Like breaking your neck," Mara says. Her cheeks are flushed; I can feel the anger coming off her like fire. "Why are you doing this?"

"*I'm* not doing this," Stella says. Her rage is cold. "You are."

"That's bullshit, and somewhere in there, you know it."

"Stop," Leo tells Mara, holding out his hand. He walks toward Stella. "Let me pull you back. All of us, together, we can make it go away—"

Stella's eyes frost over. "I made a video to make sure it *wouldn't* go away. Now everyone will know what we are, that we exist, and they'll stop what's happening to us."

"Or stop *us*," Mara says, without pointing out that Stella didn't actually name anyone to stop.

A twisted smile forms on Stella's lips. "Yeah. Maybe they will. I hope they do."

It doesn't matter. Reality doesn't even matter—only what's

in Stella's mind, and I don't know that any of us have the right words to change it.

If we could get more *time*, though . . .

"Stella, don't," Sophie calls out, interrupting my thoughts. "We can fix this."

"No, *we* can't. Maybe *they* can," Stella says, indicating Mara, me. "But *we* can't. They're the Originals. We're just copies."

Mara starts to say, "That doesn't mean what you think—"

"You're not helping," I tell her.

"What's she talking about?" Sophie asks me. "Originals, copies?"

"Just a little something I heard Felicity think before she died," Stella says. She takes one hand off the fence, the muscles flexing in her arms, her core, as she wipes her hand on her shirt. Her muscles must be on fire. She's stronger than she looks.

Or something's making her stronger.

"Noah knows, I bet. Jamie, too." She pauses. "And Mara, of course."

I'm wary of latching on to anything she says for fear that she's already so far gone I can't trust it, but my conversation with Daniel surfaces regardless. He was the one to first bring up Stella's type—"suspected original." Stella just called herself a copy. What does she know now that she didn't know before?

I wonder if Daniel's caught it. There's movement in the corner of my eye. It's him, backing up.

"Stella," I say, feeling every second as it's lost, grasping for more. "You weren't there when my father said the things he said."

"I didn't have to be there. It's in your head. I can see it."

"You can see his *memory* of it," Mara says. "Memories are tainted. Unreliable. If you bothered to look at my memory, I bet it would be different."

Stella smiles again, coy. "What makes you think I haven't?"

I look reflexively at Mara. Her face reveals nothing, her expression almost as still as the paused officers'.

"That's why I made the video," Stella goes on. "So everyone can see who you are, what you do. Obviously, memories can't be trusted. I mean, look where I am right now."

"You don't have to be here," Mara says.

"No, I don't have to be *here*. I could be in some basement with a gun in my mouth—it probably would've taken people a while to find me. A quieter death would've been a lot more convenient for you."

Leo looks at me, his hands balled into fists. "Why aren't you stopping her?"

"Stopping whom? Stella's in control here. Aren't you, Stella?"

She looks around, up at the frozen police, the paramedics. Then at each of us, landing on Mara, last.

"Am I?"

I follow her gaze—the bodies of everyone who isn't Us shimmer and blink. And then—gone. It's elegant, the way they're wiped away. Replaced with blank space. The pieces don't completely fit—the pavement shivers, miragelike, where they once stood.

"She's in your head too," Stella says to me, but it's Leo I look at.

"What are you doing?" I ask him.

"I'm trying to make it so we focus on Stella, because I can't hold the rest of them for long."

I turn to Goose, who's sheet-white, with Daniel next to him, speaking in a low voice. Mara takes a step toward Stella. "What am I saying to you, in your head?"

"You're not saying anything. You're just there, crouching like a tiger." Stella laughs, which is especially disturbing, considering the fact that there's nothing between her and a 135-foot drop. When she rights herself, she steadies her gaze on Sophie.

"You're next, I think." She blinks slowly. "I think you're safe for a while, Leo. I'm glad."

"I'm begging you," he says to her. "Don't do this." I try and focus my energy on him, on listening to his heartbeat, to hear if he's lying to all of us or telling the truth, but all I hear is a swarm of flies. I look back and see Sophie, but instead of her face, I see a skull.

"Stop," I say to Leo through clenched teeth, but Stella thinks I'm talking to her. She's about to say something back when Mara says—

"Let go, then."

The words echo, then flatten, then become part of the swarm.

"Stella," I say quickly, "this isn't happening the way you think it is." I turn back, looking for Daniel, for Jamie, for help, and the bridge behind me vanishes, rubbed into white space.

"You said you wanted a cure," I hear Mara say. "You could be fighting for one. Instead, you're giving up."

"Fuck you," Stella spits. "I'm not giving up, or letting go. I didn't get to choose my own adventure, but I can choose my own ending."

I don't know if it's a trick of my eyes, of Leo's, or if what I'm seeing is real, but Stella doesn't fall from the bridge, or jump.

She dives.

41

STRONG AND VALIANT NATURES

THE LAST CONSCIOUS THOUGHT THAT STELLA has, that I can hear, is

Your move

It's stunning, watching the river swallow her body. The closest person to her, proximity-wise, was Mara. But I was the one she was thinking about as her neck broke. A white sear of pain and then, nothing.

I hadn't noticed that dawn had risen, that it was morning, until now. The police are back in motion, talking to us, coming toward us, and Jamie's in gear, leading the way with Leo. The illusion's broken, Daniel and Goose are by my side. Goose is leaning on to the rail, weakest of all of us.

"Drained" would be a better word, I suppose. I twist back, looking for Mara, but the only person I see behind us is Sophie. She's crying, silently.

"Have you seen Mara?" I ask her.

She looks up at me through dark blond lashes. "She left as soon as soon as Stella . . ."

"The cops are going to want to talk to all of us," Daniel says. "There are cameras on the bridge, not to mention the helicopters—"

"Did any of them get audio, do you think?" I want to replay what just happened. Make sure my own memory is untainted.

"Who *cares*?" Leo turns, faces me. "Who the fuck cares?"

"We all should," Daniel says, though not for the reason I expect. "Especially us, seeing as we're eighteen."

"And that's relevant why?" Leo asks.

"Because it means we can be questioned without a guardian present," Daniel says flatly. "Because we can be charged as adults."

"Charged for what? She committed suicide," Sophie says quietly. "No one's going to be arrested for murder."

"Even though *one* of us should be," Leo says. He turns his assholic stare on me as Mara's not here.

"Shut up," I say as Jamie talks us past one of the cops, but I don't say it out of anger. I stop at the railing, threading my

334 · MICHELLE HODKIN

fingers through the fence. A boat arcs through the river, its wake curving like a smile.

Beneath the cars, beneath the trains, beneath the voices and sounds of every living thing in New York—

Beneath the water, there's a heartbeat.

42

HOWEVER MEAN

SHE'S ALIVE." I'M STARING DOWN AT THE WATER, watching the boat, but it's as though someone took an open palm to an unfinished oil painting and smeared it. I can't tell if her body's floated up, or if they've sent divers down for her, and my mind can't reach simple facts I should know.

Leo steps beside me, looks down. "How—"

"I need to get to her."

"Noah." Sophie puts a light hand on my arm. "She's gone."

I don't shake her off. She's barely there, flickering in and out. I call out to Jamie, "Can you get us through?"

I have to shout it—it's deafening up here, now that the illusion's broke. The cars and trains and the city—we would barely've been able to hear ourselves speak.

"I'm trying!" Jamie calls back, just as Goose falls to the pavement.

Daniel's voice tugs at me as he crouches over my friend. "Can you do anything?"

I try and let it all in, every sound I can usually hear; lungs expanding, blood rushing through arteries, hearts like metronomes, but instead it's everything else; pistons firing in engines powering cars, a garbage bag being stepped on, glass breaking, the ticking of Leo's watch.

I'm bent over Goose—I can see his chest move, but can't hear him breathe. I tilt my head, my ear to his mouth, and still I can barely hear a shudder of a breath, even though I can see it. It feels like I'm backing into a corridor, the lights going out one by one. Someone's calling my name, but I'm on the pavement, deaf, but not blind. A drop of blood wells up in Goose's nostril, then drips down the side of his cheek. It drips to the ground. I can't hear that, either. The air stirs his hair, the collar of his shirt.

Daniel's mouth is moving, but no words are coming out. Goose blinks out of my field of vision even though I'm kneeling over him. When he blinks back in, *his* hand is on my shoulder and I'm the one on the pavement, on my back, shouting for everyone to shut the fuck up.

I watch two pigeons take flight between the suspension cables. The colour leaches out of the sky; the world is grey and white before I black out.

43

PAINT THE VERY ATMOSPHERE

HER VOICE CURLS AROUND MY NERVES.

An instantly familiar alto with a slight growl that gives her words a faintly sarcastic edge. I first heard her in a thick, pulsing crowd at a club. The tourist hordes descend on South Beach in December like beasts, but I glide past bouncers one, two, and three without effort. This Croyden idiot named Kent's toted two of his Pine Crest friends along; I've already forgotten their names. They're staring openmouthed at the girls—models, mostly—writhing to music in a haze of fake smoke.

I feel the notes beneath my skin. Atrocious, but they drown out the sound of things I shouldn't be able to hear but can, chords of life blending together in a discordant soup of noise.

I open my eyes to find two tall, angular blondes—twins, perhaps—twining around each other and dancing feet away from us. One tosses me a look, then speaks to the other in Russian. Kent and his friends are spellbound; I am relentlessly bored. I rest against the seat, legs stretched out in front of me, and wonder if I could possibly sleep. But one of the girls moves in closer. Watching me to see if I'm watching her.

I lift my glass and take a slow sip of scotch. The girl is now dancing between my legs. If I don't break eye contact, in six seconds she'll kneel.

At four, I look away.

The girl moves back into the crowd, but throws a look over her shoulder. She's hurt.

Better this way. She wants connection, and I can't connect.

Kent says something obscene over the music, and I consider hitting him to break the tedium. I manage to resist, barely, and take another sip. I haven't been able to get properly drunk in years, but I like the burn.

That is what I'm thinking when I hear her voice for the first time. Fear and rage twisted into three words:

"Get them out."

Her voice brings pain with it; my head throbs and aches and every muscle feels sore. Then I go blind.

I would panic, if this were the first time this had happened. But it isn't, and I know that I'm still with Kent surrounded by tourists, though when I try and look down at myself out of habit, I see nothing at first. Then out of the darkness, hands come into focus. Pressed up against something—a wall, a ceiling perhaps. Not my hands, though—the fingernails are small, dirty, the fingers slender, feminine. But I see them as if I'm looking through the lenses of my own eyes. They push against the wall, and I can feel the texture of the cinderblock and dirt even though my hands are clean.

The waking nightmare ends, eventually, but now, nearly two months later, I hear that same voice again. Those same words.

The sun is shining aggressively, and I'm staring at the thatched roof of one of Croyden's absurd tiki huts, avoiding it and class. I don't look up to see who happens to be beating the shit out of the vending machine until I hear that voice. I would know it anywhere, in any dream or memory, but I never imagined I would hear it in reality.

When I do, I lean up and watch her. The girl's more angry than annoyed, as if the malfunction is personal.

"You have an anger management problem," I say. She whips around.

My psychic disaster seems to have developed a life outside my psyche. She stands there in dark jeans that would be indecent if she didn't wear them so casually, with a loose, faded black T-shirt that sets off her skin. Not from Florida, clearly new, and so beautiful I nearly laugh out loud. And with this look on her face like she doesn't give a fuck what I think of her. Perfection.

She considers me for a long moment, her eyebrows drawing together.

"Get him out," Mara says. It's her voice, but her mouth doesn't move. And the tone is off—oddly tinny, and far away.

"What?" I ask, or try to, but something's wringing the air from my lungs. The sun pierces the shade of the roof.

"He's waking up; I'll call you back." Those words come from nowhere. And that is definitely not Mara's voice anymore. It's Jamie's.

WHAT I LIVE FOR

I BLINK, AND THERE'S A FLARE OF LIGHT. THE SUN
in my memory becomes a fluorescent tube light in
reality.

"Noah, come on, we gotta go."

It's Jamie, shaking my shoulder. I gasp for air, and Florida
sheds its skin; the picnic table shrinks into a hideous chair, the
thatched roof bleaches out into a white ceiling. The vending
machines are still here.

"Where is everyone?" I ask him.

"Where we need to be."

"Where are *we*?"

"Mount Sinai," he says, and the pieces fit together.

We're in a waiting room. "You insisted."

"*I* insisted?"

"They brought Stella here, but." Jamie shakes his head. "It's not good."

An image comes to me, a memory, possibly, of people pulling her out of the water—one of her shoes was still on.

"Is she alive?"

Jamie nods, but his eyes dart away. "For now."

"Can you get me to her?"

He shakes his head, his dreadlocks flicking his cheeks. "No one's getting near her right now. Her neck's broken and she's on life support, I overheard."

I can choose my own ending.

She didn't, though, seeing as how she's still alive. Seems especially cruel.

"Noah, we *really* need to go."

"Where's Daniel?" I say as I get up, swaying on my feet. I steady myself on one of the chairs. Jamie's not watching— he's looking at the front entrance.

"At the precinct," he says. "Waiting for his parents."

"What? What *precinct*? The fuck—why?"

"Because he doesn't want to talk to the police without a lawyer. And neither do you."

"I've got enough to go round," I say. "But it would be simpler for you to just get us out of it."

"I can't get us out of anything. You can't *do* anything. Are you listening to me?" He faces me, fake smiling, speaking through clenched teeth. "Someone cut the power. Like literally, in our case—our abilities are gone. We *have* to *go*."

45

UNSURVEYED AND UNFATHOMED

JAMIE TRIES TO FILL IN THE GAPS IN MY MEMORY
as I walk numbly out of the hospital with him.

"Goose passed out on the bridge as I was trying
to get us out of there," he says. So that happened in
truth. Good to know. "Daniel was getting paranoid,"
he finishes.

"For good reason, it seems."

"As it happens, yes. So when Goose passed out, you tried to
heal him, but I guess you couldn't."

"He's all right though? When you said someone cut the—"

"He's fine. I don't know what the fuck happened up there,
but none of us seems to be able to do what we can do anymore."

"*None* of us?"

"None," he says, shaking his head. But he stops midshake. "Well. One assumes."

"One should never assume," I say, mostly to myself. "Anyway, I'm sure it's likely temporary."

"Sure, why not," Jamie says, head down, hands in his pockets. I notice he's been avoiding the main streets. "Anyway, I realised I couldn't do what I usually do, and the cops stopped us. Sophie started talking to them while we were still on the bridge. Offered to explain everything. She doesn't seem to do well under pressure."

"Christ."

"So that's where she, Leo, and Daniel are. If they haven't destroyed each other yet."

"And I insisted we get to the hospital," I say. "To help Stella."

"Actually, you had the presence of mind to say to the cops that you needed to go because of Goose. Being English and all, him not having family here, blah blah. It worked, they brought him to Mount Sinai too. I got to tag along because I said I was sick too. Felt pretty shitty, TBH."

"He's not still at the hospital, is he?"

Jamie shakes his head. "No, checked himself out."

"Where's he, then?"

"On his way to a hotel, I believe."

"And Mara?" She'd been there until Stella dove. After that . . .

Jamie pauses before saying, "Not . . . entirely sure."

"How's that?"

"Because she didn't say."

"But you saw her leave?" I have no memory of it.

Jamie appears to though. "Yes, but I didn't ask where she was headed. We have a sort of a Don't Ask, Don't Tell policy with each other." He looks up for a second. "I recommend it."

Instead of his face I see Goose, unconscious, a drop of blood running from his nose to his cheek to the pavement.

I think of Stella's last words:

Your move.

I withdraw my mobile. No texts from Mara, no calls from her. About a thousand others I still haven't returned, though. "What's the play, here, then?" I ask Jamie, feeling adrift.

"Well, you probably have an army waiting for you at the apartment. I'm going to my aunt's place."

"You don't live there."

"It's probably better if I do right now. Speaking of," he says, looking up at the clock tower.

"Right," I say slowly. "Catch up later?"

"Yeah," Jamie says. "Definitely."

I don't need my ability to know that he's lying.

Part III

"And ever," says Malory,
"Sir Lancelot wept, as he had been
a child that had been beaten."

—T. H. White, *The Once and Future King*

TO LIVE DELIBERATELY

I DON'T KNOW WHAT I'M EXPECTING TO FIND WHEN I walk into the building, but it isn't nothing. Which is exactly what I find. Nothing.

No doorman. No detectives. No one.

My stomach drops as the lift rises, and as the doors open, I hesitate. I force myself forward, key the lock.

I feel her in the space even though I can't see her. My feet carry me toward the room that holds her.

She's standing in the study, not sitting amongst the trunks and the boxes. Standing at the window.

"I missed you," she says without turning around.

I mean to say it back, but the words that come out are different. "You vanished, on the bridge."

"I wanted to get here first."

"Why?"

She turns around. Her eyes are glassy; she's been crying. "Because."

"*Because?* What did you do?"

She looks startled by the question. "What?"

I'm thinking the words *Don't ask, don't tell,* even as I say, "What. Did. You. Do."

She swallows. "When?"

"*When?*"

Her expression hardens. "Yes, *when?* What did I do today? Five months ago? Before we met?"

"Start with today," I say, growing more aggravated by the second. I'm the one in the dark, here. She has the advantage, and she knows it.

"Why don't you just ask me, Noah." She steps forward. "Ask me."

"What did you say to Stella, on the bridge?"

"What do you think I said?"

"You told her to let go. That she was giving up," I say, searching Mara's face for anything to hold on to, any hint that I'm wrong.

But she says, "Yes."

Part of me expected her to deny it, and splits off from the

half that always knew. I let that one take over. "She's in a hospital. Her neck is broken and she's on life support."

"I know," Mara says, calm as anything.

I'm so far beyond anger I'm mental. "You might as well have pushed her off the bridge yourself."

"No. What she did wasn't my fault," Mara says.

"It's not your fault, Mara. Say it."

That's what I said to her when my father forced me to choose between saving her and killing Daniel or the other way around. Mara begged me to give her a shot to stop her heart, and I wouldn't do it. Not until I heard her compare herself to Jude.

"I can't let Daniel go," she'd said desperately. *"I can't let what happened to me happen to Joseph. They've done nothing,* nothing *wrong. I've done everything wrong."*

"Not everything."

"You haven't been *here! Your father isn't lying. I did* those *things. All* of them.*"*

And then I said next, *"I'm sure they deserved it."*

How many other people had died because Mara thought they deserved it? "Is anything *ever* your fault?"

"Yes. Your father."

"What about him?"

"I killed him."

She announces it. Just like that.

I laugh because it's fucking gorgeous outside and Stella's broken body was just pulled out of the river and the girl I love is announcing that she made my sister an orphan. "He killed himself," I say like an idiot, knowing it's not true.

"It *looked* like he killed himself," she says. She's studying me, spine straight, stare direct. Not hiding. Not crossing her arms, not defensive.

"Because you made it look that way."

"Yes."

I blink and see Sam Milnes, hanging from the buttress. "Like the others."

"No," Mara says.

Beth steps off the platform in front of the train.

"Not like the others," she says.

Felicity burns herself alive. It's all I see when I look at Mara now. That and my fucking father. Stabbed himself, they said in the fucking obituary, and that piece—"What the fuck was that about the poisoning?"

I regret the question as soon as I ask, watching the words shatter against the stone of her skin. No guilt, no remorse, no fear—there's nothing there. Nothing anymore.

"Everything Stella said . . ." I let the sentence trail off, thinking of her in the hospital, alone. "I defended you."

"I never asked you to defend me," she says. "Not to anyone."

"You asked me to *help* you. You asked me to fix you, for fuck's sake!"

"That's true, I did, once. And you told me I wasn't broken."

What else had gotten twisted up in her mind in the past

nine months? She'd endured trauma beyond torture, I always knew, but *that* doesn't lead to *this*?

"My father," I start, grasping at what I can understand. "How did you do it?"

"I stabbed him in the neck."

I think back to my conversation with Stella, to just the other day with Mara, in our bedroom. To walking out of the room, my hand dripping blood on the floor after I found—

"The scalpel? The one you kept after stabbing Dr. Kells?"

She shakes her head. "I didn't keep that one. The one I have is different. From a hospital."

"Have you murdered anyone with it?"

"No."

I think back, revise. "Have you *killed* anyone with it?"

"No," she insists.

"Then why keep it?"

"I told you, it makes me feel safe," she says, and now her arms are crossed, and she is defensive. "I haven't lied to you. You never asked, so I never told."

"I'm asking now," I say.

She shrugs. "And I'm telling you now."

"A bit fucking late."

"You told me you saw me," she says. "So many times. You said you loved me anyway, no matter what I'd do. I thought you understood."

"I want to." God help me. "*Help* me understand," I beg

her. "My father . . . you were defending yourself—"

"No, I wasn't," she says, but this admission costs her. "I waited. I knew it would hurt you even though you said more than once you thought that he should die for what he did. I mostly wanted to make sure he could never come after my family again."

I do understand that, I do. But the others . . .

"Why everyone else?"

Her silence is horrifying. The flat is so quiet I should be able to hear our hearts beating, but I can't hear anything at all.

"There were twelve who showed up," she finally says. Her voice is toneless, robotic. "Jamie and Daniel were in a chamber beneath the factory. Then it was just me, holding you, and Jude begging to die. I killed him because he killed you, which was what he wanted, it turned out."

"No great loss."

"No. But you were." Her voice tightens. "I was still holding the knife I killed him with when the police came. I wasn't thinking about them. I felt the breath leave your body. I listened to your last heartbeat. And then I was surrounded by people who would do their job and then go home to their families and laugh around their dinner tables and read their children bedtime stories and you and I were never going to get that because you were dead and I was alone." Her voice breaks, and a cold finger traces the nape of my neck.

"I would have given anything to bring you back." She

looks at me then, reining all feeling in. "So I did."

There are a thousand words circling my mind, but none can escape my throat.

"My grandmother wrote me a letter," she says, and I vaguely remember reading it, but nothing in it to explain the expression on her face. "She said, 'You can choose to end life or choose to give it, but punishment will follow every reward.' I can reward people, did you know?" She says that almost to herself, looking over my shoulder out at the city. "It's one of the things she wrote, in her suicide note. One of her memories I have. Along with your great-great-grandfather discovering her. Her moving to England to live with your family."

"The letters you were reading, the journal"—I gesture to the trunks, the boxes, newly raging—"you knew what it was all about, yet you were giving *me* shit about keeping things from you?" Everything in me turns in on itself. "Who *are* you?"

"I didn't know I could bring you back that way. I didn't know it would work." She shrugs. Like she's not talking about having murdered innocent people, but thought she'd try getting high because she was curious. "But I'm not sorry it did. You're here."

"And they're not," I say in my newly hollowed-out voice.

Her eyes glass over, hard and fathomless. "I would do it again."

It's unreal that we're standing in the same room, in the

same universe, having this conversation. "I suppose it doesn't matter now that the power's out, as it were."

"Mine isn't."

"How do you—no." I nearly laugh. "I literally don't want to fucking know. You'll never do it again," I manage to say, at full volume and without hesitation.

"I'll have to do it again. Because you don't heal anymore. And it's not temporary. I've been reading up." She looks at the trunks. "Your father was right about some things."

"Not this," I say. "Not *ever* this, not ever again."

"I'm not apologising for saving your life."

"It's *my* life!"

"And how many times have you tried to end it? Would *you* let me die?" she asks, but I'm not ready for it, so I say no.

She leans back against the desk, jagged and unmovable. She's a rock I want to break myself against. Her expression clarifies that she thinks this is a victory of sorts, and I'm so furious and consumed by shame that the last thing I say to her is, "But I never want to see you again."

47

NO OTHER LIFE BUT THIS

I F SHE REPLIES, I DON'T REMEMBER IT. I DON'T remember her packing and leaving. Only the sound of the door as it closes behind her. I stare at it for a moment and then lean my forehead against the wood and scream.

In that forever moment there's a storm inside me. When I can breathe again, I move to the window and stare at the street below. The day's escaped, somehow—at dawn, Stella's spine was intact and my life was unbroken. Now the dark street's empty but for a black car. And then I see her. Mara strides down the cobblestones, a small speck, a dot, moving farther away until she turns the corner.

I need to stop staring at the space where she used to be, but when I force my eyes from the window in a minute that feels like an eternity, I'm *still* here, in this *fucking* room, somehow fantastically unchanged since she's left. It's beyond fathoming—how did I get here? Pacing alone in a room of relics, so completely fucking lost?

I can't stand still and I can't seem to leave, so I unlock one of the other trunks, small and brass, and start furiously looking through it, searching for a distraction, a diversion. I find one.

An envelope, large and black, with gold calligraphy addressed to me at the North Yorkshire address. A condolence card, likely—the others seemed to be—but this is unique enough to divert my attention, which desperately needs diverting, so I rip it open, tearing a bit of the thick card that bears only two sentences.

Condolences on your loss. Congratulations on your inheritance.
—A.L.

I throw the card like a disc, giving in to the fresh wave of disgust. I'm about to crush the envelope and bin it when I notice something peeking from the fold. Another paper, which I unfold as well, knowing I'll regret it, but what's one more regret to throw in with the lot?

It's a page torn from a book—some sort of history book. The title isn't on it. A section about priest holes, the sixteenth-century secret passages created when being a Catholic priest was high treason.

There are rooms in this house even I don't know about.

I crush the paper in my fist, toss it back into the trunk. The lid slams shut on its own, and with it, everything I've faced, to bring me to exactly this moment. He engineered what we are. I knew it, ignored it, and still ended up playing a hand of cards dealt long before I existed, without even knowing the game.

"*Only play the games you can win,*" Jamie had said. I didn't realise that the mere fact of my existence makes me a player. How do I win at someone else's game, with someone else's rules?

I check my mobile, because it hasn't sunk in, quite, that she's gone. I check our texts, e-mails, expecting that little (1) to show up in the account I've got just for her, but there's nothing new. Realising that there might never be anything new again—that I've *told* her I don't *want* anything from her again, and she listened—that pain is next level. I can't take my words back. I also can't give back the lives that she took.

My hands round into fists, and I dig my nails into my palms. They bleed.

That's never happened before; the fact of my not healing hasn't quite sunk in either, I suppose. I consider it.

I don't have to live without Mara if I don't want, not anymore. I can finally stop, put an end to it, reach the oblivion I'd been chasing, cut myself and bleed until there is no blood left. That would be an ending too.

That's when I see the little grey pouch on the floor, where Mara had been sitting. I know what's inside before I untie the knot, before the single pendant spills into my palm. Mara's taken the other with her.

I know, then, that I won't choose to die, not yet, at least. I wagered my heart on her and lost, again and again, but still I would do it. I could never bet on anyone else. I know how you love endings, Mara. But this isn't ours.

I fasten the chain around my neck.

I won't quit the game. I'll destroy the fucking board.

EPILOGUE
THE MEETING OF TWO ETERNITIES

HE AIR THINS BY THE SECOND. I LEAVE, FACE the lift, see the button, and know instantly that I can't press it. I stride down the hall until I see the door, nearly hidden, for the stairs. I take them two at a time, penthouse to ground floor. I'm breathing hard, fast, my lungs bursting, my heart racing to catch up with my roaring mind. I explode out of the tower using the service exit, and then—

"Got a light?"

My head swings toward the voice: female, an alto, intimate with a familiar sarcastic edge, brandishing a South London accent. It belongs to a woman standing at the corner where

I last saw Mara. A black car idles some paces away. Police? Someone sent from my family to find me? My mind's running in a thousand directions, but her voice is an anchor, her question a command.

She's wearing a dress—silk, ivory, and the hem curls toward the East River in the warm breeze. I flick open my lighter when I'm close enough, and she bends slightly, dipping her cigarette in the flame, the tip turning amber. The light changes her face enough to leave an imprint that I will never forget for the rest of my life, however long or short it is.

A fall of thick ink-black hair tumbles forward, and when she leans back, reveals skin the colour of burnished bronze, and one black iris fringed in thick black lashes. A wave of hair shades the other half of her face. She takes the cigarette between her first two fingers and bends a delicate elbow, wrist up, against her hip. Every movement of every joint is perfect and graceful, as if she's been practicing for centuries, though even in darkness, she looks only a decade older than I at most. Her smile is like the glare of headlights, and I'm a deer caught.

"Thank you."

The words curl around my nerves.

A rush of feeling—nostalgia, déjà vu, inevitability, incredulity—forces words out of my mouth. "I have to—"

"What?" she asks. "What do you have to do?"

"Go," I say, my voice fading at the edge.

"Shame," she says. "I was hoping you could help me."

That shakes me back into myself a bit, forcing out a mirthless grin. "I can't help anyone."

"It's a matter of life and death," she says.

The ridiculously dramatic gravity of the sentence shoves off the weight of her force. "If it's mine, you're wasting your time."

"It isn't."

"Whose, then?"

She tucks the wave of hair back behind her ear. "Someone we love."

I've seen this woman's face before, captured in black and white, in a photograph I found in a trunk of my mother's things, with my mother standing beside her. I've seen her painted in bold, bright brushstrokes hanging on a wall in Mara's house, sitting alone, commanding the attention of everyone who saw her. She is beautiful—stunningly, familiarly, and I know. Even as I ask the question, I know.

"Who are you?"

"Call me Mara," she says, adding that fully grown smile. "Everyone else does."

ACKNOWLEDGMENTS

THIS BOOK WOULDN'T EXIST WITHOUT THE READERS who read and loved Mara Dyer's story, and wanted to read more of it. I'm deeply grateful to you for giving me the chance to share Noah's story, and to the team at Simon & Schuster for their enthusiasm and help in getting The Shaw Confessions out into the world.

Special thanks to my editor Liz Kossnar, who jumped onto this project midstream and got it to the finish line, to Christian Trimmer, who helped me get it out of the gate, and to Lucy Ruth Cummins for making it look beautiful. I'm also always and especially grateful to my agent, Barry Goldblatt, for everything you do for me.

Thanks also to Holly Black, Sarah Rees Brennan, and Kat Howard for helping me find my early footing with this book, and to Libba Bray, Nova Ren Suma, and Justin Weinberger for your encouragement along the way. Most of all, my forever-thanks to Stephanie Feldstein, who did the heaviest lifting, in every possible way.

Last but never least, I am indebted to and beyond grateful for my growing family. I couldn't do what I do without you, and I wouldn't be where I am without you.

MICHELLE HODKIN GREW UP IN SOUTH FLORIDA, went to college in New York, and studied law in Michigan. You can visit her online at michellehodkin.com.